STRANDED

Center Point
Large Print

Also by Dani Pettrey and available from
Center Point Large Print:

Submerged
Shattered

Alaskan Courage
• Book Three •

STRANDED

Dani Pettrey

CENTER POINT LARGE PRINT
THORNDIKE, MAINE

This Center Point Large Print edition is published
in the year 2013 by arrangement with
Bethany House Publishers,
a division of Baker Publishing Group.

Scripture quotations are from the Holy Bible, New
International Version®. NIV®. Copyright © 1973, 1978,
1984, 2011 by Biblica, Inc.™ Used by permission of
Zondervan. All rights reserved worldwide.

The text of this Large Print edition is unabridged.
In other aspects, this book may vary
from the original edition.
Printed in the United States of America
on permanent paper.
Set in 16-point Times New Roman type.

ISBN: 978-1-61173-880-3

Library of Congress Cataloging-in-Publication Data

Pettrey, Dani.
Stranded / Dani Pettrey. — Center Point Large Print edition.
pages ; cm.
ISBN 978-1-61173-880-3 (library binding : alk. paper)
1. Missing persons—Fiction. 2. Alaska—Fiction. 3. Large type books.
    I. Title.
PS3616.E89S77 2013b
813'.6—dc23
                                                    2013020493

To Ty:
My blond-haired, blue-eyed,
full-of-life girl.
You are amazing,
and I hope you never forget it!
I love you beyond measure.

Prologue

Abby's head swam, her vision narrowing as she stumbled into her cabin. What had they slipped her and when? Nausea rumbled in her stomach, magnified by the surging waves created by the brewing storm. How could she have been so foolish?

They must have figured out who she was and that she was close to exposing them. They were trying to silence her—though if it came down to it, she preferred death to the alternative.

She lifted the receiver and dialed Darcy's cabin.

Please be there. Darcy had said she'd wait in her room, but the phone kept ringing until it rolled over into voice mail. This wasn't a message for voice mail. Not if they knew who she was. Not if it could lead them to Darcy. She had to find a better way, a safer way to leave a message only Darcy would understand.

She scribbled a quick note. Now . . . where to put it? She grabbed the Gideon Bible from the nightstand, slipped the message inside, set the Bible on her bed, and headed for the door. Only Darcy would know Abby would have no reason to have a Bible on her bed. Turning, she spotted her purse next to the nightstand, grabbed it, and placed it atop the Bible. Never hurt to have a little added protection. Darcy would still recognize the significance.

As she walked around her bed, the ship heaved and she stumbled. She needed help. Wobbling with each step, she managed to grasp the doorknob, the metal cool inside her clammy palm. Her breath quickened. Cracking the door, she peered into the corridor, thankful to find it empty. Stepping into the hall, she moved toward the elevator.

Shadows arched around the bend halfway down the hall, where another corridor intersected it. She halted. Her breath hitched.

A man spoke, his words angry and heated. A second man responded. Her heart seized in her chest. It was them. They were coming.

She turned heel, nearly losing her footing, and braced a supportive hand against the wall, hugging it as she moved as fast as she could in the opposite direction.

The deck door. She'd slip outside and track back toward the elevator, entering on the far end of the corridor. Perhaps the fresh air would help clear her muddled brain.

Sliding the exterior door open, she stepped out onto the deck. Brisk Alaskan air slapped her face but didn't bring the clarity she'd hoped for. Heat still surged along her skin. Seriously, what had they slipped her?

Fighting to remain erect, she gripped the railing

as the tumultuous Alaskan waters crashed against the ship's hull. If she could just make it to the aft door, she'd come out right by the elevator. A few decks up and she'd be surrounded by people.

She took a tentative step, then another. Only sixty feet to the door she needed.

I can do this. For them, she'd fight.

"There." His voice sent ice water through her veins. They'd found her.

Sweat drenching her skin, she broke into a run, but her legs tangled beneath her. She flailed forward, her chin colliding with the rough deck surface. Pain and heat shot through her—her hands and face tingling with the loss of skin.

The footsteps grew heavier, nearer.

She peered through the haze swarming her brain, struggling to focus on the door a mere thirty feet ahead. Pushing up on her bloodied hands, she shot to her feet and stumbled forward. The deck bobbed with the waves, her vision swirling.

Please. Tears pooled in her eyes. She grasped the door handle as an unforgiving hand clamped down hard on her shoulder, pinching her in a viselike grip. Pain radiated down her right side.

"You really thought you could outsmart us, Abby?" He wrenched her back. Grabbing her hair in his fist, he hauled her across the narrow deck.

She scrambled to grasp onto something . . . anything. She kicked as best as her limp legs would allow, fighting whatever was poisoning her system. She mustered a scream, but the ocean's roar swallowed it.

He pressed her against the railing, her back arched over the thick metal beam, her feet dangling in the air. "What a waste."

"Please. No."

"It's too late for that." With a push, he forced her overboard.

Her feet flailed as the air rushed up to meet her. "Nooo!"

1

Darcy strode down the eerily silent corridor, heading for the elevator. Where was Abby? Perhaps, after returning from the day's excursion, she'd been called in to help with the evening's bash on Deck 9. Whatever the cause of Abby's delay, Darcy wasn't going to spend the rest of the night waiting. She had signed on with the *Bering* to aid Abby in an investigation—an investigation she still knew very little about.

Abby's calls from various Alaskan ports over the past few weeks had been brief—telling Darcy about an adventure journalist opportunity aboard Destiny Cruise Line's *Bering* and encouraging her to apply. The last call—the day before Darcy was scheduled to leave California to join the cruise —had been different. It had lasted less than a minute, and there was a heightened urgency to Abby's tone, true fear—unlike anything she'd heard in her former undercover investigation partner before. She wouldn't give any details, only frantically confirmed that Darcy was indeed arriving. Whatever Abby was on to, it was big.

For the first time in three years, the hunger of the hunt was back for her. And the beauty of it was that her adventure journalist "cover" was real.

Her adventure credentials and her ability to be on board the ship within forty-eight hours had impressed Destiny Cruise Line and snagged her the spot. She'd been on board little over twelve hours, and already she was anxious to plunge into whatever Abby needed her help with.

She pressed the Up button, tapping her foot until the elevator doors slid open. She stepped inside, hit the button for level *9,* and leaned against the rail. Who would have thought she'd ever be back on a case? When she left undercover investigative reporting three years ago, she'd vowed never to return. But this was different. Abby needed her help, she wasn't totally under-cover, and most importantly she wasn't working for Kevin—that fact alone made all the difference. Or, at least, she tried to convince herself it did.

The elevator moved slowly, or perhaps the anxiety was getting to her. She'd been so rest-less since she'd left Alaska last December . . . left the McKenna family . . . *left Gage.* She'd expected to stay in contact, but nothing had come —five months with no phone calls, no e-mails . . . nothing.

She jiggled her leg as the numbers overhead lit with each deck passed—*5. 6. 7.*

The elevator jerked to a sudden halt at *8,* jarring her hard against the back rail. An alarm whirred and the lights dimmed.

You've got to be kidding.

She pressed the *9* button. Nothing.

"Oh, come on."

Depressing the emergency call button, she held it in, trying to ward off the encroaching panic.

She was trapped.

* * *

He answered his cell on the third ring, irritated at the intrusion. "This better be important."

"We've got a situation," Jeremy said.

He stood and stalked away from the bed. "I thought you were handling the situation." Isn't that what Jeremy had promised—to take care of *his* mistake?

"I was," Jeremy mumbled. "I am, but . . ."

"But?"

"We've hit a complication."

There's a shock. It was always something with Jeremy. Why he'd trusted him to run things this long . . . That was *his* mistake. "What kind of complication?" He retrieved his whiskey glass from the wet bar.

12

"Someone sounded the man-overboard alarm."

"Where are you?"

"There's no need for you to come. Just tell me what to do."

"Obviously following orders isn't your strong suit." He finished his drink in a single draught, the golden liquid burning its way down his throat and spreading across his chest.

"But, boss . . ."

"Give me your coordinates. Now." He kept his voice even, tight. No sense losing his temper until the matter at hand was resolved.

Jeremy gave up the coordinates.

"I'll see you soon." He cut off the call.

2

Abby came to, nausea rolling in her belly. The ground purred beneath her. Muffled voices spoke from somewhere nearby. She lifted her head off the cold, damp surface as darkness swirled around her.

Her sopping clothes clung to her shivering body. *Where am I?* Peeling the matted strands of wet hair from her face, her view cleared, and reality struck like a death knell. She wasn't dead. This was much, much worse.

"I'm sorry, boss. Someone sounded the alarm," Jeremy's voice quivered.

The man whose voice set terror aflame in her blood was afraid? Who was this other man?

"That's all I've been hearing from you lately. *'I'm sorry.'* Do you have any idea the strings I had to pull to cover up this mistake of yours? I might as well be conducting a bloody orchestra." The man speaking stalked into view a mere twenty feet in front of her, but the night masked his features in shadows.

She looked up, and rain splattered her face. She was still outside. But the purring? *A boat.* Maybe a rescue boat. No, this certainly wasn't a rescue.

"You." His voice was deep, cut hard with the edge of anger.

She stiffened, fearful he was addressing her, but he stalked the opposite way, toward someone beyond her line of sight. "Get going. You've just been promoted."

Whomever he was addressing didn't argue. Didn't say a word. A moment later, a small motor sounded and quickly disappeared into the distance.

She inched toward the boat's side. If she could reach the water, perhaps she stood a chance.

"If I don't go back . . ." Jeremy spluttered.

A shot pierced the night.

Fear ricocheted through Abby's dull limbs, and adrenaline propelled her forward, the rough deck tearing at her already-battered knees.

"And where do you think you're going?" A gun cocked beside her ear as the man knelt over her.

* * *

Moisture slithered down Darcy's back as she sat, sweating, in a stuck elevator. She'd pressed every button on the control panel. She couldn't reach the elevator ceiling to see if there was a way to climb out. The rising heat . . .

What if there was a fire on board and she was trapped inside this metal box? *Don't go there, Darcy.*

She was stuck until someone complained the elevator wasn't working, and the ship's crew fixed the problem. *Malfunction.* Maybe if she repeated it enough, it would drown out the panic hissing in her ear. The air was growing stale— suffocating. She hated enclosed spaces. Hated being surrounded by darkness. The dim emergency lighting certainly didn't count as light—she could barely see her hands balled at her sides.

Uncurling her fingers, she lifted her arm and depressed the small light button on her watch, illuminating the iridescent face. *One hour, eight minutes and counting.* She'd loathed every second of it.

Finally, with a jerk, the elevator resumed rising and the regular lighting kicked back in. She surged to her feet and smoothed out her blouse. She was sweating, flushed, and going to look it when the elevator doors opened.

The doors slid open, and she was met by a worried crew member—a man, close to her age. He was tall and slender, with wavy chestnut hair and matching brown eyes. "Are you okay, miss?"

"I'm fine." She practically bolted from the elevator, gulping in deep breaths of fresher air. "What happened?"

"The man-overboard alarm was triggered, and I'm afraid when that kicks in, it's just like the fire alarm has been set off. We have one central alarm system on board, and it automatically shuts the elevators down."

"Man overboard?"

"Yes, miss."

People began to get on the elevator she'd just escaped from. Were they *crazy?* She scanned the crowd, the worried faces, and realized the problem. They were clamoring for the elevators because they wanted to check on their loved ones—make certain it wasn't them that had gone overboard. Nearly all were elderly. No doubt the younger ones had already taken to the stairs. They moved past her until the elevator was stuffed to capacity and the doors slid shut.

"Do you know who went overboard?" she asked.

The man shrugged. "No clue." He signaled another group onto the next available elevator. "I've been busy seeing to the ship's safety, and then resetting the alarm once the person was secure."

"Person . . . secure?"

"The rescue crew successfully retrieved the person who went overboard." He looked back at the diminishing crowd, relief finally settling on his brow.

"That's great."

Refusing to get back on the elevator, she headed straight for the medical clinic. If she wasn't going to catch up with Abby tonight, the least she could do was investigate the overboard incident.

Exiting on Deck 7, she headed straight for the medical clinic. Whoever had gone overboard would be brought there immediately to be checked over by a doctor.

She rounded the hall and to her surprise found the clinic dark.

Curious . . .

She tried the knob. Locked.

Surely the rescue crew would have the rescued passenger back on board by now.

She waited, pacing the corridor for several minutes, but no one appeared.

She scurried back to the ninth level, hoping the man who rescued her might have some answers by now, but he was gone. Nearly everyone was— no doubt having returned to their cabins after the frightening episode.

Moving out onto the exterior deck, Darcy

peered over the side. Rain pelted her face, cooling her skin. The spring storm that had been threatening all day had finally hit.

She scanned the choppy water, looking for any sign of the rescue crew but finding only blackness. She walked the circumference of the ship, searching all four points—port, starboard, bow, and stern—and saw nothing but the tumultuous sea. Where had the rescue crew taken the victim if not to the clinic?

She peered across the waves from the aft of the ship, at the lights fading in the distance. They'd been near land. *Perhaps* . . .

"This is your captain speaking," a baritone voice piped over the intercom. "I want to thank you all for complying so willingly with our emergency protocol. I am pleased to announce that the young lady who fell overboard has been successfully retrieved and taken to a nearby hospital. Please rest assured we are back on course and will dock in Yancey shortly before dawn. Now get some rest. It looks to be a beautiful day in Yancey tomorrow."

Darcy swallowed. *Young lady?*

She stared back at the lights nearly swallowed by the darkness. Could it have been Abby?

3

The call had come in at a quarter to one. A group of teens camping in Tariuk Island's rugged mountains had thought a late-night rafting race on Class IV rapids was a good idea.

Gage stood at the edge of the foaming waters, the sound of a young female's sobbing not far away.

"The raft is overturned and pinned against the rocks. Two of the young men went out to help and were swept away in the current. One showed up about a half a mile downstream, battered on the shore. The other hasn't been seen since," Gage's older brother, Cole, said.

Cole was head of Yancey's volunteer search and rescue crew, which consisted of all Gage's siblings; Deputy Sheriff Landon Grainger, his youngest sister's fiancé; and Last Frontier Adventures' employee and good family friend, Jake Westin. In addition, a number of auxiliary volunteers were combing the shores, but the technical rescues were up to the trained core circled around Cole at the moment. Floodlights shone down on them and fanned out across the raging water.

Sheriff Bill Slidell and the rest of his deputies had the teens corralled. No sense letting any of them near the water again. The last thing they needed was more casualties. The spring wind howling through the valley lashed against Gage's cheeks along with the dashing rain. The mid-May water temperatures were likely over freezing with all the melting snow working its way down the mountain face.

"According to the group, there were three teens and a kid in the raft."

"A kid?" Piper's eyes widened.

"Barry Moore thought he was being kind bringing his kid brother Tommy along for the weekend."

Gage watched the emotion swell in his sister's eyes.

"Two of the four made it back to shore. We're looking for Barry, his brother Tommy, and the second rescuer. Water is too shallow for divers, so this will be a swift-water rescue with no eyes on the victims, which makes you point, Gage."

He nodded. "We need to set up secure lines running from the site of the incident to a half mile downstream. We search in teams of two, always anchored in." He looked at his sister Kayden. "How long?"

She looked at her watch. "Call came in twenty minutes ago. Accident occurred at least ten before that."

Which meant the odds were high they were looking at retrieval, not rescue. Factoring in the strength of the rapids, the temps of the water, and the lack of daylight, chances were slim they'd be able to do any good. But they'd give it their best. Gage lifted his whistle. "Signal if you see anything, and we'll move to you. No one goes under without the full team in line-up position. Understood?"

Everyone nodded their consent and set to work.

The rapids' pull was strong, buckling Gage's knees as he waded in full dry suit out toward the wreckage. Piper was on lights and communication. The closer they came to what remained of the tattered raft, the more incensed Gage became. "What were they thinking?"

"They weren't," Kayden said beside him. "It's clear from the empty beer cans, they've all been drinking."

"Barry had no right endangering his little brother like that." Gage's gloved fingers snagged hold of the outer edge of the raft. Working with his sister, they peeled the battered and frayed raft from the boulder it'd been plastered to, hoping they'd find Barry or Tommy clinging to the rock beneath it—but no luck.

"Angle the light down," he hollered over the rapids, directing Piper with the wave of his arm. The beam slid down the rock's surface. "On the swell beneath," he directed, his headlamp too dim to penetrate more than a few inches below the tumultuous surface. "Pan to the right."

The shaft of light moved, and Gage's breath caught—the pale face of a little boy. Gage blew three long whistles and repeated. His team shifted to assist.

Once everything was secured and everyone was in position, Gage dove beneath the surface. Tommy's hair floated above his head, swaying with the river's pull, and his little arms swayed out at his sides.

Gage dove deeper, his headlamp illuminating only inches in front of him. He followed Tommy's small body down. His right leg was free but was being battered against the rock with each new crushing rapid swirling in. His left leg was pinned between the large boulder and a smaller one nestled beside it.

Gage surfaced, gulping in air. "He's pinned. We're going to need tools."

Cole, being the expert diver—even if they were only dealing with a depth of four feet—swapped places with Kayden and accompanied Gage back under the water to free Tommy's leg from the boulder's crushing hold.

Working together, they managed to free Tommy and bring him to the surface.

Gage handed Tommy's limp body to Cole, who passed the boy down the line toward shore.

"Noooo," a woman wailed as Tommy's battered body reached land.

Sheriff Slidell quickly intercepted Tommy's

mom, Gail, who'd arrived on the scene along with her husband, Tom. Slidell tugged her away from her son so the paramedics could work.

Gage's heart wrenched at the mother's anguished wails. He knew firsthand the torment of watching your child die.

Two hours later, Gage and the crew returned to Yancey's fire station, where the team stored the majority of their gear.

Cole's hand clamped on his shoulder. "We brought both boys home."

It was true, they'd pulled the brothers from the water, but it brought Gage little consolation. Both boys were dead. A group of teenagers' idea of fun had destroyed a family.

"They had no business being out there. They didn't have the skills."

"I agree." Cole sat on the bench beside him. "They were drinking. It impaired their logic, and what they expected would be a fun ride ended up killing Barry and Tommy, and we still have one teen missing."

"Maybe I shouldn't go tomorrow. I should stay and help find the missing boy."

"No. We made a commitment to the *Bering*. You go. There are plenty of us to comb the water and the shores. Besides, we both know that there's little chance we'll ever find him."

It was a sad statistic, but unfortunately his

brother was right. The rapids led out to the Gulf of Alaska and on to the Pacific Ocean. Unless the teen's body was pinned somewhere beneath the surface that they'd overlooked, chances he'd still be found were slim.

"You think they learned anything?" Water safety was nothing to be trifled with. Treating it lightly endangered not only your own life but the lives of others—the teen rescuer still missing had reportedly tried to warn the others of the potential dangers, and when they didn't listen, he'd been the first in the water to try and help. He'd paid with his life for their foolishness.

Cole leaned forward, resting his hands on his thighs. "I imagine none of their lives will be the same. At least I pray that's the case."

* * *

Gage pulled to a stop before his rental cabin and glanced up at the darkness overhead. It befuddled him how his intelligent siblings could worship a God that let children die so senselessly. He had to admit that last winter—being around Darcy, witnessing the passion and depth of her faith— he'd actually begun to waver in his steadfast refusal to believe, but tonight brought all his hurt and anger roiling right back to the surface.

Stalking across the muddy drive, he climbed the wooden porch steps to his cabin. Flipping on the light, he kicked the door shut behind him and dropped his gear bag on the ground, wishing he could shuck the crushing weight constricting his chest.

He'd thought he'd finally reached a point of functioning, of existing, and then Darcy St. James had strolled into his life—barreled into it was more like it. She'd stayed barely a month, but it'd been more than enough time for her to anchor herself into what remained of his heart.

When she'd returned to California, he'd assured himself everything would go back to normal— well, at least to routine—but five months and counting and he still couldn't shake her from his mind.

He glanced at the clock. Nearly five a.m. He was scheduled to report to the *Bering* at eight. Should he even bother trying to sleep?

With a sigh, he tossed his clothes on the floor and plopped on the bed, figuring a couple hours were better than nothing. Rain slashed against his windows, dripping off the gutters. Tommy's pale face would haunt his dreams.

He rolled over, incensed anger biting at him. But the *Bering* job was just what he needed. The first day of a new journey—a ten-day voyage across the Bering Sea, leading adventure activities and kayak excursions for the passengers. He hoped new places and new faces would prove enough distraction for him to finally erase Darcy St. James from his mind.

Well, maybe not erase entirely—she was

awfully pretty to think on. The problem was the *amount* of time he thought about her—how her eyes lit when she was on to something, the cute dimple that formed in her right cheek when she smiled, and the way his heart beat a little harder when she laughed.

He needed a diversion, and Kayden's on-site excursion proposal finally being picked up by Destiny Cruise Line provided the perfect one.

Kayden didn't even bat an eye when he'd so readily offered to take point on the trial run, but she wasn't the sister who would notice. Piper was the sister who saw things a little too clearly, and she'd definitely questioned his eager acceptance of the lead role. She knew he was running, but what choice did he have?

Nothing could happen with Darcy. Even if he was ready for another stab at love, it could never be with her.

4

Early the next morning Darcy returned to Abby's cabin, rapping impatiently on the door. She gulped down another swallow of her macchiato, trying to shake off the fatigue of a sleepless night, hoping the caffeine would give her the boost she so desperately needed. This had to be the sixth—no, the *seventh*—time she'd tried

Abby's cabin, and each time Abby didn't answer, her heart had dropped a little more.

Come on, Abby. Enough is enough.

It was hardly the first time Abby had missed a meeting or even the first time she'd disappeared for a short while during an undercover assignment. Abby was a bulldog, and when she caught the scent of something, she ran with it—often neglecting to notify others, especially her partner.

Darcy sighed. She wasn't technically Abby's partner, at least not anymore. Hadn't been for three years.

She knocked again, louder this time. *Where are you?*

"This would work a lot better if you let me in first."

Darcy spun around. The woman was young—early twenties, at most—brunette, and wiry.

"You're Abby's roommate?" she guessed.

"Guilty. I'm Pam." She stepped around Darcy and slid her key card in the lock. The light flashed green, and the woman stepped inside, flicking on the overhead light.

Without waiting for an invitation, Darcy followed her in. The beds were made—the right one had a series of dresses flung across it, and the left, a purse she assumed was Abby's.

"So . . . what do you want?" Abby's roommate seemed a little annoyed, but Darcy wasn't going to miss this opportunity.

"I was just wondering when you saw Abby last. I'm new to the ship, and we arranged to meet last night, but she never showed."

"Yesterday morning. I worked until one last night"—she smoothed her hair—"and I'm just getting back. I don't know"—she looked around the room—"whether Abby's been here or not."

"So . . . have you heard any details about the person that went overboard last night?"

"Nah, the *Bering* is pretty tight-lipped about anything out of the ordinary—anything that might reflect badly on the cruise line." She sat on her dress-covered bed, clearly impatient. "Is that all? I need to get some sleep before my next shift."

"Could it have been Abby?"

"No, I think I would have heard if it was her."

"But I've searched everywhere for her. Where else could she be?"

Pam released an exasperated sigh. "Look, I don't know where Abby is or who went overboard. What's your deal anyway?"

"I'm a journalist."

"Of course you are." Pam climbed into bed without moving any of the dresses. "That explains all the questions."

"I'm here to cover the new hands-on adventures the *Bering*'s offering. I set up an interview with Abby for last night—my first of interviewing everyone involved with the new excursions—but she never showed."

"Maybe she got a better offer." Pam grabbed a lotion bottle off the nightstand.

"Meaning?"

"Meaning, maybe she met some cute passenger and hooked up."

"Oh." *Not Abby.*

"As for who went overboard . . ." Pam squirted the white liquid onto her palm and began working it through her fingers. "I wouldn't worry too much about it. Captain said they'd been rescued and taken to the local hospital. Now, if you'll excuse me . . ." She set the lotion back on the nightstand and clicked off the bedside lamp.

"Right."

In the faint glow of the light over the door, Darcy glanced at Abby's purse on her bed and then to Pam, who'd rolled over with her back to her. Leaning over, Darcy snatched Abby's purse and tucked it under her arm. "Sorry to bother you." Pam didn't stir. "I'll just see myself out."

Reentering her room, Darcy flipped the overhead switch and plopped on the bed, trying to quell the butterflies darting about her belly. *She's probably just stumbled onto a new lead and lost track of time . . . maybe trying to track down whoever fell overboard.*

Taking a deep breath, she dumped the contents of Abby's purse on the bed and sorted through it.

A tube of lip gloss, a couple pens, a handful of blank index cards, contact drops . . . Nothing out of the ordinary. She shoved it all back in the purse and set the canvas bag aside.

An hour later, Darcy waited for the *Bering* to lower its gangplank and allow cruise passengers off into the port town of Yancey. She had been up all night but couldn't even think of sleeping now, and she couldn't just sit around praying Abby showed. She had to do *something*.

With the excursion meeting still several hours away, she headed into Yancey under the guise of reporting on one of the *Bering*'s port stops. Fortunately, having spent a month there last winter, she could easily come up with a fluff piece to suit Destiny Cruise Line's publicity team without having to actually put any research into it. Instead, she'd pay a visit to a friend.

During her time in Yancey, she'd come to love the town—and one family in particular—quite deeply. She'd hoped to return, but she'd envisioned it being under much different circumstances. Foolishly, she'd dreamt it would be at Gage's invitation, but after five months and still no word from him, she'd obviously misread his signals. Though, she supposed, she was partially to blame.

She could have called, but she hadn't wanted to press. Gage needed space, needed time to heal from old wounds that were still very raw. His silence had left her lonely and restless, and very much ready for a change when Abby's call for assistance had come.

Darcy hurried up the hill from the marina into town. It looked so different in May than it had in December. The snow was gone, and beautiful red and yellow tulips dotted the planting beds leading up the main walk. She headed straight for the sheriff's station, fighting the longing to at least duck into the McKennas' shop. How could she come to Yancey and not see Gage?

Her gaze fixed on their shop sign in the distance —*Last Frontier Adventures* scrolled in bold blue letters. Her resolve wavered as a wealth of memories came flooding back—one in particular tugging at her heart: Gage McKenna bent over his son's grave. Such a strong man, broken by the tragic loss of a child. She'd wanted nothing more than to race to him and shelter him in her arms, but he'd have balked at her sympathy, at her attempts to comfort him. He didn't want comforting. He wanted restitution.

So much anger and bitterness in such a tender heart—it broke her's. If only she had the power to fix things, to help Gage see how much God loved him. But God was the last "person" Gage wanted to discuss, and she was the last person he'd accept comfort from.

Taken aback by the powerful anguish that

thoughts of Gage McKenna still dredged up in her heart, she stepped into the sheriff's station praying Deputy Landon Grainger was in.

* * *

"Are you sure you don't want one of us to go with you?" Piper asked, not relinquishing hold of Gage's duffel just yet.

They stood huddled on the front porch of his cabin, his sisters hemming and hawing over what he'd packed or possibly forgotten.

"Piper, I'm not four. I can handle this." He tugged his duffel back.

"Of course you can." She smiled. "I just thought you might like . . ."

He cocked his head with a knowing grin. "Someone watching over me?" He slipped the duffel strap over his shoulder.

"Someone to help." She crossed her arms, leaning against the porch rail as the sun rose higher in the sky.

"You will be helping every time we dock in port." It would only be a day before he'd see them again.

"He's a big boy," Kayden said, hopping onto the rail. "He can handle this."

"I know." Piper nibbled her bottom lip.

She did *know*. That was the problem. She saw things, heard things beyond the spoken. Not in any magical sort of way. She could simply read people, knew when they were hurting. She

32

claimed it was a gift from God, but he preferred to view it as an annoyance—especially when it centered on him. Piper knew Darcy had gotten to him, and it was clear she didn't like his response, his running from his feelings. But there was nothing else to be done. Piper would eventually understand that or she'd at least have to learn to live with it—because, as tantalizing as the prospect might appear during his greatest moments of weakness, nothing would be happening between him and Darcy St. James.

"Any word on the missing teen?"

Kayden shook her head. "Cole and Jake are out there with a full team of volunteers, and a swift-water-rescue team from Kodiak arrived early this morning to lend a hand."

Gage shook his head, knowing they were in for a long and most likely disappointing day.

"Are *you* guys all set?" he asked, shifting the conversation to the upcoming cruise. "Land part of the package ready to go?"

"Jake says we're good to go," Kayden said with the trace of indifference that lingered whenever she spoke of Jake.

"Good, then I know it'll be done right." It was true, and it allowed him a jab at his sister.

"Very funny. We both know I'm in charge of details," she said.

And completely skeptical about Jake's ability, though the man had never proven anything less than stellar in his work since coming on board with LFA nearly three years ago.

"Trust me, we all know what a *boss* you are." Piper nudged her sister with a smirk.

"Just like we all know what a mom you are." Kayden nudged back.

"I just want to make sure everyone is taken care of," Piper huffed.

"So do I," Kayden said. "Just in a different way."

"You're both mother hens, and I'm fleeing the coop." Gage bounded down the porch steps with a grin.

"Just remember if it hadn't been for these mother hens, you'd have been without socks for the duration of the cruise," Kayden called after him.

He tried to muster a retort, but she was right. It was a highly annoying habit.

* * *

"Darcy St. James, is that you?"

The sound of Landon's voice filled her with relief. She turned and smiled at the deputy—tall, chestnut brown hair, and every bit as ruggedly handsome as she remembered.

"What are you doing back in this neck of the woods?"

"Another investigation."

"Here I was hoping you'd come back to visit."

"I wish that were the case."

"Come on into my office." He signaled for her to follow. Deputy Earl Hansen eyed her from the front desk, clearly trying to place where he recognized her from.

She followed Landon down the hall to his office on the left. He shut the door after them and gestured to the open chair. "Take a seat."

"Thanks." She sat as Landon stepped around the black metal desk and sank into his swivel chair.

"How can I help you?"

She quickly brought him up to speed. "It's probably nothing. The ship is large—well, fairly large—and Abby . . . When her scent fixes on something . . . It's just the timing of a woman going overboard and my not being able to find Abby . . ." She was rambling. She always rambled when nervous.

Landon leaned forward. "What cruise ship did you say?"

"The *Bering*. Why?"

He sat back, shaking his head with a grin. "You're not going to believe this, but Gage is starting work on the *Bering* today."

"What?" Gage McKenna on the same cruise ship as her?

"Kayden got this idea a couple seasons back about staffing an excursion leader on the ship, so once they dock they can get on with the excursion quicker. The prep, safety instructions, and

35

paperwork are all done on the ship ahead of time."

"I've seen different themes like that on cruises—golf, photography, wine . . ."

"Exactly. That's what gave Kayden the idea in the first place. Then it was simply a matter of getting a cruise line to give the idea a shot. Destiny Cruise Line agreed and slotted them on their signature Alaskan ship, the *Bering*, for their photo-and-adventure cruise. Gage is in charge of adventure activities aboard the ship and several overnight excursions while they're docked."

"So he'll be on the ship today?" She tried to ignore how her heart quickened at the thought of seeing him again.

Landon nodded. "What are the chances?"

Slim to none, which meant God was involved. But why? Why Gage? He didn't want anything to do with Him.

Though, it would be nice to have at least one friendly face on board—that is, *if* Gage chose to be friendly. The two of them were always setting off sparks. It was simply a matter of what kind —intense attraction or WWIII. Only time would tell.

"I'll give Kodiak Hospital a call." Landon lifted the receiver. "I just need Abby's full name."

"Her real name is Abigail Tritt, though she's always gone by Abby. But she was using the name Abby Walsh."

"Okay, I'll give them a quick call while you're

here, see if we can't get her on the phone for you."

"That'd be great." But the gnawing in her gut said it wasn't going to happen. She simply couldn't shake the feeling that something was very off.

She fidgeted with her purse strap while Landon placed the call. Her hand stilled when his face fell and then tightened around the strap as confusion filled his handsome features.

"What do you mean no one was brought in after falling overboard last night?

"Are you certain?

"What about for near-drowning? Maybe the cruise staff tried to downplay the fact she'd fallen overboard.

"The records show that no young woman was brought in last night?

"Can you check with the doc on call last night just to be sure? Thanks. You can ring me back at the station." He hung up and looked at Darcy.

"I heard." Exactly what she'd feared.

"Maybe they took her somewhere else."

"They didn't bring her back to the ship's clinic, and Kodiak was the nearest hospital."

"The nurse I spoke with wasn't on duty last night. She was just going by the computer. She's going to check with the crew from last night's shift and get back with me. I'll get word to you if I hear anything."

"Thank you."

"Is there anything else I can do?"

"Not at this point."

"So what next?"

"I show up at the excursion meeting and pray Abby is there."

5

Gage followed Employee Liaison Theodora Mullins to the Caribou meeting room. "The excursion team has use of this room for the next hour. That should give you plenty of time to coordinate with the team."

"The team?"

"The *Bering* caters to a luxury crowd. If they are going camping, they'll want to do it in style—which is why our activities director, in conjunction with our usual excursion liaison, has coordinated a support team for you."

"Last Frontier Adventures provides a complete land support team that will be meeting the *Bering* at each excursion port."

"For the adventure portion, yes. I'm referring to your camping support team."

You pitched a tent and made some grub. How much support was required?

"You'll be assigned a medic."

"We're all first-aid certified."

"Yes, but Clint Walker is also a certified

personal trainer and massage therapist. He can assist the passengers with any aches and strains they may encounter after their day of *roughing* it."

He didn't particularly care for the tone Mullins used when talking about his living.

"You will also have a gourmet chef and two activities engineers escorting you."

"A gourmet chef?" These people really did travel in style.

"Yes. Unfortunately we've had a recent shift in our excursion support team," she said, rounding the bend.

"Shift?" Gage asked with hesitation as he spotted the meeting room at the end of the corridor. A carved scene of a caribou surrounded by evergreens graced the wooden door.

"Our excursion chef and one of our activities engineers have recently departed the *Bering*. Didn't even bother giving proper notice . . ." She took a deep breath and exhaled. "But no matter. Replacements have already been found. Oh, and I almost forgot . . ." she said, opening the door. "You'll have a reporter joining you."

"A reporter. For wha—?" He took a step into the room and froze. *Darcy St. James.*

She stood, and his heart seized, his mouth going dry. *It can't be.* "What are you doing here?"

"I'm covering the exciting new hands-on adventure angle for the *Bering*."

Of all the reporters in all the world . . .

Mullins looked between the two. "You two know each other?"

"We—" he began.

"I covered the Midnight Sun Extreme Freeride Competition in his hometown this winter," Darcy cut in.

There'd been so much more. "And—"

"And"—she thrust out her hand—"it's great to see you again, Gage."

He cocked his head. What was going on? Why was she so exuberant, and why did she keep cutting him off? He clasped her hand in his, trying to ignore the softness of her skin.

She pulled her hand back and shoved it in her pants pocket.

"Now that we're all caught up . . ." Mullins pushed a red folder toward each of them and shifted her attention to the door. Two men entered—both tall and fairly athletic in build. "Ted, have you brought George up to speed?"

Ted nodded. "We're good to go."

"Wonderful." She turned to Gage. "These are the activities engineers I was telling you about. Ted Norris has been with us since the *Bering* first launched, and George Cooper is joining us for the first time, just like you." Turning to Ted and George, she waved toward Gage. "This is Gage McKenna."

"Nice to meet you both." Gage shook each man's hand in turn.

Mullins glanced at the clock over the door and frowned. "Looks like Clint is late, as usual. Let's get started. Ted, you can catch him up."

Ted settled into his seat with a nod.

Mullins tugged the hem of her navy blue jacket and began. "As you all know, this is a new venture for the *Bering*. One that a lot of weight is resting on. It's no secret that the *Bering* hasn't been performing at peak levels. Our numbers are down, and headquarters believes these hands-on adventure experiences are the answer to drawing in a new, vibrant crowd and thereby boosting our numbers. To that end, they have hired Last Frontier Adventures to handle the kayak and adventure excursions. Alaskan Adventure, our normal provider, will still be outfitting and running the photography excursions, as well as providing support personnel."

The door opened and another man entered. He was tall like the other two, but much more muscular. Had to be the personal trainer.

"Clint . . ." Mullins rested her hand on her hip, the motion exposing the gold braided belt at her thick waist. "So nice of you to join us."

"I was catching Phillip up on how the excursions run." He looked over his shoulder at the robust man trailing behind.

"Phillip," Mullins said as the squat man entered, "thank you for being so flexible. Trent has assured me he'll have a replacement on board by the next cruise."

"It's no problem." Phillip plopped into the first open seat. "Might actually be fun to spend some time outdoors."

Clint paused beside Darcy's chair and smiled. "And, who do we have here?"

"This is Darcy St. James," Mullins said. "She's a reporter."

"Journalist," Darcy corrected.

Gage arched a brow.

"Clint Walker, at your service." Clint slid into the open seat beside her. "A journalist with who?"

"I freelance. Primarily with adventure magazines like *Ski Times*, *Adventure World* . . ."

"Ms. James will be accompanying you all on the adventure excursions," Mullins explained. "She'll be giving a firsthand account of what future passengers can experience and enjoy. Headquarters thought it would be great for publicity."

"Wonderful." Clint smiled at Darcy in a way that made Gage uneasy. "Looking forward to getting to know you better."

Darcy smiled. "You too."

"Well, now that we're *all* here . . ." Mullins said, reaching for the stack of papers on the table in front of her, "let's proceed."

"All here?" Darcy tilted her head, a mixture of confusion and worry clouding her vivid blue eyes.

Gage had forgotten how startlingly beautiful she was.

"I briefly met the excursion chef when I came aboard yesterday. Abby . . . I believe," Darcy said, her tone relaxed—a stark contrast to the brief flash of worry he'd seen in her eyes but a moment ago. "She isn't here yet."

Mullins lifted the stack of papers. "Ms. Walsh has decided to leave Destiny's employment. Phillip here"—she indicated the robust man with a lift of her chin—"will be taking over her role as excursion chef until a full-time replacement can be found."

"Left?" Darcy frowned. "But I just saw her yesterday. I was supposed to interview her last night, but she never showed."

"It was a very recent decision." Mullins tapped the stack of papers against the table, getting them perfectly in line. "Phillip has graciously agreed to transition from the ship kitchen to the excursions for the time being, so we're all set."

Darcy shifted forward, leaning toward Mullins across the oval table. "May I ask why Ms. Walsh left?"

Mullins chuckled with a shake of her bottle-red head. "You're definitely a journalist." The other men joined in her laughter.

Darcy smiled, but Gage didn't miss the tightness edging her mouth. "This doesn't have anything to do with the woman who went overboard last night, does it?"

"Someone fell overboard?" Gage asked, his brows arching. *Not a great start.* This was supposed to be the trip that erased Darcy from his mind, that gave his heart a break and let him immerse himself in ten days of full-on adventure. If some woman had gone overboard . . . His mind flashed back to the rapids and Tommy Moore's lifeless form.

"The woman who fell overboard is perfectly fine," Mullins said with utmost confidence.

"Yes, but was it her?" Darcy pressed. "Is that why Ms. Walsh isn't here?"

Mullins' shoulders squared. "Like I said, Ms. Walsh decided to leave Destiny's employ, and that is all you need to know."

Darcy opened her mouth, but Mullins held up a hand. "I realize you are a journalist and overly curious by nature, but who went overboard has nothing to do with the job we hired you to do. I suggest you focus on the task at hand. The first excursion heads out bright and early tomorrow morning, and we have plenty of items to go over." Without giving Darcy a chance to respond, she continued, "Now if everyone will turn to the first page of your orientation glossary, you will see the activities and excursion schedule for this cruise."

* * *

Darcy didn't hear another word Mullins said. Exhaustion eroded her focus, and concern for Abby's safety consumed her thoughts. Either

Abby had fallen overboard or she'd gone missing by some other means—in any case, they were covering up the truth with this "decided to leave" story. There was no way Abby would call her in to help with an undercover investigation and then just take off. Something had happened to Abby.

Darcy had a difficult decision to make and precious little time to make it. She could stay on the ship and try to continue Abby's investigation with what little she knew about it, *or* she could get off and hope to track Abby on her own.

She knew the prudent course was to stay on board, to track Abby by her last whereabouts, by following the story she'd been working. If she got off the ship, she could completely lose the trail.

If Abby had fallen overboard and was safely recovering at Kodiak Hospital, she'd want Darcy to continue and would find a way to get word to her. On the other hand, if something sinister had happened to Abby, the people responsible were on the *Bering*, and that made her decision clear. She needed to stay the course.

Darcy shifted, trying to ignore Gage's gaze resting on her. He was scrutinizing her. He sensed more was happening than she let on. She could see it in his stare, read it in the tautness of his broad shoulders.

She shifted. Her real intentions aboard the *Bering* were none of his business. As far as he was concerned, she'd come to report on the adventures and was curious about a missing excursion chef. The fact that the hunger of the hunt, the urge to dig, was nipping at her heels once again could remain her secret. He'd only judge her for it. He'd made it abundantly clear when they met last winter in Yancey that he loathed what she did for a living—loathed the lies reporters told, loathed anyone fake or overly ambitious—and after meeting his ex, she understood why.

Of course, she'd tried explaining she was different, but in the end, it had taken more than words. Finally, throughout the murder investigation, when they'd awkwardly been paired to work together, she'd begun to prove she truly was different, that she had morals and that there were lines she refused to cross, even if it meant her job. But *now* . . .

She stiffened. Nothing had changed. She still had lines she wouldn't cross. If he was too bullheaded to see that . . .

She exhaled. She was getting ahead of herself. Gage hadn't said a word, and already he had her twisted in knots. How did he do that? And why did she care when he hadn't even bothered to pick up the phone in five months?

"All right," Mullins said, slipping the papers back into her leather attaché case. "I think that covers everything. Any questions?"

6

Darcy had barely made it around the corner when Gage's hand clasped lightly on her arm. His palms were calloused—no doubt from his daily kayak rides. But his touch felt incredible all the same. "We need to talk."

Pulling her thoughts from the warm, innately protective touch of his skin on hers, she glanced around, her gaze fixing on Mullins, Ted, and George headed in their direction. "Fine, but not here." She spotted the stairwell door out of the corner of her eye and moved toward it. Tugging Gage inside, she shut the door quietly behind them. With every inch blanketed in a dull grayish-white—like a dirty blank canvas long neglected—it was the only space on the ship she'd seen devoid of cheery color.

"I knew it," he blurted. "You're on a case, aren't you?"

"Shhh," she hissed, stepping to the metal rail. Leaning over, she glanced up and down, and relief filled her at finding no one present. She spun back to Gage, a mix of irritation and attraction heating her limbs. "Do you think you could tone it down a bit?"

Gage leaned against the wall, one knee bent, the sole of his Merrell boots braced against the textured concrete. "I thought you gave up undercover reporting." Disapproval clung to his tone.

Of course it did. He'd been judging her since he'd stepped foot in the meeting room. She only prayed no one else picked up on the fact that they knew each other far better than she'd let on. Explaining her prolonged stay in Yancey and the active role she'd played in a murder investigation would only highlight the truth and depth of her reporting background. As far as anyone on the *Bering* was concerned, she was an adventure journalist and always had been—and she needed to keep it that way.

"Darc?" His voice was as deep and warm as she remembered it—like rich, cascading caramel. "You were saying . . . ?"

Of course he wasn't going to let this drop. "I had . . . I have . . . I mean . . ." She took a steadying breath, trying to compose her thoughts. What was that tantalizing scent? She inhaled again, forcing herself not to lean into his muscular body. *Spicy vanilla aftershave?* The man was flat-out dizzying.

"Had?" he pressed.

"My friend Abby . . ."

"The woman who left the *Bering*?"

She blew a stray lock of hair from her face. "Supposedly."

"Supposedly?" He linked his arms across his

chest, his sculpted forearms front and center. "She is your friend?"

She diverted her eyes while trying to decide exactly how much she wanted to confide in him, or rather, how much she *should* confide. "Look . . ." She shoved her hands in her pockets. Why couldn't she concentrate around the man? It was utterly ridiculous. "I'm not comfortable discussing this here."

"Fine, let's go to my cabin."

"Now?" *Great.* The two of them in even closer quarters—the exact opposite of what her heart needed. After five months apart without a word, she'd thought she could manage her emotions better. Frustration bubbled inside. She needed to be focused on finding Abby, not explaining herself to Gage.

He smiled. "No time like the present."

Gage walked with Darcy to his cabin, his pulse increasing just being in her presence. He balled his hands into fists. It was going to be a grueling ten days.

She kept her shoulders stiff, irritation lacing her brow. She clearly didn't want to explain, but if she planned on using LFA's excursions to conduct her investigation, at the very least he deserved an explanation.

Opening his cabin door, he gestured with his arm. "After you."

She glanced up at him as she stepped past, the top of her head not quite reaching the bottom of his chin. She was a petite thing, but he'd never met anyone more full of fire—with the exception of his sisters, perhaps.

He shut the door. "So, what's this all about?"

She strolled about the tiny confines, clearly stalling.

"Darcy."

She stopped and plopped down into one of the sitting area's egg-shaped chairs.

He leaned against the desk's edge, trying to keep some distance between them. "What's really going on, and who's Abby?"

"Abby is my old undercover reporting partner."

"Reporting partner?"

"Yeah."

"So you've decided to go back." He didn't bother trying to mask his disappointment.

"Abby and I haven't seen each other in years, but she asked for my help." She explained how Abby had called out of the blue and asked for Darcy's assistance on her undercover investigation, told her about the adventure journalist job she could use as a cover.

"But I thought you'd given that all up?" That's what she'd claimed last winter in Yancey.

"I had." She leaned forward. "You don't understand. . . . Abby and I have been friends since the first day of college. We roomed together at Baylor. Got our first reporting gigs together. We worked at the *Times* and then the *Watch* together."

"And then?"

She sighed, crossing her legs. "And then I decided to leave undercover reporting."

He inched closer to her, shimmying along the desk's edge. "But . . . Abby stayed?"

"Right."

"And you two . . . ?"

She shrugged. "Remained friends, but . . ."

"It wasn't the same."

Darcy nodded.

"Then why did you agree to come join her investigation? Why agree to go back to under-cover reporting?"

"Because . . ."

He scooted closer still, moving to the far edge of the desk, stopping only when his leg was nearly brushing hers. "Because . . . ?"

"She needed my help."

There was more to it. He could see it in her eyes—hunger, ambition. It was masked by real concern for her friend, but it was nestled in there nonetheless.

Taking a deep breath, she stood, shaking out her hands. "It looks like I made the right decision, because something's clearly happened to Abby."

"Are you certain she didn't just leave, as Mullins said?"

"She wouldn't do that." Darcy shook her head. "Not after asking me to come. Besides, I only saw her for a minute when I first boarded yesterday. She was headed out on an excursion, so she couldn't talk, but she looked scared."

"And that's unusual?"

"For Abby, yes."

He hopped up on the desk, his legs dangling as Darcy paced. "What do you know about the case she's working?"

"Not a lot. She didn't want to explain over the phone—was going to fill me in once I got on board. We were supposed to meet last night, but she never showed."

"And the woman that went overboard? Was that her?"

"I don't know. I had Landon call Kodiak Hospital, but—"

"Wait . . ." Gage cocked his head. "Where does Landon come into this?"

"When the *Bering* docked in Yancey this morning, I went to see Landon."

And she hadn't bothered to drop by and say hi? How could she have visited Yancey without seeing him, even if the visit had to be brief? Guess he knew where he stood. "Was Landon of any help?"

"He tried, but there is no record of Abby, or

52

anyone for that matter, being brought in after falling overboard or nearly drowning last night."

"How can that be?"

"I don't know. That's what I've got to figure out."

"You think it was Abby that went overboard?"

"I'm not sure. I mean, it's the only thing that makes sense timing-wise, but why isn't there a record of her at Kodiak Hospital?"

"Have you talked to the onboard medical clinic? Surely they'd have some kind of record."

"Not necessarily. Not if she was treated elsewhere."

"Okay, but there has to be a record of the rescuers. Can't you just talk to one of them?"

"I'm going to try, but I have to keep my cover intact. I can't go around demanding answers the cruise line's clearly not in any hurry to provide. I mean, did you see the way Mullins cut me off when I tried to gently press?"

Sadly, for Darcy that *was* gentle. To most, it was dogged. "She's just trying to protect her ship's image. The last thing Destiny's going to want is the adventure journalist they hired to garner good publicity shifting her focus onto someone going overboard."

"Yeah, I suppose you're right. It would be bad press, but how hard is it to simply acknowledge if it was Abby or not?"

"Do you have any information about what she was investigating?"

"Pretty much nothing."

"You agreed to help without knowing what the case is?"

"On Abby's last call, which was super brief, she told me she'd initially thought it was like San Diego, but she was wrong. She said it was much worse." Darcy bit at her thumbnail.

"What does that even mean?"

"San Diego was the last undercover investigation case Abby and I worked for the *Watch*."

"And what kind of case was it?"

"A nasty corruption case involving drug running."

"So Abby suspects some of the *Bering*'s crew members are running drugs?" It happened on Caribbean cruises all the time, but Alaskan?

"She said it was much worse."

"So . . . what's worse?"

"I don't know." Darcy ran a hand through her hair as she stalked back and forth. "I don't know if she meant it was worse because of who is involved, the amount being trafficked, or if they are running something a lot more dangerous."

"Like what? I mean, what could you smuggle on a cruise ship? Everyone has to go through security when they board, crew included. The metal detectors would pick up any weapons."

"Any traditional ones."

"Meaning, what? Chemical, biological?"

"The ship runs between the United States and Russia. The black market in Russia is huge. Mafia practically runs the country."

"So what are you going to do?"

"Try to pick up where Abby left off."

"And Abby?"

"I'm praying when we dock in Eagle Cove tomorrow that Landon's sent word she's in fact safe and sound at Kodiak Hospital. Better yet, I'm hoping Abby gets word to me herself."

"Why do you think Landon will hear anything different tomorrow? You said he'd already spoken to the hospital?"

"He did, but he said he was going to dig deeper. He was going to talk with the night crew when they came on duty tonight. See if any of them remember Abby."

"And if they don't?"

"Then, I have no idea where she is." She looked at him so starkly, tears welling in her eyes, that it nearly broke his heart.

"Come here." He tugged her to him and enveloped her in his arms.

Slowly, apprehensively, she nestled into his embrace. She felt so good, like she was made to be held in his arms.

"It's going to be okay," he whispered, feeling the odd need to comfort her, to protect her. All

57

the feelings he'd felt in Yancey were still there, despite his attempts to forget about her—still there and, to his surprise, far stronger.

"I pray that's true"—her voice was more tentative than he'd ever heard it—"but my gut says something's very, very wrong."

7

He glanced at his cell, at the number blinking across the screen. It was the burner satellite cell he'd gotten for his lead man aboard the *Bering*, which until yesterday had been Jeremy.

"What now? Don't tell me I'm going to regret promoting you."

"No. I . . ."

"Aren't going to waste my time."

The caller cleared his throat. "Of course not. I just wanted to keep you apprised of a new situation."

"What kind of *situation?*" He loathed the word. It was simply another way of saying someone had screwed up *again*.

"There's a reporter on board."

"Another one?"

"No. Not like that. She's an adventure journalist. Some bigwig over at headquarters hired her to drum up publicity for the ship. They're all pumped about this new adventure angle."

"Okay . . ." He drew the word out, wondering where the problem was.

"I only thought you should know because she'll be tagging along on the excursions."

"I see."

"Does that change anything?"

Was he kidding? "What do you think?"

"I . . . I just wanted to check."

He wanted to be sure he didn't get his head blown off, like Jeremy had. "Are we good?"

"Yes, but . . ."

His impatience flared. He wasn't the hand-holding type. Maybe he'd chosen the wrong man. "But . . . ?"

"She's still a reporter. What if she catches on?"

Please, she was a fluff adventure journalist. "Then we get rid of her like we did the other."

* * *

After returning to her cabin and writing up a few notes, Darcy realized she'd neglected to ask Gage what Mullins had said in the meeting. She'd considered taking a quick nap, but if she was to cover the excursions, she decided she ought to at least have some idea of what was planned. She splashed water on her face, freshened up her makeup, and headed back to Gage's cabin, only to find him gone.

Great.

Landon had said something about Gage being

57

in charge of adventure activities aboard the ship. Perhaps he was up on Deck 9, where the bulk of the ship's activities seemed to take place. Not eager to get back on an elevator anytime soon, she took the stairs and exited at the end of a corridor.

The carpet—the same cobalt blue as the rest of the ship, chosen no doubt to mimic the crisp blue-green Alaskan waters—was extra plush beneath her feet. They'd recarpeted the hall recently. The head of Destiny's publicity department, Megan Nash—who'd given her the journalist job—had mentioned something about recent upgrades occurring throughout the five-year-old vessel.

As she entered the main hall, she glanced up at the enormous model of a humpback whale suspended from the ceiling three decks above. It appeared to be gliding through the ocean-mosaic dome above it.

The noise of the hall was nearly deafening as passengers milled about—parents pointing out the two-story-high pillar aquariums to their excited children, couples leaning arm in arm with exotic umbrella drinks in hand.

"Hey, Darcy," Ted said, passing by her with a wave.

"Hey, Ted. Have you seen Gage?"

"Yeah, he's running the rock-climbing wall," he called over his shoulder, not slowing his pace.

"Great. Where is that?"

Ted stopped and turned with a smile. "Didn't Mullins give you the red packet?"

Red packet? "You mean the folder thingy?"

He chuckled. "She'd kill you if she heard you call it that."

"Oh. Sorry."

"No apology necessary. I think she's incredibly uptight insisting we all refer to it as an orientation glossary."

"Yeah, that was . . ."

"Ridiculous."

The two exchanged a good laugh.

"But," Ted said, "it does contain a detailed map of the ship that you might find helpful."

She smiled. "Guess I better check that out."

"In the meantime, the rock wall is that way." He pointed across the hall to the south corridor.

"Awesome. Thanks."

"No problem. See you bright and early tomorrow."

"Right." She still had no idea exactly what was happening tomorrow. Some sort of excursion. But after hearing Abby was gone, she hadn't heard much else—her mind racing to remember every little thing Abby had told her leading up to her arrival on the ship, anything that might be of help in finding her friend.

The corridor banked right, and Darcy followed it until it flowed into an enormous open space. The vaulted ceiling went up three full decks, just as in the main hall, but at the moment this space was much quieter. A variety of activity stations were dispersed throughout the area.

The rock wall, standing almost the full three decks high, was positioned at the rear of the room. She moved toward it, catching sight of Gage's muscular arm reaching up, his hand closing on a rung. She stepped around the punching bag obstructing her view, and her breath caught. Gage was climbing freehand, moving at an incredible pace toward the top of the wall—though *gliding* would probably better describe the ease of his motions. She followed his trajectory and saw a child—a boy no more than ten—clinging as if for dear life at the top rim of the wall.

"It's okay, Isaac. Gage is coming," a woman in her thirties, blond and wearing a pink velour jogging suit, called up.

Isaac whimpered at his mom's voice, his fingers white-knuckled on the rubber knobs mimicking rock handholds.

Darcy stopped at the base of the wall as Gage reached the child, his hand resting on Isaac's back. "It's okay, sport. I'm right here. First time letting go is always a little unnerving."

She'd actually found it liberating, but she'd been a young adult at the time. For a ten-year-old, a forty-foot distance between him and the floor had to be terrifying.

"He's holding everybody up," a teenage boy

sulked—clearly the self-absorbed older brother.

"Marcus Sterling, not another word."

Marcus obviously thought about continuing until his mother held up a perfectly manicured finger, hot-pink polish matching her jogging suit.

"Not another word," she said between clenched teeth.

Marcus kicked at the matted ground with the toe of his rock-climbing shoe but remained sullenly silent.

Darcy turned her attention back on Gage, who had positioned himself next to Isaac. "We can do this, bud. One hand at a time."

Isaac shook his head.

"Isaac, look at me."

After a moment's hesitation the boy did so.

"You can do this. I have faith in you."

Faith. Odd choice of words for Gage.

"Just follow me movement for movement. I'll show you the way. You just have to follow."

Isaac sniffed and nodded, following Gage slowly back down the rock wall.

Gage hopped to the mat and helped Isaac unharness. "You did great."

Isaac smiled as his mom rushed over and enveloped him in a hug.

Darcy lifted her chin with a smile as Gage's gray eyes locked on hers.

"Everyone, five-minute water-and-bathroom break. Ben, you're up next."

Ben—a gangly teenage boy—smiled broadly.

Gage retrieved his water bottle and stepped off to the side with Darcy. He was wearing a sleeveless navy Under Armour shirt and a pair of khaki cargo shorts dusted with chalk. He looked *good*—vibrant, masculine, fit.

"What's up?"

"I forgot to have you bring me up to speed on what Mullins said in the meeting."

He swallowed a slug of water. "Sure. Which part?"

She pulled her bottom lip into her mouth. "All of it."

"You weren't paying attention?"

"I was distracted by Abby and the case."

"Right." He took another sip.

She frowned at the edge in his voice. "I think you'd be distracted, too, if your friend were missing."

Gage tightened the cap back on his bottle. "You're right." He glanced back at his rock-climbing group waiting for him. "But I can't talk now."

"Okay, after?"

"I've got two more groups after this, and then I'm meeting with the excursion passengers to brief them about tomorrow. You should be there. We're meeting at five, in the Caribou room again."

"All right. I'll be there."

He winked. "Until then."

8

"Did you find Gage?" Ted asked as she passed back through the main hall.

"Yeah. All good."

"Mullins thought you should get a tour of the ship, and since I'm not doing anything . . . I volunteered."

"That's really nice of you, but I don't want to take up your free time."

He smiled. "I insist."

"Okay." It'd be good to get a firsthand tour of the inner workings of the ship.

Ted started with the main social areas, all crammed with passengers—hundreds of people. It was nearly enough to make her feel claustrophobic. "That restaurant"—he pointed to the steakhouse—"has the best food on board."

"Thanks, I'll remember that." She tucked a strand of hair behind her ear.

He smiled, gazing down at her. "So . . . are you and Gage an item?"

She laughed. "No. I barely know him."

Ted's brows arched. "Really? You two seemed . . ."

"Irritated by each other?"

He laughed. "I was going to say *chummy*."

Exactly what she feared, that they'd appear

closer than the loose association she'd hoped to convey.

"Nah, I just covered an extreme-sport event in his town."

"Well, you must have made some impression, because he stared at you all through the meeting."

If only it were out of attraction instead of judgment on his part. "We're both a bit strong willed, so we tend to butt heads."

"Strong willed." He smirked. "I'll remember that."

She smiled. Ted was flirting with her, and if she weren't so worried about Abby and so distracted . . .

Ted was exactly the type of guy she could be interested in—tall, athletic, handsome, kind, interesting. But who was she trying to kid? She was head over heels for Gage.

"So did you know Abby, Ted?" Now that she and Ted had reached a comfortable level, it was time to start digging.

"The excursion chef?"

She nodded.

"Yeah." He took a sip of the coffee they'd picked up at the espresso café on Deck 7 while making the rounds.

"Weird she just left like that."

"Nah. Happens a lot."

She nearly choked on her macchiato. "It does?"

"Sure." Ted shrugged, waving at a group of

passing crew members easily identified by their crisp white bottoms—a mixture of pants and varying length skirts—and both long- and short-sleeved dark navy tops with the Destiny Cruise Line emblem, a gold merman holding a trident, emblazoned on the right-hand side.

Ted finished off his coffee and tossed the paper cup in the trash. "People think working for a cruise ship will be exciting. They romanticize traveling the world, but when they get here they realize it's not all it's cracked up to be."

"It's not?"

"It's work, just like anyplace else. Long hours. A lot of time away from your family." He held the door to the spa open for her.

"Sounds like you aren't a big fan."

"Me? Nah, I love it."

Fresh fruity scents of coconut, mango, and pineapple swirled in the air.

"But you just said . . ."

"That people expect it to be this grand adventure, and in a way it is, but not everyone is made for a life at sea."

"And you are?" she asked as they stepped to the counter.

"Sure. I love traveling, meeting new people every cruise." He lifted his chin at the gal behind the desk. "Just giving the resident journalist the grand tour," he said as the woman's gaze raked over Darcy.

"Enjoy," she said with a clipped nod.

"Thanks." Darcy nodded back.

Ted led her down the back hall. Soothing music piped over the speakers. "I don't mind the hours and the time away from home," he continued, "but I've always been an independent guy." He pointed out the yoga room as they passed. "And I don't have a lot of family to begin with. None I'm really close to. I've got a sister, but she's busy with her job and her kids. We see each other for the holidays and that's enough."

Not so different from her. With her parents retired and traveling the world, and her brother, Peter, having died three years ago, she didn't have much in the way of family to spend time with. Most of the time she was okay with that, or at least she had thought she was until she'd spent a good portion of the winter with the McKennas.

Being part of a close-knit family on a daily basis had been really nice. It'd become comfortable, and near the end expected, which made leaving all the more difficult. The thought of spending time with some of the McKenna siblings on tomorrow's excursion lightened her devastated heart a little, and she silently thanked God for that. For *them*.

"You'll find that's pretty common around here," Ted said, opening another door.

"What is?"

"Lack of family." He led her into the steam bath. A large, shallow pool commanded the center of the space, the glass windows covered with shadowy mist. Two people sat in the crystal blue water, perspiration and contentment on their brows.

She and Ted quietly stepped back out, leaving the two to their solitude.

"I don't understand," she said, once back in the hall.

"You're a good reporter. Always inquisitive."

"Just curious by nature." She shrugged.

"So . . . curious *and* strong willed?" He chuckled.

She smiled. "Curiosity's a great way to get to know people."

"I suppose it is."

"So . . . you were saying something about lack of family . . . ?"

"Right. Most folks can't hack being away from loved ones for so long, so the cruise line ends up employing people who are desperately in need of the money and are only here until they find something better back on land, don't care much for their family and are looking to escape them, or most often don't have family period."

"No family? How sad."

"Depends on the person and the family, I suppose."

"So you think that's why Abby left so suddenly?

Because she decided cruising wasn't for her?" she asked, though she knew better.

"Who knows why she left? And honestly . . . not to be rude, but who cares?"

She stopped. "No one cares that she left suddenly?"

"Like I said, I wasn't trying to be rude but—"

As he came around the corner, Clint almost barreled into them. "Are you forgetting your manners again, Ted?" he asked with an apologetic smile at Darcy. "You have to forgive Ted. He doesn't always have a filter between his thoughts and his mouth."

Why didn't anyone seem to care that Abby had seemingly just up and left midcruise? And why on earth wasn't that considered unusual?

* * *

Darcy returned to her cabin thoroughly frustrated. She'd spent all day speaking with crew members, digging for answers under the guise of wanting the inside scoop of the *Bering*'s new adventure angle, but found only a general lack of concern for her friend's absence. While Ted and Clint had proved to be the most talkative, neither appeared to have any concern about Abby's sudden departure.

When she shifted from the adventure focus to a simple question about Abby's disappearance, every single crew member shrugged it off as no big deal. All she had managed to get was irritation and indifference—not leads. And to top it off, she'd lost track of time and missed Gage's excursion meeting. Now she'd have even more annoyance and irritation to deal with on his end.

She shrugged off the navy *Bering* sweater she'd been given by Mullins upon arrival, replacing it with her cobalt-and-black-striped American Eagle one. It was soft and cozy, and allowed her a small touch of home. She also swapped out the white slacks she'd been wearing and pulled on her favorite pair of faded jeans. If everything around her was going to feel foreign, at least she could be in comfortable clothes during her time off.

She ran a brush through her hair, touched up her makeup, and moved to grab her lip gloss from her purse. Opening the closet where she'd left her purse hanging next to Abby's, she froze. Only hers remained. Her gaze dropped to the floor, thinking perhaps the purse had, too, but it wasn't there—only her own neatly lined-up shoes.

She sifted through her hanging clothes, thinking maybe Abby's purse had somehow gotten tangled in the garments, but still nothing. Grabbing hers off the hook, she riffled through it, panic setting in. Everything appeared to be in place, but she couldn't shake the feeling something was very off.

She set her purse on the bed and began searching the room. Everything was where she'd left it—only Abby's purse was missing.

Taking a deep breath, Darcy studied the room. The bed was neatly made, fresh towels hung on the rack in the bathroom—housekeeping had been by. Had one of them taken Abby's purse? But why not hers? Who else would have access to her room?

The question was, how did she proceed without drawing even more attention to herself and her interest in Abby? How could she possibly explain that she'd taken Abby's purse in the first place? And, worst of all, had she missed something of significance when she'd searched it?

9

Nervousness wracking her, Darcy smoothed her hair for the third time since leaving her cabin en route to Gage's. Who had taken Abby's purse and why? How would Gage react to her absence at his meeting? She'd been investigating—he'd have to understand. But, this was Gage. . . .

She sighed. How crucial could the information have been? He could easily fill her in. The more important question was—how could she head off on a fun-filled excursion while Abby was still missing?

Biting her bottom lip, Darcy climbed the stairs to Gage's floor, her heart fluttering in her chest. If she didn't go on the excursion, she'd lose her gig, and that would be of no help to Abby. She didn't have a choice. She had to go.

She exited the stairwell, made her way down the corridor, and stopped in front of his cabin door, forcing herself to take several calming breaths before knocking.

He answered wearing a long-sleeved white T-shirt and comfortable-looking navy sweats. "Missed you at the meeting."

"I was investigating."

He nodded but didn't remark.

"Can you fill me in on what I missed?"

He stepped back. "Come on in."

His cabin was similar in size to hers, and the walls were the same cheery yellow with white shells painted along the top border. He had the same double bed, recessed dresser and desk, but also had a quaint seating area with a low, round side table between two egg-shaped chairs. She sat in the one she'd sat in earlier.

"So what's the deal with tomorrow?"

Gage sank into the other chair, his eyes narrowing. "Is something wrong? You seem edgier than usual."

Great. He was still able to read her. Could he also tell that just being near him made her tingly? Her friend was missing, she was getting nowhere on the investigation, and yet she was still managing to fall head over heels for a guy who, at best, only humored her with a charming flirtation. *Am I crazy?* The man hated her profession and wanted nothing to do with God. And other than an occasional soulful smile, she couldn't even be certain he liked her. *Get your head in the game, Darcy.*

Gage leaned forward, jiggling her knee with his hand. "What's going on?"

She took a breath, worried that if she spoke too quickly, it'd all come pouring out—her fear of not being up to the task of the investigation, of never finding her friend, and of her deepest fear that Abby could already be . . .

She shook off the thought. She refused to go there. Abby was alive. *She has to be.*

"You're starting to freak me out." He squeezed her knee. "Did something happen?"

"Yes . . . No . . . I mean, it wasn't anything, I don't think."

"You don't think . . . ?"

His hand remained on her knee, and she struggled to ignore how good his touch felt. Considering the circumstances, his touch was the last thing she should be thinking about. "Abby's purse is missing from my cabin."

"Meaning someone broke into your room and stole it?"

"It seems that way."

"Did you report it?"

"How can I?"

"Someone broke in your room and stole something."

"Yes. A purse that didn't belong to me in the

72

first place. How do I explain that one? I took the purse from Abby's cabin, but now I'm reporting someone for taking it from mine?"

"Yes, but you had a reason. You're trying to help."

"But I can't share that."

"Right." He sat back, removing his hand from her knee—the warmth of his touch dissipating. "Your cover."

Here came the censure. "I know you don't understand, but . . ." *Wait.* Why was she explaining herself to Gage *again?* She didn't owe him an explanation, and yet she so desperately wanted him to understand, which in itself irked her even more. Why did she care what he thought? *Don't answer that one.* Sadly, she knew exactly why. "Look, the fact is I'm trying to find my friend, and this is the way I have to go about it."

"Can't you just be up-front? Explain who you are. Question them outright about Abby?"

"You don't understand. I'm getting nothing but resistance, and they believe I'm only an adventure journalist. If—"

"Only?"

"You know what I mean."

"Sounds like you think being an adventure journalist somehow isn't enough."

"That's not the point." She exhaled. How did he turn her around like that? "The point is, I'm barely getting anything now. If they find out that

73

I'm investigating Abby's disappearance, I'll get a one-way ticket off this ship."

"You sound awfully confident about the ineffectiveness of something you haven't tried."

"I believe someone aboard the *Bering* found out the truth of who Abby was—that she was a reporter—and now she's missing. Do you really think whoever made her disappear wouldn't come after me?"

He sank back, concern marring his brow. "I don't like it. It's a dangerous game you're playing."

"I don't have a choice."

"You keep saying that."

"Because it's the truth." Why couldn't he see that? "Look, just fill me in on tomorrow's excursion and we can both call it a night."

"Fine." He exhaled with a grunt. "We're taking a group of fourteen passengers on an overnight kayak excursion."

"Overnight?" He was kidding, right?

"The *Bering*'s docking in Eagle Cove for the night. It's part of the new adventure angle. Instead of giving folks only a few hours, they get chartered from spot to spot to enjoy overnight camping experiences."

"Camping?"

"We'll be spending the night on Kesuk, a small island off the southwest coast of Aukaneck."

"Aukaneck?"

"The island where the community of Eagle Cove is located, where the *Bering* will be docked. We'll take off by kayak from there."

"By kayak?" Her eyes widened, her pulse skittering.

"You really weren't paying any attention, were you? Kesuk, the island where we'll be camping, is only reachable by boat or floatplane. There are no facilities there. That's why Mullins put Ted and George with us. They're in charge of the passengers' accommodations and will be bringing them by supply ship."

Supply ship. Her heart settled. She'd be transported by supply ship—no need to panic.

"It's apparently their job as activities engineers to cater to the passengers while they're 'roughing it.' " He used air quotes, clearly finding the entire notion of activities engineers absurd.

"Wait, did you say there are no facilities?" Meaning no bathroom? No running water? Things just kept getting better and better.

"Afraid not." He smiled.

Of course he'd enjoy this. She squared her shoulders, refusing to give him the satisfaction of knowing how much she hated the prospect of spending the night with no facilities. "I'm sure if the *Bering* is providing accommodations, they'll be far above what one can expect with traditional camping."

"The *Bering* is providing the passengers'

accommodations." A smirk tugged at the corners of his mouth. "LFA is providing the staffs'."

"Charming." She could just picture the rustic tents now.

"You sure you don't want to make up an excuse to stay behind? We both know you aren't the 'roughing-it' type."

"Need I remind you that I'm an *adventure*-athlete reporter?" She spent plenty of time outdoors and loved it, but when the day was done she wanted a hot shower and a comfy bed.

His smirk widened into a grin. "First time I met you, you were wearing three-inch heels in Yancey. In the middle of *winter*."

"They were boots."

"*With* three-inch heels."

She shrugged a shoulder. "I adapted."

"Yes, you did, but that doesn't make you an outdoor enthusiast."

"I love the outdoors and the sports competitions I cover. I simply enjoy being comfortable." Was that so unreasonable?

He linked his arms across his chest. "Uh-huh."

"Trust me, I'll be fine. But I wish I didn't have to waste time out on the excursions when I should be investigating on the ship."

"Then stay on board."

"I can't. I was hired to cover the excursions."

"Well," he said, kicking his feet up on the coffee table, "if nothing else, this ought to be entertaining."

He answered his cell. This was getting old. He'd clearly promoted the wrong man. "What?"

"I took care of the bag."

"So you're calling me to tell me you did your job?" At least Jeremy'd had some pride. This guy was ridiculous.

"No, there's something else. . . ."

"You going to tell me, or do I have to chat it out of you?" *What a pansy.*

"I thought you should know that the cruise line's journalist is asking questions about the under-cover reporter."

He stiffened. "What kind of questions?"

"Why she left so suddenly . . . That sort of thing."

He tapped his glass. "And what are people telling her?"

"As far as I can tell, everyone's simply brushing it off as not being out of the norm."

Which, unfortunately, could prove more problematic than if they'd expressed concern. He shifted his glass to the side and leaned forward, lowering his voice. "Keep an eye on her. See who she talks to. Find out what she learns. Even better, dissuade her from asking."

"Meaning?"

"Be creative." Though he doubted the man possessed the capacity. He straightened, brushing a piece of lint off his lapel. "In the meantime,

I'll do some digging on this adventure journalist."

"You think she's not who she claims?"

"Let's just say I haven't gotten where I am by ignoring possible threats—slight or otherwise." And Darcy St. James was beginning to sound like a viable threat. One best nipped in the bud.

10

Darcy met up with the excursion team on the dock as instructed. The air was crisp, but the sun, thankfully, was remarkably bright. The photo excursion groups—which made up the bulk of the passengers participating in excursions—had headed out while it was still dark, apparently wanting to get great shots of the sunrise over the bay. While she appreciated a beautiful sunrise, she appreciated the extra couple hours of sleep even more.

Mullins bustled her way. "Ms. St. James."

"Good morning." Darcy glanced about the marina. "Where do I meet up with the supply ship?"

"Supply ship?" Mullins' penciled-in brows arched.

"I was told we have a transport vessel to ferry supplies over to the campsite."

"Supplies, yes." She waved over to where

George and Phillip were loading supplies onto a sturdy utilitarian boat. "You, no."

"I don't understand. I thought you wanted me on the excursion."

"That's right. *On* the excursion."

Surely she wasn't suggesting . . . ?

"You were hired to provide potential cruisers with a *firsthand* look at the adventures they can experience. The only way to properly do that is to experience the adventures firsthand."

"But . . ."

Mullins frowned, the lines around her mouth deepening. "Is there a problem?"

Darcy rubbed the back of her neck. "I just thought—"

"This is what headquarters wants, what they hired you to do. If you're not able or willing, we can always get another journalist."

"No. That won't be necessary. I'm just surprised is all."

"Good. Then I suggest you scurry over to the vans before they leave without you."

Darcy followed Mullins' outstretched hand to the two white vans waiting in the parking lot at the end of the pier. Gage's sister Kayden stood by one, Deputy Sheriff Landon Grainger by the other. *Why is Landon here?* Maybe he had good news about Abby and wanted to share it firsthand. *Or* . . . Her heart sank. Maybe he had bad news and felt the need to deliver it in person.

She hesitated, wanting answers but suddenly afraid of what she might be about to learn—of how the news Landon held could permanently change her life. Gage's sister Piper made eye contact with her, and an enormous smile filled Piper's face. Excusing herself from the group, she darted toward Darcy.

Darcy moved to greet her.

Piper wrapped her in a big hug. "So good to see you again."

Darcy reveled in the warmth of friendship but pulled back, glancing around. Fortunately Mullins had already headed back aboard the ship.

Piper straightened, glancing about too. "I'm sorry. Am I not supposed to know you?"

"No. It's fine. The employment liaison, Ms. Mullins, knows I worked an event in Yancey, but . . ."

"You want to keep your connection to us subtle," Piper said. She had a gift for observation and deduction.

Darcy felt horrible saying it but . . . "Yeah." It was best for the case.

Piper took a step back, shifting her hands to her pockets. "Totally understand."

"Thanks."

Piper leaned in. "I'm really sorry about your friend. Anything we can do to help?"

"Thanks. I appreciate it. I'm anxious to hear what Landon's learned."

"Gage says you're riding to the launch point with us?"

"Apparently I'm kayaking with you too." Darcy prayed the fear dancing a jig in her stomach didn't show on her face.

"That's what Gage said."

Gage knew and hadn't said anything to her? Maybe he'd assumed—just as Mullins had—that, since kayaking was part of the job she'd accepted, she'd be good with it. But Abby most certainly hadn't mentioned kayaking when she called, nor had headquarters brought it up. They'd gone on and on about firsthand experience and accompanying the excursions, but she'd assumed she'd be on a boat . . . with a motor . . . that was difficult to capsize. She'd been so anxious to get on board, to work the case with Abby, she hadn't bothered asking questions or even paying much attention to what was being said. That was not like her at all. What had she been thinking?

As they approached the group, Piper leaned in to whisper, "We've situated the vans so you can ride with Landon to the launch point."

"Thanks."

Gage addressed the group. "My sister Piper will call out your name and direct you to the appropriate van. We'll take a quick ride to the northwest coast of Aukaneck, where the kayaks are waiting, and we'll launch from there and paddle across to Kesuk Island."

Within minutes, everyone was settled in the vans and they were pulling away from the parking lot.

Piper had worked it so Darcy was strategically placed in the front passenger seat of the first van while Landon drove.

Piper and Gage sat in the two bucket seats located directly behind them, affording a small barrier of privacy between them and the passengers in subsequent rows.

Gage and Piper swiveled around, addressing the passengers.

"So, who's excited about today?" Piper asked.

Darcy ignored the conversation and various replies, fixing her attention on Landon instead. "So?"

"Having seen how upset you were, I wanted to be thorough, so I flew over to Kodiak to talk to the night staff."

"And . . . ?" She could barely sit still as they drove through the town of Eagle Cove, along the coast toward the northwestern tip of Aukaneck Island. The main village was quaint and would no doubt make a nice destination for the passengers opting not to join one of the excursions.

Landon cleared his throat as he banked right, heading away from the central village.

"Turns out a woman *was* brought in to Kodiak Hospital late last night."

Hope welled inside her. "Abby?"

"That's the name that was given. . . ."

"But . . . ?" Her eyes narrowed.

Landon's grip tightened on the steering wheel. "She was gone, apparently left rather abruptly soon after being brought in."

"How abruptly?"

"The triage nurse spoke with her briefly. She identified herself as Abby Walsh, told the nurse she was fine, and took off before she could even be registered, let alone assessed by the doctor."

"So that explains why the day shift didn't know about her."

"Right."

She shifted, the seat belt pinning her uncomfortably. "If it was Abby, then why hasn't she sent word?"

"I don't know, but the entire thing seems odd."

"Because she left the hospital so quickly?" If it was Abby, she was probably hoping to get back to the ship or at least to get word to her.

"That's one thing." Landon tapped the steering wheel as she slackened the belt cutting across her midsection. "You said you heard the alarm go off around ten thirty?"

"Yes."

"The woman wasn't brought in to Kodiak Hospital until nearly one o'clock."

"I don't understand." She frowned as noise swelled in the rear of the van. "Why so long of a time gap?"

Landon glanced in his rearview mirror at the commotion. "I don't know."

"We've got an instigator back here," Gage said, leaning forward.

"What?" Darcy turned with a start. "How so?"

"Heath thinks he's the life of the party. We'll have to keep an eye on him."

Landon smiled at Darcy's confusion. "What Gage means is when you have a show-off, they are likely to make stupid choices out on the water."

"Or prod others to do so," Gage added.

"Like the popular kids in high school, always egging one another on?" she said.

Gage tapped the back of her seat. "Exactly." He turned back to the commotion, and she redirected her thoughts to Abby.

"So do you think it was Abby?"

"There's no way to be certain. A man dropped her off, saying he had to hurry back to the ship before it was too far gone, but after nearly three hours, he'd have to meet up with it at the next port."

"I don't like it."

"Neither do I."

"We need to show the nurse Abby's picture and see if she can confirm whether or not it was in fact her."

"I already did. I pulled Abby's driver's license photo after you left the station."

"And?"

"The nurse said the ER was hectic that night. The woman had the same hair color, same basic build, but she couldn't be certain one way or another."

"Why such a long time delay? What were they doing for three hours?"

"I don't know. Their decision to take the woman to Kodiak rather than back on the ship indicates they were close to the island."

"And I could see the town lights in the distance when I finally made it out on deck."

"The hospital sits barely a block from shore. They should have reached it in well under an hour."

"So why did it take so long?"

Landon pulled the van to a stop. "I don't know."

11

Gage watched Darcy climb from the van, frustration etched on her beautiful face. Whatever news Landon held, it wasn't what she'd hoped for. With the noise in the rear of the van, it'd been nearly impossible to hear what she and Landon were discussing up front—which was probably for the best. He needed a clear head today. Not the distraction of Darcy. Not when he was responsible for more than a dozen lives.

Kayden clapped him on the back. "Let's go, bro. Looks like a stellar day."

He eyed the sky, took a moment to feel the wind on his skin, the warmth of the sun. It was a gorgeous day, but they still had to be wary. The ocean temps wouldn't be over forty degrees this time of year. Winds could strengthen in the blink of an eye, and by nightfall they'd be looking at a low near thirty.

He'd covered all of these concerns with the participants during the excursion briefing, but men like Heath Donovan didn't really listen. They exuded a confidence that often fell short when danger surfaced. He just hoped Heath's bravado didn't prod others—especially his fiancée, Amber, who appeared a bit timid—to push their limits. Not when kayaking an area as untamable as the Aleutians.

Jake waved from the water's edge and, once he had Gage's attention, gave him the thumbs-up signal. The kayaks were set.

Darcy's countenance brightened at the sight of Jake, and she quickly moved to greet him. *Odd.* Gage hadn't recalled them making a particular connection during Darcy's time in Yancey. In fact, Darcy's curiosity over Jake's silent past seemed the entire scope of her thoughts of him. Why would his presence on the excursion please her so?

Shaking off the thought, Gage set to work. He

double-checked to be certain everything was properly secure and ready for launch before addressing the group. "As discussed, I'll be taking the lead. Heath, Amber, Cal, and Brett, you'll be in my group." Where he could keep a close eye on them. "Piper . . ." He looked to his sister and she waved her hand. "You'll have Howard and Jillian."

"Jill to you, dear," the sophisticated woman informed Piper.

"Jill it is." Piper smiled.

"Sarah and John, you'll also be with Piper."

The thirty-something couple nodded in Piper's direction.

"Kayden."

She raised her hand.

"You'll have Whitney. . . ." He pointed to the only single woman in the bunch and noticed both Cal and Brett zero in on her. They were clearly aboard the *Bering* to meet women and had set their sights on Whitney for the duration of the excursion.

Gage's only concern was the signed waiver he had from both of them stating that they possessed kayaking experience. Sea kayaking was no place for a novice kayaker, especially if they were only there in some lame attempt to pick up or impress a lady.

His gaze shifted to Darcy still hovering at Jake's side. *Curious.*

He hoped she was focused enough to put Abby to the back of her mind, at least until they were safely on land.

"Gage?" Kayden snapped her fingers. "You still with us?"

"Right." He cleared his throat, thoroughly frustrated by how easily Darcy seeped into his thoughts, stealing his focus.

"I've got Whitney and . . . ?" Kayden prodded.

He glanced back at the clipboard in hand. "Luke and Kelly."

The young newlyweds smiled at Kayden.

"Cool." Kayden cinched her pack, clearly pleased with her athletic and eager group.

Gage tapped the clipboard. "Which leaves Jake with Henry and his sons—Greg and Cody."

Henry stepped across the open space and shook Jake's hand, introducing his college-age sons.

With such a large group, it was essential that each team member knew exactly which clients they were responsible for should a situation arise. Distributing the numbers equally by reported skill level helped keep the stronger paddlers near the front and the less experienced near the rear, where they could take their time without feeling pressured. The order he'd assigned kept him and Jake near the front with the stronger paddlers, Kayden in the middle, and Piper pulling up the rear with the potentially slower, less-experienced ones.

"Any particular place you'd like us?" Ted asked.

"I've been assured by Mullins that every crew member accompanying this excursion, including our journalist, has kayak experience, but she had no idea how much." None of the crew members had been present for the excursion training. When he'd complained to Mullins, she'd assured him that all members were more than qualified, including Darcy.

"I got my fair share," Clint commented.

"Same," Ted said.

"Okay, why don't you two hang near the center of the group." He could spread them out if necessary.

The men nodded their agreement.

"Ms. St. James?" He glanced at Darcy.

She quickly shifted her attention to grabbing a life vest. "I'm good."

Not what he'd asked. "Everyone climb on in and get comfortable with the craft." Once everyone else's attention was focused on the task at hand, he stepped close to Darcy. "You okay?"

"Fine." She struggled with the straps on her vest, trying to line up the clips.

"Come here." He tugged her to him, trying to ignore the supple curve of her neck and the golden tendrils of hair slipping from her ponytail.

He secured the first clip and paused. Was she *trembling?*

Clamping his hands on her shoulders, he stooped to look her in the eye. "Why are you shaking?"

She wiggled in his hold. "I'm not."

"Yes. You are. I'd like to think it is my charm setting you aquiver, but—"

"Ha!"

"Ignoring the insult. But seriously, what are you afraid . . . ?" The words died on his lips as understanding dawned. "Please tell me you've kayaked before. Mullins assured me . . ."

She bit her bottom lip.

"You realize you can't go on this excursion."

"I have to."

"I'm sorry, but you can't. It's not safe." He turned to step away, but she grabbed his arm.

"You don't understand," she pleaded, her voice low but urgent. "If I don't go, Mullins will fire me."

"I understand your case is important to you, but—"

"Not the case. *Abby*. If I get fired I may never find her."

"Something wrong?" Piper asked, coming up beside them.

"Darcy's never been kayaking."

"Shhh." Darcy quickly scanned the crowd. "Would you please keep your voice down? Last thing I need is for Ted or Clint to overhear and tell Mullins. If she learns I'm not qualified for

90

this gig, for *all* aspects of this gig, I'll lose the job, and my cover will be blown."

"I thought Abby was your concern, not your cover."

"The two go hand in hand."

Right. "If you say so."

"Look," Piper interrupted. "It's not a problem. Darcy can hang in the back with me. I'll keep an eye on her."

"Which will pull your attention from your charges. Everyone else on this excursion has at least some experience." It wasn't a beginner's route.

"We work with beginners all the time," Piper said, always trying to be the peacemaker.

"Not out here." The weather in the Aleutians was unpredictable—fog, wind, quickly shifting currents.

Landon came up behind Piper, snaking his arm around her waist and resting his head on her shoulder. "What's up?"

"Darcy's never been kayaking," Gage said.

"I told you," Piper said, her tone placating, "I'll keep an eye on her."

"Then you'll be neglecting the rest of your charges, who will be moving at a much faster clip, since they're more seasoned," Kayden said, joining the pack. She tilted her head toward the surf. "Everyone's getting restless."

Gage followed her gaze to the clients waiting

impatiently aboard their crafts. "Be right there." He waved.

The idea of a longer wait, no matter how brief, settled irritation across most of their brows—especially Heath's. The guy was going to be trouble—Gage just knew it. And now he had Darcy to worry about too. He turned to Kayden. "Thank you for understanding the predicament this poses."

"I'll stay with her," Landon offered. "I wasn't even supposed to be on the excursion, so it won't take anything away from the paying customers if I help Darcy."

Gage mulled that over, irritated Darcy had put him in this position in the first place, that she was forcing him to make this call—all to protect a cover he wasn't even convinced was necessary. Being up-front was always the best course of action.

"Gage?" Piper prodded.

He gritted his teeth. "Fine, but you two"—he pointed between Landon and Darcy—"had better keep within a reasonable distance. I don't want you guys so far back that we're forced to come after you."

"Don't worry." Darcy linked her arms across her chest, the life jacket hiking up with the motion until it was cresting her stubborn chin. "I won't hold you up."

Funny how someone so frustrating could be so

adorable. He sighed. "Come here." He grasped the loose strap of her safety vest, tugging her once again to him. "Let me finish fixing this."

Everyone else stepped back, refocusing on the excursion ahead. Darcy's breathing was hurried. *Good.* He'd flustered her as much as she'd vexed him. Surprisingly, the thought warmed him. He liked that he could get her heart racing, even if it was from frustration rather than his charm. He slid the last clip in place but didn't slacken his hold. "I'm not trying to be a jerk."

"Uh-huh." Her jaw tightened.

"Really, I'm not. You just need to understand that these folks and their safety are *my* responsibility."

Her shoulders slackened slightly. "You know I'd never want to cause any trouble for you or your family."

His eyes locked on hers at the deep sincerity of her words, and his frustration ebbed. "It's not only *their* safety I'm concerned about." That's what had him so irritated. It was because he knew his attention would be divided today—that Darcy's safety would consume his thoughts, regardless of who hung back with her.

"Meaning?"

Pleasure tugged at the corner of his mouth. Of course she'd make him *say* it. He slipped a loose strand of hair behind her ear, momentarily reveling in the silkiness. He held her gaze and, lowering his voice a notch, whispered, "I'm concerned about *yours.*"

Her blue eyes widened. "You are?"

He nodded, amused and touched at her surprise. *More than you know. More than even I understand.*

"That's . . . kind of you," she spluttered out. "But I'll be fine." She stepped from his hold, determination emblazoned on her stiff posture.

He refrained from reminding her what *fine* stood for. *Freaked out. Insecure. Neurotic. Emotional.* He genuinely hoped she was none of the above, but the weary expression sneaking past her resolute guard left an uneasy feeling in the pit of his gut. Not what he needed today. Today he needed to be on his game, not worrying about Darcy St. James.

* * *

Darcy stepped into the kayak, utterly terrified. Her heart still pitter-pattered from her heated encounter with Gage, from the secure feel of his strong hands on her shoulders, and the intensity echoing in his soulful eyes. Unfortunately, the encounter had done little to calm the nervous energy already pulsating through her.

She was determined to find Abby, but she could not screw up this excursion for Gage and his family. If her actions brought anything negative upon their company, she'd never forgive herself.

94

The kayak wiggled beneath her, and she quickly dropped to her bottom.

She could do this—could face her fear. She was in a floating vessel with a life preserver. She wouldn't drown.

Landon waited until everyone else had cleared out before instructing Darcy to push off. Push off into *water.* Her hands clammy, she gripped the metal cylinder of the paddle with her left hand and clutched the plastic hand plate with her right. Ignoring the world spinning at dizzying speed around her, she bore down, digging the paddle into the wet sand below, pushing off from shore.

Noise warbled in her ears as the current quickly grabbed her in its greedy clutches, tearing her away from shore and yanking her out to sea.

She blinked, trying to focus on the shore of the island in front of her. Panic clawed at her chest—tightening, suffocating until she couldn't breathe.

Flashes of tumultuous waves and the unyielding grasp of the ocean's pull flooded her mind—being dredged and tumbled along the sandy bottom in a whirl. The relentless tug of the sea ripping her away from safety and those she loved.

"Hey." Landon's hand clamped hard on her shoulder. "You okay?"

She stared at his worried expression, blinking back to reality, to the moment. She wasn't on the ocean floor having the breath pummeled from her lungs, wasn't having her best friend ripped from her life, from this world. That was the past. This was now. She had a chance to save another friend, and she *wouldn't* let go. Not this time.

"Darcy."

She looked up at Landon, at his kayak butted next to hers. "Sorry. I'm fine."

"You don't look fine."

She sheltered her eyes from the sun with her hand. "Really, I'm okay." A cool breeze wafted over her perspiration-drenched skin. "I'll be okay."

Landon assessed her. "Are you scared . . . of *water?*"

She wasn't scared of water; she was *terrified* of drowning in it. "I can do this." She had to.

"You sure?"

She tightened her hold on the paddle to the point her fingers burned. "Positive. Now we better get going before we fall too far behind. I don't want another lecture from Gage."

Landon exhaled. "All right. If you're sure you're okay."

"Positive." It was a bold-faced lie, but what choice did she have?

"Slow, easy strokes—like this." He demonstrated.

That looked easy enough. *Don't think about where you are. Just focus on the motion.* She prayed for God's protection, for His strength. There was no way she could do this without Him.

Following Landon's lead, she mimicked his

movements—her paddle cutting through the blue-green water in sure, even strokes.

"You got it." Landon smiled. "Now, let's catch up. I'll lead the way. Let me know if you need anything."

She nodded, terrified to look anywhere but straight ahead. She had no idea how far away the rest of the team was. She simply kept her gaze fixed on Landon's back and the horizon in front of her.

Don't look down. Just keep paddling.

The waves crashed against her kayak as they headed toward Kesuk's northern shore. She prayed the waves would settle, but the myriad of whitecaps dotting the expanse ahead dispelled her hope. The rocking didn't bother her, but the water sloshing up over the kayak was a constant reminder of where she was, and of what was surrounding her.

She fought another wave of dizziness, taking deep breaths through her nose and wiggling her toes as her dad had instructed in times past, though he'd never managed to actually get her back in the water. It *was* strange how such simple motions could distract her brain from the reality surrounding her, even if only momentarily —but even a moment's reprieve from the panic threatening to overtake her was better than nothing.

Please, Father, carry me through this.

A verse she'd memorized from Psalm 93 filtered through her mind.

" 'Mightier than the thunder of the great waters, mightier than the breakers of the sea— the Lord on high is mighty.' "

You are greater than the danger surrounding me.

She paddled on.

12

Darcy had never been so thankful to be on solid land. Her legs were wobbly, unsure beneath her as she took her first steps onto the hard-packed sand of Kesuk's southern shore. The pent-up anxiety she'd wrestled all day as they paddled along the island's northern and western shores now left her body in a burning adrenaline rush. She fought the urge to lay prostrate on the shore and kiss the ground. She'd made it. God had carried her through.

"What a rush!" Clint smiled beside her.

"That's one word for it," she mumbled.

"You did good," Landon said, setting his pack in the pile forming beside the unlit fire pit.

"We've still got a lot of work to do," George said, greeting Ted. "I've started setting up camp in a half circle with our backs to the hills."

Ted nodded and moved to assist.

"I've got Phillip's supplies set by the cooking pit," George said. "Hopefully he'll start soon. Looks like the passengers are hungry."

"Starving," Heath chimed in.

"Passengers aren't the only ones." Gage rubbed his stomach. His damp shirt clung to his mid-section, hugging his well-defined abdomen. Heat rushed Darcy's cheeks.

"I'll get the cooking fire started for him," Jake offered.

"Piper and I will get the staff tents up." Kayden pulled the tent roll from the base of her pack.

"Unless you need me, Gage, I'll help the girls," Landon said, inclining his head in the sisters' direction.

"Nah, I'm good. Thanks." Gage shifted his attention to Darcy. "You good?"

"Fine." She was just thankful to be on land.

His gaze bore into her—so much emotion dwelling there.

"I . . . better get started interviewing the participants about their first day out."

"Right."

* * *

Gage approached Darcy at the picnic table while everyone else was otherwise occupied, settling into the tents George and Ted had so master-fully erected. Though *tents* hardly seemed the appropriate word. What they had set up looked more like the luxury safari tents of the early

1900s, bordering far too close to what many referred to nowadays as *glamping* for Gage's tastes. The only difference between true glamping, as Piper explained it, and what stood erected around him was the lack of actual furniture. Each passenger had an inflated air mattress on a raised frame, upon which high-loft goose-down sleeping bags were spread. A small battery-lit lantern hung from the overarching beam, bathing the faux-linen tents in soft light. He had to admit the overall effect was quite nice—like fireflies dancing in the coming dusk of twilight. The sun wouldn't be fully setting for a bit, but the pink already streaking across the Alaskan sky indicated it was going to be a gorgeous one.

He sank down beside Darcy on the picnic bench. Somehow Chef Phillip had enlisted her to help with dinner, putting her to work on the potato skins—which she'd clearly never made before, though watching her attempts to cook them over the fire had proved highly entertaining. "How'd your interviews go?"

"Fine until I got to Phillip." She poked at the limp skins arranged on the platter before her.

He fought back a chuckle. "How'd he wrangle you into helping?"

"I'm not really sure. One minute I was talking to him about Abby, asking if he'd ever worked with her, how he felt about her leaving and his taking over her job, and the next thing I knew, he'd put me to boiling potatoes over the campfire."

The distinct smell of smoke clung to her fleece jacket—he leaned in—and to her silky blond hair.

"Hope I'm not interrupting."

They turned to find Clint standing behind them.

"Not at all." She sat back from Gage. "Please, join us."

"Just wanted to sample one of those amazing-looking potato skins. May I?"

"Of course." She smiled.

Clint reached in between them and grabbed one. She stiffened as he popped it in his mouth.

He swallowed. "Delicious."

"Really?" Relief filled her face. "Thanks."

"No. Thank *you*." His appreciative gaze lingered on Darcy far too long for Gage's liking. "Hope all your interviews went well."

"Yep. Everyone's really enjoyed the excursion so far."

"That's great." He shifted his weight, resting his boot on the bench between them and leaning in slightly toward Darcy. "And did you enjoy it?"

She nodded.

"I'm glad to hear it. There's nothing like the wind in your hair, the sea air on your face." He smiled. "Such a beautiful face."

"Thanks."

Gage leaned around Clint, fixing his displeased gaze on Darcy.

Clint straightened. "Guess I should let the restless natives know dinner's about ready."

"Yeah. Shouldn't be long now," she said. "I think Phillip is just about done with the steak."

"Great." Clint popped another potato skin in his mouth, then turned and headed back toward the campers.

Gage cocked his head. "What was that?"

"What was what?" She fidgeted with the arrangement of the potato skins.

He jutted his chin toward Clint's retreating back. "The two of you all flirty."

"We weren't flirting."

He arched a brow.

"*I* wasn't flirting."

"Uh-huh."

"I was simply trying to establish a connection with him."

"I'd say connection established." He linked his arms across his chest. Why was he getting so worked up?

"It's vital I make connections with as many crew members as possible. I don't know which of them may be of use to me in finding Abby."

"So you're using them?" Why was he getting combative? And why did he feel so territorial all of a sudden? Maybe it was simply that Clint rubbed him wrong, or maybe it was the way she'd just led Clint on that bugged him so.

"I'm just getting to know the people Abby

worked with leading up to her disappearance."

"In case they can be of *use* to you?" Isn't that what she'd just said—they'd be of *use* to her? Was he simply of use to her too?

"I'm not *using* them." She fanned the stack of napkins out beside the tower of plastic plates. "I'm just getting to know the people that knew Abby."

"So, let me get this straight. You form a *false* attachment with Clint, for example"—though it could just as easily be him—"in case he can be of *use* to you in finding Abby?"

"Yes . . . but it's not how you're making it sound."

"How am I making it sound?" He was only repeating what she'd said, though he recognized he was making the situation far too personal.

"Wrong and manipulative."

"Just call it like I see it." He shrugged. "But that's me. I prefer to be up-front."

"I'm doing what I need to do to find my friend."

"By using other people." Just as his ex, Meredith, had. He was falling for another woman who led people on and lied. What was wrong with him?

While Meredith's and Darcy's professions weren't the same—lawyer and reporter—the means they used were far too similar for his tastes. It showed the heart of their character.

While in Yancey this winter, Darcy had tried so hard to convince him she was different, that she wasn't the type of reporter who lied and manipulated to get ahead, and about the time she'd left for California, he'd actually started to believe she was different.

Now . . . he feared the truth was showing through. Darcy might be kinder than Meredith, she might even have great intentions for her actions, but the end result was the same—she did what she needed to do to get what she wanted.

It wasn't like he didn't understand. He'd been there—wanting to do everything possible to protect a loved one, to prove his brother's innocence, but he'd never lost sight of who he was and of what mattered.

"You think I should simply walk away?" she asked at his silence—her tone less assured than it had been moments before.

"No, but I still believe there's a straightforward way to go about it."

"You don't understand. People lie. They cover their tracks."

"So, what . . . you *have to* lie to catch them?" That was convenient.

"That's not what I said!"

Kayden cleared her throat.

They both turned.

Kayden tilted her head in the direction of the group. "You're starting to draw an audience."

Darcy's eyes widened. "Could you hear what we were discussing?"

"No, but your voices were rising. A few more seconds and . . ."

"We don't have to worry about that." She pinned a glare on Gage. "This conversation is *over*."

It wasn't the only thing that was over. He had to keep his distance. Darcy had worked her way into his heart, and he had to do whatever it took to work her out again. Even if it meant being combative, blowing things out of proportion, making it personal. Because the truth was, if he didn't stop his deepening feelings for Darcy, it would become intensely personal, and he couldn't go back there.

13

Darcy sat on the open spot on the log beside Piper, her dinner plate in hand, her ire fully riled. She watched Gage across the flames laughing with one of the passengers—the single, female passenger. Frustration boiled inside. Not at his conversation with the beautiful lady, though she wasn't thrilled with the way Whitney smiled at Gage. She was frustrated by a pricked conscience.

What am I to do, Lord? I know that to do my job and to find Abby, I'm going to need to lie about who I am and my reasons for being here. I can call it something less negative, but I am lying, and I'm wrestling with that.

It was the reason she had left undercover reporting in the first place—having to compromise to get to the truth. But this was an entirely different situation—she was trying to save a life. Why couldn't Gage understand that?

And why do I care what he thinks of me? It hurts when he assaults my character. Can't he see I'm just trying to help Abby?

But in all honesty, she was energized by the hunt for the truth, enjoyed tracking down leads.

Why can't he see I'm not Meredith? I'm not self-serving. I'm trying to save Abby. Lord, don't let her die until I reach her, until she knows you. Nothing matters more.

She cut into her steak with all the force of a lumberjack attacking a giant redwood, glaring at Gage across the fire.

Piper studied her but didn't say a word. She didn't have to. Darcy knew she understood completely.

Darcy jabbed a piece of her meat. "Is he always so—?"

Piper sighed. "Yes."

"Don't you just want to—?"

"Occasionally." Piper smirked.

"Only occasionally?" Darcy set her plate aside, too rattled to eat. "Then you're a better woman than me."

"I'm just related by blood. There's a certain level of innate love and forgiveness woven into that."

"I suppose it would have to be innate."

"I think it's God's gift," Piper continued. "We drive each other crazy, but we'd do anything for each other."

She would have done anything for her brother —and had until the day he died. Even Peter, in his limited understanding, showered her with unbounded love. He treasured her as his sister, and that love still permeated her heart. But she wasn't related to Gage and wasn't bound by the same innate forgiveness, and right now he was being a downright judgmental pain, when what she longed for was his support. "He thinks so poorly of me." It broke her heart.

"That's not true. Gage thinks very highly of you."

Darcy nearly choked on her cider. "Yeah, right."

Piper angled to face her better. "I'm serious. Whenever he talks about you . . . I can see he feels something for you."

"Yeah, annoyance."

Landon wrapped his arms around Piper from behind. "Ahhh . . . she's not that bad." He pressed a kiss to the top of Piper's head. "Somehow I manage to put up with her."

"Very funny, mister." Piper jabbed her fiancé playfully.

"Mind if I steal my gorgeous fiancée away to see the sunset?"

"Not at all." Darcy smiled, so happy to see them together, especially after all they'd been through over the winter. God was present in their lives, in their relationship. Their trial had brought them closer when it could have so easily torn them apart. Most definitely God's handiwork.

Darcy wrapped her fleece more snugly about her as the warmth slipped from the air. Someone needed to stoke the fire.

As if on cue, Jake rose and, grabbing a stick, stoked the flames, adding another log to the fire.

Darcy studied him in the light of the flames—tall, slender, dark hair, hazel eyes . . . the weight of sorrow permanently etched on his face.

When she'd left Yancey last winter, she hadn't been able to resist digging into the past of the man who had intrigued her so. Now she understood why he displayed such an intricate knowledge of criminal proceedings during the case she'd investigated for the McKennas, but she also understood why he'd chosen not to tell anyone about his past, and it certainly wasn't her place to do so. She felt rotten about looking him up, now that she knew the truth.

She waited until Jake settled back on the log at the far end of the gathering, as usual seeming content to hang on the outskirts and observe.

Grabbing another cup of cider, she approached him. "Mind if I sit down?" She indicated the empty spot on the log beside him.

"Of course not. Take a load off."

"Thought you might like something hot to drink."

He took the cup she offered. "Thanks."

"Looks like it's going to be a cold night." Small talk was always a good way to ease in.

Jake assessed the sky. Piper had told her that in the time he'd been in Yancey, he'd come to be known as the best tracker in Alaska. It probably came as a natural extension of his background she'd uncovered, but whatever the cause, Jake lived up to the nickname he'd earned with Alaskan Search and Rescue—Hawk.

"I'd say mid-to-low thirties tonight." He took a sip of cider.

"I see why Piper calls you the human weather station."

He chuckled. "You spend enough time outdoors, looking for signs, you begin to see them everywhere."

"I hope that's true." She hoped people left signs too—didn't just disappear, didn't evaporate. She prayed God would give her the vision to see the signs, follow the trail, to find Abby and to bring her home.

"Piper told me about your friend." He looked at her with such compassion in his eyes—

compassion only a fellow sufferer could understand. "I'm sorry."

She nodded her thanks. "I was hoping to pick your brain a little, if that's okay?"

He shifted. "Why me?"

"You were so helpful on the last investigation. . . ."

"Beginner's luck." He took another sip of cider.

"Right, but I was still hoping I could run some things by you—see if you have any more luck in you." She needed his expertise.

He stiffened slightly beside her, clearly trying to figure out if she knew more than she was letting on.

"Please. I'm so worried about my friend."

"All right, but I can't promise I'll be much help."

"Thanks."

"Why do you want *his* help?"

Kayden. Darcy exhaled. Not now. Not when Jake was willing to listen.

"He was so helpful with Reef's case, and—"

"He was, wasn't he?" Kayden cocked her head. "Makes you wonder where he got such knowledge." She was the steadfast doubter when it came to Jake. She didn't trust him—couldn't accept a man who wouldn't admit his past.

"Hey, Darcy," Clint said, striding up. "The sunset is going to be amazing. I know a great vantage point. Care to join me?"

"Uh . . ." She glanced over at Jake.

"We can catch up later," he said.

She looked back at Clint and smiled. "Sure." She'd hoped for help from Jake, but maybe she'd find some from Clint instead. He knew Abby—brief as their time working together might have been. Clint was open and easygoing, and clearly feeling more and more comfortable around her. Maybe he was ready to share a bit more.

Near the top of a rocky rise, Clint extended his hand.

Darcy took hold, and he guided her up the final steps. She gazed across the northern expanse of the island to the strait and beyond, and her breath caught. The sun was setting to her left, and straight ahead, two snow-covered peaks glistened in the evening light. "It's stunning."

"Yes," he said, stepping closer. "You are."

She glanced over to find his gaze fixed on her. "Thanks."

"It's the truth." He reached out, caressing her jaw with the back of his hand.

"Thanks for bringing me up here." She shifted her attention back to the view, hoping he'd do the same. "So, what am I looking at?"

"Those are the Pavlov volcanoes. That spit of land that they sit on divides the Pacific Ocean from the Bering Sea."

"Wow. You sure know this area well."

"It's not my first excursion here. After a while, you learn where the best vantage points are."

"Did Abby come on excursion here too?"

"Sure. On the last cruise."

"Did you show her this view?"

"Nah."

"How come?"

"We never really connected."

"Connected?"

He smiled. "I like you, like your style. Thought you'd enjoy a good view."

"And Abby?"

"Never really thought about Abby. Then again, I only worked a few excursions with her."

"This is the first excursion *we've* worked together."

"Yeah, but we connected. Clicked. Ya know?"

She smiled but didn't feel any true connection, though it would hardly help her cause to let Clint know that. He was a nice enough guy—she just had pressing matters at hand.

Gage's words of condemnation raced through her mind, and she tried to shove them down, needing to focus on finding Abby. "Kind of odd, though, isn't it?"

Clint stepped closer, his full attention on her. "What's that?"

"Abby just leaving like that."

He frowned. "You're sure putting a lot of

thought into this. Did you know her or something? Before the *Bering*, I mean?"

If someone on the ship had discovered Abby's true identity, and she claimed to have known Abby outside of the *Bering*, then they'd know she was a fake as well. "No. Just met her once, when I boarded."

"You're awful curious about someone you've only met once."

She needed to tread carefully. She didn't want Clint spreading the word that she was asking questions. "You're right. I guess I'm just surprised."

He popped a mint in his mouth and offered her one.

"Thanks." She slipped it in her mouth, the overpowering cinnamon burning her tongue.

He slid the tin mint case back in his shirt pocket. "What's to be surprised by?"

"I met Abby when I boarded the *Bering* one day, and the next day she was gone without any word."

"So?"

"Seems like she would have said something to somebody."

Clint smiled. "You're assuming she cared enough to leave notice. Most people in this industry don't."

"Care about their jobs?"

"Have much loyalty to the cruise ship. People come and go as they please."

"Mullins had me sign a three-month contract for the spring season."

"Yeah. We all do. So what? You leave and they stop paying you. End of contract." His eyes narrowed in amusement. "What do you think, they're going to go through the trouble of tracking you down and force you to return to the ship? Employees are a dime a dozen. The cruise line doesn't care as long as the slot is covered."

"That doesn't sound very cheery."

"Cheery." He laughed. "This is obviously your first gig on a cruise ship. What you need to do is stop worrying about some gal you didn't even know"—he stepped closer, trailing his hand down the length of her arm—"and enjoy the view." He gestured to a large bird gliding overhead, nearly a shadow in the darkening sky. "We're in a beautiful place, and you're with a man that finds you absolutely captivating. What's not to like?"

If he only knew. . . .

"Come on, Darcy, let's get to know each other." He nudged her arm. "Tell me something about you. Anything."

"Okay." She smiled. *Something safe.* "I hate pickles."

He chuckled. "Well . . . that's a start."

"My turn," she said, narrowing her eyes. "Massage therapist-medic—the combination is intriguing."

"That's not actually a question, but you're certainly not the first to comment."

"So how'd you get started?" It was quite the job combination.

"Well, I began on the *Bering* as a massage therapist, but having to stay on the ship all the time got boring, so I diversified. Took my rotation off and got my medic's license. Now I participate in most of the excursions."

"You seem to enjoy them."

"It's great getting to meet new people." He stepped closer. "Captivating people like you."

She smiled but focused her gaze on the view, not him.

"You and Gage seem to have an interesting dynamic."

"That's one way to put it."

"I'm not stepping on any toes, am I?"

"Me and Gage?" She laughed but felt no humor on the subject. "No." There would never be a "her and Gage."

"Good." Clint smiled. "Because I'm enjoying getting to know you."

As nice as Clint was, she needed to keep a tight rein on things. She wasn't who he thought she was, and as soon as she found Abby, she was out of there. Which meant she needed to be very careful not to lead Clint on, as Gage suggested she was doing. Nothing beyond a casual friendship was going to happen with Clint, but at the same time, she needed to find out what he knew. Abby's life could depend on it.

Everyone was a potential suspect or witness— even if they didn't realize it. Any one of them could have seen or overheard something they didn't think anything of at the time but could prove vital to her investigation. She had to keep digging until she found it.

14

Gage stretched out before the fire, trying not to think about how long Darcy and Clint had been gone. There was no harm in a walk, but uneasiness filled him and no doubt would until her return.

Whitney shifted beside him. "I'm going to grab some more coffee. Would you like a refill?"

"Sure, that'd be great."

Whitney had a great sense of humor, was intelligent and very athletic. She reminded him a great deal of Kayden.

She returned, handed Gage his cup, and was about to sit down when Ted approached. "Hey, Whitney, I hear the sunset is gorgeous."

Interesting. Gage had expected Cal or another of the other single passengers to hit on Whitney, not one of the crew.

Whitney glanced up at the darkening sky. "I think we've already missed it."

"Even better to see the stars from the rise. Wanna join me?"

"Thanks, but I'm good right here." She settled back down on the log beside Gage.

"You sure?" Ted smiled. "I promise, I don't bite."

"I'm good. Thanks."

Ted glanced between her and Gage and then nodded with a look of understanding. "Maybe some other time."

Gage waited until Ted walked away before glancing at Whitney. "Not into walks or not into Ted?" He took a sip of his coffee.

She shook her head. "Not into disappearing."

Gage spluttered on the liquid. "I'm sorry. What did you say?"

"Not into disappearing."

"That's what I thought, but I don't understand. Are you suggesting Ted . . . ?"

"I'm not suggesting anything. I'm simply being safe. I'm a single female alone on an excursion. It would be foolish of me to leave the group with anyone, no matter how cute he may be."

"You make it sound like people are disappearing from cruises all the time."

"Nearly twenty last year alone."

"From the *Bering*?"

She shook her head. "No, worldwide, but the *Bering*'s not free of its problems."

"What do you mean?"

"Last August some honeymooners, Drake and

Christine Bowen, disappeared while on an excursion."

Bowen? "Wasn't that the man who murdered his wife and then ran?"

"That's what the media claimed."

"Claimed?" The media certainly wasn't bias-free, but it had sounded as if the husband was downright guilty.

"I had a friend on that cruise—Melody. We used to work together at our old law firm. Anyway, Melody said she spent some time with one of the men who'd been on that excursion, and he said the whole thing was strange."

"Strange . . . how?"

"They'd made camp, and everyone had gone to bed. In the morning, Bowen gets up and can't find his wife. The team starts searching, but they can't find her anywhere."

Gage remembered the news coverage—it not being far from their backyard. "I think at first they thought she'd wandered off, but then someone discovered blood in the Bowens' tent."

"Right, but this guy told Mel that Bowen freaked and claimed it was planted there."

"Planted there? Oh, come on." Gage sat his cup aside.

"That's what everyone thought—that he was just trying to cover up his crime."

"He took off. Proves he was guilty if you ask me."

"That's what everyone believed, but the guy told Melody that Bowen seemed genuinely distraught —that when he took off, he said he was going to find his wife."

"But he never did."

"And no one ever saw him again."

"Because he ran."

"Yeah, probably." She sighed. "They'd drunk a lot the night before, so who knows? Alcohol does strange things.

"But the guy Melody talked to said it had shaken him to see how loving the Bowens had seemed that night around the campfire, and then . . ." She shook her head. "Probably why I'm not so keen on marriage." She laughed. "One of the reasons at least."

"Did you say they'd been drinking?"

"Yeah."

"On an excursion?"

She nodded. "I know, stupid. Yet another one of my safety rules. No alcohol while traveling. It's just an invitation for some guy to take advantage."

"Beyond stupid of them." He'd never allow it. Too much risk. It would cloud people's vision, and a foggy brain was the last thing a person needed when sea kayaking.

"Apparently the land excursion outfit provided the alcohol."

If he recalled correctly, the cruise line had, in an effort to save money, gone with an unestablished excursion company. *Company* was actually too flattering a description for the mishmash group of kayakers who thought they'd make some summer cash by catering to the cruise lines and under-bidding all the established companies in the area.

No wonder the ragtag venture had quickly folded and the kayakers involved dispersed.

"It prompted Destiny to announce they'd be way more stringent with their excursion provider choices in the future—though that might have just been a PR number."

The incident had put a lot of unwanted heat and bad press on legitimate excursion companies like LFA. But they'd weathered the storm and proven their worth, and now they were the first excursion company in the area to lead an *onboard* excursion component.

"They were pretty stringent with us," Gage said. They'd done an extremely thorough background check on Last Frontier Adventures before allowing them to conduct even half-day land excursions.

He turned to Whitney. "I think it's very smart of you to take the precautions you do."

"Thanks. You're definitely in the minority."

"Really?"

"Yeah. Most folks fall into one of two camps. Either they think I'm paranoid or they think I'm an idiot for going on excursions alone. I'm traveling with my aunt, but she's not up for the excursions. I don't see why I should miss out on the adventures out of fear something might happen, so I take precautions and enjoy the excursions I want to take. But, and at the same time, it's nice to know Aunt Ellen is on the ship waiting for me."

"Makes a lot of sense."

She smiled up at him. "Thanks. That's refreshing to hear."

Darcy and Clint came through the clearing, the moon now full in the sky. Clint pressed a kiss to Darcy's cheek and headed toward the crew's tents.

Gage finished off his coffee and stood. "If you'll excuse me . . ."

"Sure." Whitney stood beside him and brushed the debris off her pants. "About time I turn in. See you in the morning."

"Bright and early."

"Don't remind me," she said, heading for her tent. "I love adventure, but definitely not early mornings."

Darcy turned as Gage stepped to her side. "Looks like you made a friend."

Gage watched Whitney slipping inside her tent, the shadow of her athletic form illuminated by the battery-operated lantern.

He lifted his chin toward Clint's retreating back. "I could say the same. . . ."

"We were just catching the sunset. Clint found this amazing—"

"Cliff at the top of the rise?"

"Yeah." She cocked her head, curiosity fluttering her lashes. "How'd you know?"

"I lead excursions out here all the time."

"Right. So how come you didn't head up there?"

"Wasn't feeling it tonight." In truth, he'd very much wanted to show Darcy himself, but after their argument . . . "Clint obviously was."

She smirked. "Do I detect a note of jealousy?"

"Of Wonder Hands?" He laughed.

"Wonder Hands?" Her brows pinched together.

"That's what the ladies were calling him earlier."

"Really?"

"Interesting nickname."

"Probably because he's a massage therapist."

"I'm sure."

"Are you trying to suggest that Clint gets personal with the female passengers?"

"I'm not suggesting anything. Just stating what the ladies are calling him."

"Calling who?" Kayden asked, tossing Gage an apple.

"Darcy's new friend Clint." He bit into it.

Darcy's eyes narrowed on Gage. "Did you want something, or did you just come over here to annoy me?"

He'd come over because, as loath as he was to admit it, he wanted to know how her time with Clint had gone. "Actually, Whitney was telling me something that I thought might interest you."

"Really?"

They took seats by the dying embers of the fire as Jake, Landon, and Piper joined them. All the passengers had turned in for the night, settling into their luxurious tents, while the remainder of the *Bering*'s crew were dispersed about their own business—most likely preparing for bed.

"So what *helpful* information did Whitney share?" Darcy asked.

Gage bit back a smirk. She clearly wasn't a fan of his time with Whitney. *Interesting.*

"She reminded me of a disappearance involving the *Bering*. The couple disappeared during their excursion here."

"Here?" Darcy's eyes widened. "As in literally *here?*"

He went on to relay all that Whitney had shared, as well as some details he remembered from the media coverage.

Darcy shook her head. "I definitely need to do some digging on the *Bering*'s history. This all happened so fast, I didn't have time to prepare, to do the typical background research I normally do. I was relying on Abby to catch me up, and then . . ."

"Whatever you do, don't use the *Bering*'s

computers to search for it," Jake said, leaning forward and rubbing his hands together.

"Why not?" Kayden asked.

"Because everything is monitored."

"What do you mean, *monitored?*"

"All the computers in the cruise ship's Internet lounge are linked and can easily be monitored through their browser history."

Kayden linked her arms. "And I suppose that's just another random fact of knowledge you possess?"

"What can I say?" He shrugged. "I read."

"So do I, and I don't know the things you do."

Jake kicked back the last of his cider and tossed the paper cup in what remained of the fire. "Guess you're reading the wrong books." He stood. " 'Night, everyone."

"'Night, Jake," Gage said along with the rest —except Kayden.

He exhaled. "Every time, sis?"

"I can't believe I'm the only one who finds Jake's storehouse of knowledge strange." She shifted to Darcy. "You're a reporter. Surely you find his criminal knowledge suspect."

"He said he reads a lot."

"Seriously. You're buying that? You were way more curious when you were in Yancey." Kayden's eyes narrowed. "Wait a minute. . . . What changed?"

"Nothing. I've just stopped thinking about it."

"Just like that?"

Gage studied Darcy's guarded expression. He was with Kayden on this one. Darcy simply walking away from something that had intrigued her so . . . Something was off.

Darcy stood and stretched. "I think I'm going to hit the hay. It's been a full day."

Gage and Kayden exchanged a look. Something was definitely up with Darcy when it came to Jake.

" 'Night," he said as she slipped into her tent.

Kayden looked over at him. "That was weird."

He shrugged. "Never know what to expect with Darcy." It was part of what unsettled him so much about her.

Kayden stood. "See ya in the morning, bro."

"Yeah, see you." Gage remained after Landon and Piper turned in too. Content to just sit and watch the embers die out. His heart was restless, stirring, and it scared him. He was much more comfortable feeling numb.

15

Darcy settled in her sleeping bag and rolled to face Piper. They'd dimmed their lantern, but the full moon shining through their canvas tent illuminated the small space between them enough that Darcy could make out Piper's worried expression.

"How's Reef?" Darcy asked. She'd been introduced to the McKennas through Reef's home-
coming, his murder charge, and the subsequent
investigative ordeal.

"Good, I hope. It's been a while since we've
heard from him."

"What? I thought he'd decided to stay."

"He did. For about a week after you left."
Piper shifted, nestling into her inflatable pillow.
"You know Reef—can't sit still for more than a
minute."

"Will he be back for Cole and Bailey's wedding?"

"I pray so."

She did too. "I'm glad I got to bunk with you."
She'd missed Piper, missed all the McKennas,
especially Gage. "Who's Kayden bunking with?"

"Whitney Castle."

Kayden was in one of the glamping tents?
Darcy wondered about Gage's influence on that
decision, when she was the one who was supposed to be writing about the excursion
experience from a participant's POV.

"Ah, Gage's new friend," she said with a little
more bite than intended.

"What?" Curiosity danced in Piper's voice.

"Nothing." She was being petty. Whitney
seemed perfectly nice, and there was no reason for
her and Gage not to converse. It wasn't like *she*
and Gage would ever be an item. They couldn't.

His disapproval of her profession and questioning of her character were the least of their problems. She'd been praying about his utter lack of desire for a relationship with God ever since she'd first met the man. And she prayed still that God would bring healing—for only He could.

Though he frustrated her more than anyone she'd ever met, he'd wrestled a part of her heart away, and she feared it would always belong to him. As much as she hated to admit it, she yearned for his understanding, his assurance, and his . . . *love?*

"You okay over there?" Piper asked in the silence.

"Yeah, I'm just . . ."

"Deep in thought?" Piper propped her head on her hand. "Are you making any progress?"

Darcy sighed. "Not nearly enough." Although Whitney's conversation with Gage might have given her the first viable lead—a place to start digging on the *Bering*.

She needed to get back into Abby's room without the roommate present and snoop some more, needed to see if Abby had hidden away anything containing more detail or more elaborate notes. For all she knew, the Bowen case Whitney mentioned was nothing more than what the media and law enforcement deemed it to be— that the man killed his wife and somehow escaped—but maybe there was more to it, something connected to Abby's disappearance.

Piper shifted to face her better in the small confines. "Tell me about her."

"About Abby?"

"Yeah."

There was so much to say, so many memories. . . . Where did she start? "I met Abby freshman year of college. We were assigned to room together."

"Did you hit it off right away?"

"More or less. Abby was a go-getter, smart, savvy . . . destined to be a reporter."

"Sounds an awful lot like you."

"People always said we were two peas in a pod."

"Which is why she reached out to you when she was in trouble."

Darcy let the comment slide, unsure how to answer. After she left investigative reporting, her relationship with Abby had changed. Abby had pressed forward while she'd gone to heal. Things hadn't been the same since. They still talked— occasionally—still remained friends, but at a greater distance than ever before.

"I think it's wonderful that you dropped everything and went to her aid."

"She was my best friend." Or at least she had been for years. Until that last case. "We were hired by the same paper out of college, both worked our way up to investigative journalism."

"Like undercover reporting?"

Darcy nodded.

"Wow. That must have been exciting."

"That's one word for it."

And for a while it was absolutely exhilarating, but then the cases began to wear on her—the heartache, the lies, the ugliness she was exposing. She was bringing the criminals to justice, but it began eating away at her. She'd wrestled with the idea of taking a breather but didn't want to leave Abby hanging. She and Abby were the Starsky and Hutch of the undercover investigative world.

Then a case turned her world upside down, leaving her no choice but to walk away, to get out while she could still maintain her dignity, her character, everything she stood for—bruised as it may have been. Abby said she understood, but things had never been the same between them since.

Darcy moved on to covering the extreme sports circuit, reporting on the events and the athletes she'd grown up around. It was an entirely different world—one that didn't leave her satisfied—but for a while she'd been content to remain in a holding pattern until God showed her the next step, the new direction and plans He had for her. This—Abby's undercover case and disappearance—was an unexpected detour, but it was one Darcy had to take.

"You must have worked some pretty intense

cases," Piper said, never one to lack curiosity.

"I could tell you stories that would curl your toes. Which makes Abby's fear of this particular case all the more frightening. I've never seen Abby so scared. The way she looked at me when I boarded the ship . . ."

"Which is why you're willing to ignore your fear and push forward regardless."

Darcy swallowed. "My fear?"

"You're scared of water—you can't swim, can you?"

"What?" Darcy sat up. "How . . . ?" How did she know?

"I've seen the fear before—recognized the panic on your face when you climbed into the kayak. We had a client at Last Frontier Adventures a few years back—Pete Baker. He'd grown up in the Aleutian chain surrounded by water but was terrified of it."

Having grown up in southern California less than a mile from the beach, she knew the feeling all too well.

"He decided it was crazy to be scared of the water surrounding his home, so he decided to face it. He knew Cole from his competitive skiing days, so he came in the shop and asked for Cole's help in overcoming his fear."

"And did it work?"

"Yeah. Pete's a scuba fanatic now. His passion for the sport nearly rivals Cole's."

"Impressive." Clearly he was much braver than she was.

Piper swung her legs around to sit cross-legged and leaned forward, resting her elbows on her knees. "You know you're going to have to tell Gage."

Darcy sat up. "I can't. He won't let me continue with the excursion. I'll lose my job and any chance of finding Abby."

"I'm sorry, Darcy. I understand how desperately you want to help your friend, but it's not safe."

"I managed just fine today."

"Today, yes, but tomorrow we'll be cutting across the south side of Kesuk on the Akalux River, and Class IV conditions are the norm, not the exception."

Darcy swallowed.

"I can't let you endanger your life like that."

"But . . ."

"Maybe we can come up with some excuse for why you have to travel back on the supply boat."

"Mullins won't care about excuses. She'll just hire someone else."

"I know you are worried about your friend, but so am I."

"What?"

Piper leaned across the space separating them and clasped Darcy's hand. "You. I'm trying to protect you. I don't want to lose my friend."

131

How could she argue with that? But she still had to find a way to stay with the excursions. Her cover had to remain intact until she uncovered the truth behind Abby's disappearance.

16

The charcoal-gray sky held none of yesterday's warmth. A chill bit at Darcy's cheeks as she stood on the soggy ground, mustering her courage to seek out Gage.

She glanced at the group settled around the fire, noting Ted, George, and Phillip's absence. Perhaps they were busy loading the supply ship.

Gage stalked out of the woods at the north side of camp, frustration evident on his creased brow. *Great.* He was already irritated. That would make the conversation they needed to have go so much better.

Taking a deep breath, she started toward him. "Can I talk to you?"

"What's up?" His breath shone like a swirling cloud in the cold morning air.

"Is something wrong?"

"Chef Phillip injured himself."

"How?"

"He wandered too far off for his morning bathroom break while it was still dark and ended up stepping into some poacher's trap. Nearly cut his foot clean off."

How had she slept through the commotion? "Is he going to be okay?"

"George had gone for a predawn hike and heard Phillip hollering. Good thing, because he'd gone well beyond earshot of camp. If George hadn't been out there, Phillip could have easily bled out before any of us found him."

"But he's all right?"

"I hope so. I haven't seen him. Ted and George made the call to head straight back for the *Bering* with Phillip on the supply ship."

"They're gone?"

"Left over an hour ago. Clint was waiting to tell me when I stepped from my tent." He was clearly irritated he had been left out of the decision-making process.

"What about the tents, the supplies?"

"We'll bring what we can safely carry on the kayaks—at least the personal stuff—and the *Bering* will have to send the supply ship back out to pick up the rest, or figure out something else if they don't have time before the cruise continues."

Piper and Kayden hurried toward them.

"Clint just told us what happened," Kayden said.

"Is Phillip going to be okay?" Piper asked.

"I think so. Clint said they moved quickly because of the amount of blood Phillip had already lost. But they should be able to get him stabilized in the ship's clinic."

"They've already headed back with the supply ship," Darcy said to Piper, hoping, since nothing could be done anyway, that she'd let her off the hook, not insist she tell Gage about her fear of water. He had so much on his mind with the circumstances . . . surely it could wait.

"He still needs to know," Piper said.

"Know what?" Gage asked, his eyes narrowing.

Darcy exhaled, anticipating the blowback that would no doubt be coming. "I can't swim."

He dipped his head. "Excuse me?"

She swallowed. "I can't swim—I'm terrified of water."

"And you didn't think that was worth mentioning before climbing in a kayak?"

"I was wearing a life preserver when I was in the kayak. Not everyone that steps aboard a boat knows how to swim."

"Yes, but you're talking about kayaking Class IV rapids. If you get tossed from the craft . . ."

"Then I'll have my life preserver on."

"What's going on?" Clint asked, stepping into the huddle. "Something else wrong?"

Darcy grimaced. The guy had impeccable timing. She looked at Gage, pleading with her eyes for him to not out her to Clint.

Gage's jaw tightened. "Just discussing how we're going to get the supplies back to the ship."

She mouthed *thank you,* but he simply turned and walked away.

* * *

Gage, Kayden, and Clint distributed the participants' packs evenly among the kayaks, while Jake saw to loading what he could of the McKennas' supplies. Jake worked with efficiency and great care to assure the integrity of the equipment remained—equipment they'd be relying on to keep them dry and protected for the remainder of the voyage excursions.

"You should wear a water-repellant fleece beneath your life vest," Gage said, finally speaking to Darcy after an incredibly tense hour. "It's going to be a cold and damp one today."

All she'd brought on the cruise was her regular fleece.

"You don't have one, do you?" he asked.

"I didn't know I'd need one." Everything had happened so rapidly, it was a wonder she'd managed to pack what she had.

He slid his jacket off and handed it to her. "Here. It'll be loose, but it's better than nothing, and we'll adjust your life vest accordingly."

"No. I couldn't." He'd have nothing but his long-sleeved T-shirt to keep him warm.

"I've got a windbreaker that'll work fine."

But wouldn't keep him nearly as warm.

"I insist." He tugged her to him—he had the most annoying habit of doing that—and slipped her arms into the warm fleece. It was the same heather gray of his eyes and smelled like him—a sensual mixture of sandalwood and the sea. He zipped her up and rolled the sleeves so her hands showed, then stood back and assessed her. "It'll do. Let's get your preserver on. We need to make sure you stay safe, considering the circumstances."

She didn't bother fighting him, just let him adjust her accordingly, securing her in the life vest with great care. Gage's attention, even though focused on her safety rather than her person, felt enthralling.

"What?" he questioned at her staring.

"Just watching you work."

He tightened the last strap. "You're all set."

She nodded, reveling in the warmth of his fleece and of his tender care. How could he be so caring one moment, and so judgmental and frustrating the next?

"Stick close to Landon. Yesterday's conditions are going to seem like splashing in a kiddie pool compared to today's."

She clasped her hand on his before he could pull away. "Thank you."

"Not like I have a choice. Supply boat's gone."

"But I . . ." There was so much she wanted to say—where did she even start?

Gage lifted his chin. "Here comes your friend."

She turned to find Clint strolling toward her, then back to find Gage walking away.

"Looks like you've got an admirer," Clint said.

"Gage? Nah, he's just making sure we're all safe."

Clint studied Gage double-checking the rest of the passengers' vests. "Seems to have spent a lot more time with you."

Landon joined them. "You ready, sport?" He squeezed Darcy's shoulder.

She nodded, feeling anything but.

"See ya out there." Clint winked and headed for his kayak.

Landon leaned in, lowering his voice to a whisper. "Piper and Gage apprised me of the situation. Don't worry, I'll stick close. We'll get through this."

"Thanks."

"We should get out there before we hold anyone up."

Stepping in her kayak, she fought to ignore the terror rushing over her. Once again she dropped into the boat and breathed a deep and heartfelt prayer. She looked at the mushy sand with frustration. She'd left her paddle on the beach.

Gage spotted it and headed toward her before she could climb back out of the red kayak.

"Forget something?" He handed it over.

She gripped the metal as if it were her only hold on life. "Thanks."

Gage nodded, clearly hesitant to leave her side.

"We ready?" Kayden asked.

Gage shifted his gaze to the group, once again waiting impatiently on him and Darcy.

"Yep. We're set." He glanced back at Darcy one last time. "Stay safe out there."

"Will do."

Once they'd pushed off from shore, Landon butted his kayak against hers. "Be sure to stick to me like glue. If you need *anything,* you let me know. Okay?"

She nodded, following him into the bay. Last night's rain still lingered in the burgeoning waves and whitecaps. Gage had said they'd paddle a quarter mile along the shore to where the bay met up with the Akalux River. She could do this.

* * *

Gage eyed the rapids ahead with trepidation. For an experienced kayaker, they were going to be a blast; for an intermediate, a challenge, but for Darcy . . .

He glanced back. She shouldn't be in the water, *period.* But at this point, they had no choice. He could, however, reshuffle. He'd have Jake take over his group at the front, move each of the other leaders up a group, move Landon up to Piper's group, and lead Darcy through himself.

He waved Jake forward during the calmest passage they were likely to encounter. Time was short. They had a couple minutes max before they'd be within the rapids' pull.

He stalled slightly as Jake paddled to his side. "I need you to take lead with my team. I'm going to help Darcy through the rapids."

"Should she even attempt it?"

"*Should* and *will* are two different matters."

With a slight shake of his head, Jake pushed forward without any further complaint.

He continued his way back to Kayden and then Piper, garnering the stares of the passengers as he passed.

"Everything okay?" Clint asked.

"Just giving the others a taste of the froth." He lifted his chin toward the rapids. "I'm going to cover the rear."

"Stinks to be you." Clint smiled, clearly enamored with the day's ride and the action ahead.

Shuffling Piper up was easy. She'd already assessed the situation and, as always, was eager to help in any way she could. Piper glanced back as Gage approached her fiancé.

He lifted his chin to Landon. "Move up to Piper's group. I'll take Darcy through."

Landon nodded, a measure of relief crossing his brow. Landon was a fine kayaker, but he'd never led a beginner through such a challenging pass. The rain had knocked the rapids up. It was going to be one bumpy ride.

"You can stay up front." Darcy continued to paddle, determination evident on her perspiring brow. "I'll be fine." A shaft of sunlight beat down through the clouds, but its warmth wasn't causing the moisture on her brow. He watched her chest rising and falling, studying her hurried breaths. She was scared.

"Settle down. I'll get you through this."

"I told you, I'm fine."

His brow dipped. "I'm not sure if you're being arrogant or ignorant."

"I'm holding my own."

"So far, yes, but we've had a pretty smooth path. The road's about to get real bumpy."

She shifted her gaze past him, and her eyes widened at the rapids swirling thirty yards ahead.

"We've got a strong current along with pounding surf where the river dumps out on the island's eastern shore. You're going to need my help if you hope to make it through this passage in one piece."

17

Gage instructed the entire excursion team to circle up before the current pulled any of them into the section of the rapids called the Crush Zone. "The important thing to remember going through this passage is to avoid the hole."

Darcy looked at Gage.

"The flow in the hole forms a recirculating vortex that if you're pulled into can prove extremely difficult to escape from. This area is particularly tricky as we have the white-water rapids mixing with the ocean current beneath the vortex, flushing up through the sea caves."

"Sea caves?" Heath's face lit. "Cool!"

"Not cool." Gage shook his head. "The wave height might not be that high out here, but in the caves they compress. You could be entrapped or smashed against the rocks."

Amber's eyes widened.

"He's just trying to frighten you." Heath chuckled at his fiancée.

"You're right," Gage said. "I am. This is serious. Avoid the hole at all costs. Take the upper route around its edge, where the current is weakest." He pointed out the direction he wanted them to go.

"You mean the boring way around," Heath grumbled.

"The safe way," Gage reiterated. "Stick with your team and follow your guide's lead. Everyone understand?"

Everyone nodded, but Darcy didn't miss the irritation on Heath's face. Gage was right. He was going to be trouble, but she couldn't worry about him. Her job was to stick like glue to Gage through the pass. She wouldn't risk getting pulled toward the caves.

"I'm going to send the groups through in a different order," Gage said. "Kayden, you'll take your group through first."

Darcy watched as Henry and his two sons studiously followed Gage's sister in a wide arc around the hole's path, as Gage had instructed.

Landon went next with the two married couples. Again they followed Landon's lead and Darcy breathed a slight sigh of relief after they'd safely made it past the danger zone. Jake's group made it through cleanly as well—even Heath moderated his daredevil posturing and maintained a safe route. She could do this. She could trust Gage to lead her through.

Gage signaled for Piper to go next with Whitney, Clint, and the newlyweds. Piper led while Clint took the rear of the tiny group. As Piper and the newlyweds crested the far end of the Crush Zone, Gage readied to signal Darcy to move.

"Now?" Her chest tightened.

He smiled. "Now or never. Just follow me. Stroke for stroke."

She nodded and gripped the paddle until her fingers burned. She followed Gage along the edge. The vortex grew closer with each stroke, and she could feel the current fighting to drag her under. Fear pricked her spine, her vision narrowing.

Not now. Don't panic. You will get through this. It's not the same. It's not the same.

Gage angled against the current, and she struggled to do the same, her craft not cooperating nearly as smoothly as Gage's. Panic rose in her chest, heating her limbs as rain began to fall.

A piercing scream tore from Whitney's lips.

Darcy's gaze flashed to Whitney flailing in her kayak, smacking at the water with her paddle. *What is . . . ?*

Before she could finish her thought, the current grabbed hold, swirling her craft around at a dizzying speed. She'd given up her attention for one second, and that's all it had taken.

Her name tore from Gage's lips.

The current pulled strong, yanking her toward the swirling vortex.

No. Not again. Please, God, not again.

She caught sight of movement ahead. Was that Clint coming for her? He rounded the far side of the hole only to be smashed against the rocks. A guttural moan escaped his lips.

Movement swirled all around, the colorful kayaks and life vests moving toward her, but it was too late.

The vortex sucked her in, the waves swelling over her as her kayak rolled, pinning her beneath. Salt water stung her eyes; water filled her throat, burning her nostrils.

A whoosh rushed around her, and the kayak shifted, the front end nose-diving and then jettisoning up with frightening speed.

Gage grounded his kayak and ran into the water after Darcy, with Jake following. One minute Darcy's red kayak was visible, the next it upended, and now only the smallest tip showed above the surface. She was being sucked into the sea caves. The wash was strong; it would pin her down. He only hoped it would pop her above the surface once inside instead of smashing her against the rocks.

Kayden moved to assist Clint at the far end of the wash as Gage waded into the swirling rapids. Grabbing the guide rope Jake tossed his way, he wrapped it through the safety loop of his vest and triggered the strobe mounted just above it. Taking a large gulp of air, he dove beneath the surface into the heart of the vortex.

The swirling whirlpool drew him down, pulling him to the bottom and then propelling him up into the sea cave's wash. The strobe illuminated Darcy's kayak—nose down, embedded in the sand of the sea cave floor. She was struggling to free herself. He swam to her side and, pulling the utility knife from his pants pocket, worked to cut her loose. Her eyes widened and quickened in the flash of his strobe—but not on him, rather on something over his shoulder. He kicked, swimming up above the cave's waterline with Darcy practically limp in his arms.

"Body," she gurgled, gulping for air.

"You're hurt? Where?"

"No." She spluttered. "Down there."

"What?"

"There's a body. A person." As she pointed, her eyes widened again.

Gage followed her outstretched hand, directing his strobe at the head of a person bobbing above the water's surface. "We need to get back up top."

"But . . ."

"I'll get you to safety, and then we'll contact local search and rescue to help us retrieve the body."

She was shivering beside him, and he feared she wasn't registering what he was saying.

He cupped her face. "Darc, look at me." He caressed her cold cheeks. "Let's focus on getting you back to the surface, and then we'll see to the body. Do you understand?"

She nodded, her lips paling in the cold water.

They needed to move fast; hypothermia was no doubt already setting in. "We're going to have to dive back under and then swim up through the vortex."

"What? Are you crazy?"

"There are only two ways out of here, and the way we came in is safest."

"How on earth can you say that?"

"The other end of the cave system is littered with boulders and is pummeled by surging waves."

"And the way we came in was a picnic?"

He smiled. At least she was getting her fight back. That was a good sign.

"See this?" He lifted the guide rope attached to his vest. "Jake's got the other end. We tug twice to signal we're ready to come up, and he'll make sure we get there."

"You're saying . . . ?"

"I swim you back under and out."

She shook her head, her skin pearly white in the strobe's light. "I can't."

"We have to, honey. I'll do all the work. You just have to hold on." He stepped behind her. "I'm going to latch you to me."

"What?" She squirmed as he secured her vest to the guide rope and locked his arm under hers and across her chest in a secure hold.

"I'll swim you out as if you're unconscious."

"If you do, then everyone will know I can't swim."

"Darcy, you could have died and you're worried about what everyone else will think?"

"I have to."

"No. What you have to do is live. Now, take a deep breath."

He didn't give her time to argue, just tugged on the rope twice and dove back under the water, fighting his way to the surface, his hold on her steadfast and unwavering.

18

Darcy breached the surface, gulping in air and coughing up water. She flailed, trying to free herself from Gage but knowing she couldn't—not until she had something solid to grasp hold of.

"That wasn't . . . ?" she asked, praying he understood her question without her having to say it outright.

He shook his head.

Not Abby. He was saying it wasn't Abby down there. With the level of decomposition on the head, it seemed unlikely.

It had been so fast and so disturbing below the surface—caught in the swell, her heart in her throat. It had sent her back to terrorizing snapshots of being pulled under the surge all those years ago, seeing Stacey's panicked eyes right before they were dragged under. Seeing the corpse. It was all too real, all too terrible.

She couldn't stop shaking.

What if Gage was wrong and it *was* Abby?

Jake moved to assist, to pull her from Gage's arms, but Gage refused to let go. "I've got her."

His arms held her tight, secure, and if it weren't for the circumstances, she'd have been content to simply nestle deeper into his hold and rest awhile.

"She doesn't look so good," Jake commented.

"Is she going to be all right?" Whitney called from the shore.

"She's pretty shaken up, but I've got her," Gage said, keeping a firm grip on her.

Darcy liked the sound of that. Gage's sheltering embrace reminded her of her dad's all those years ago. Passing from near death to his strong arms. . . . She could never describe the absolute trust and surrender she felt toward her dad in that instant—the same, although so much deeper, surrender, trust, and security she experienced when she gave her life to Christ.

And now, in Gage's arms, she gave her safety fully over to his capable hands.

Moving her to shore, he gently laid her on the sand and she missed the security of being wrapped in his arms.

"Any injuries?" Piper asked, kneeling.

"Amazingly, I don't think so," Gage said, grabbing the blanket Kayden handed him.

His hands trembled as he wrapped it snugly around her. Was he trembling from the frigid water, the tense situation, or the emotion of saving her?

Piper gazed up at him. "You okay, bro?"

He nodded, shifting into leader mode. "If everyone could gather around."

His sisters had clearly seen to the other passengers, and one of them must have rescued Clint, because he sat among them, his shoulder bandaged.

"Thank you," Darcy said, looking over at Clint, "for trying to rescue me."

He winked. "Anytime."

"I'm sorry you got hurt."

"This . . ." Clint glanced down at the bandage on his shoulder. "Nothing but a flesh wound."

"If you're done thanking your *rescuer*," Gage said a little too grouchily even for him, "I suggest we formulate a new plan."

She hadn't meant to imply Clint was her rescuer in any sense of the word, only that she appreciated his attempt to help, and that she felt bad he'd gotten hurt in the process.

Gage was her rescuer. Her *hero*.

A tumult of emotions reeled through her, but the hollow eyes she'd seen beneath the water's depths stole any warmth—she'd stared straight into the face of death, and it left her haunted.

"New plan?" Heath asked, breaking through her thoughts.

Gage rubbed the back of his neck. "There's been a complication."

Heath snorted. "Yeah, Darcy can't handle her kayak."

She cringed. Here came the questions about her ability, her qualifications.

"It was my fault," Whitney said.

"What?" Heath said. "How?"

"If I hadn't screamed . . ." Whitney shook her head. "I totally distracted her." She looked at

Darcy with genuine remorse. It touched Darcy deeply. Gage was right—her lack of experience could have jeopardized all of their safety.

"I thought that stupid stick poking out of the water was a snake," Whitney continued. "It freaked me out. I hate snakes."

Heath snorted. "For future reference, Whitney, there are no snakes in Alaska—it's too cold."

"Oh." Whitney's cheeks flushed with the tell-tale hue of embarrassment.

"It wasn't your fault," Darcy said, choking up. It was her own, for not being able to kayak, let alone swim.

"There's no need to assign blame," Gage said.

"You'd better figure out whose fault it is," Clint said, "because Mullins is going to expect not only a full report but some serious answers."

She swallowed, making eye contact with Gage as she pulled the blanket more tightly around her. If she cost LFA the cruise-line contract . . . she'd feel horrible.

"Accidents happen," Gage said, determined to cut off further discussion on the matter. "The complication I was referring to has nothing to do with Darcy's accident, but rather with what she found in the cave."

Heath's eyes lit. Clearly he was hoping Gage would follow up with the word *treasure* or something of the adventurous sort.

"Or"— Gage swallowed—"should I say who."

"You found a *body?*" Heath asked with a mixture of reality-TV awe and borderline disgust.

Gage nodded. "I'm afraid so."

Heath's face scrunched. "Gnarly."

"Okay." Cal shrugged. "What does that have to do with us and our plans?"

"We can't just leave the body down there," Gage said, disappointed with the man's attitude.

"You don't actually expect us to retrieve some corpse?" Cal said, aghast.

"We need to head back to the *Bering* as planned," Clint said. "We can alert the authorities when we reach Eagle Cove."

"I don't expect you passengers, or any of the *Bering*'s crew, to retrieve the body, but we"— Gage gestured to the LFA crew—"volunteer with Yancey Search and Rescue, and Landon here"— he pointed to his future brother-in-law—"is a deputy sheriff."

Clint lifted his chin. "What's a deputy sheriff doing working a kayak excursion?"

"He's my fiancé," Piper said. "I asked him to join me for the trip."

"Here's what's going to happen," Gage said, taking charge. "Landon, Jake, and I will remain to assist the local authorities when they arrive." He looked to his younger sister. "Piper, you and Kayden head back with the passengers. We're past the rough spots, so it should be fairly easy

151

paddling from here out." He looked to the sky, which seemed a bit lighter. "And the trip across the strait to Eagle Cove should be relatively smooth."

He had full faith his sisters could handle leading the trip. They were strong women and strong kayakers. His gaze shifted to Clint and his bandaged shoulder. "You okay to paddle?"

Clint nodded. "No problem."

"Great, then you can help my sisters lead the passengers back. Landon's got a satellite phone, so he'll call ahead to the *Bering* and apprise them of the situation, as well as get in touch with local law enforcement. We'll meet back up with you at the ship. The *Bering* isn't scheduled to disembark until eight o'clock this evening, so we should be back in plenty of time."

Everyone agreed, though Heath, in typical fashion, grumbled.

"Darcy, you stay here," Gage said as she moved toward the kayaks with the others.

She frowned, clearly confused but not wanting to question him in front of everyone.

"We can see she makes it back fine," Clint said.

"I appreciate that, but after the trauma she's endured, I'll feel better, as the excursion leader, seeing to her myself."

"Not to mention she was first to see the body," Landon cut in. "Local authorities will want her statement."

"Statement?" Clint scoffed. "What kind of

statement can she possibly give? She went under and saw the corpse. Not much to say there."

"I'm good staying," Darcy said. "Really. I appreciate Gage's concern for my safety."

He tried not to laugh outright at the irony of that statement. The woman couldn't even swim and she'd tackled Class IV rapids. Adhering to safety precautions was the last thing on her mind.

"All right," Clint said with an edge of disappointment. "If you're sure."

Why did Clint care so much whether Darcy stayed or went? He'd have her back on the ship and in Clint's sights soon enough. He tried to ignore the jealousy tugging at him. It was petty and ridiculous. What did it matter if Clint took a liking to Darcy, or even if she took a liking to him in return?

He and Darcy would never be an item, but seeing her engaging in even a casual flirtation bugged him. And the fact that it bugged him, bugged him even more.

Within minutes his sisters had everyone organized and in their kayaks, and he stood on the river—Jake, Landon, and Darcy beside him— watching the colorful kayaks as one by one they disappeared around the river's bend.

Darcy sank down on a boulder, shivering. "Mullins is going to fire me."

Gage sighed. He wanted to assure her that wouldn't be the case, that it would all be all right.

But Mullins valued planning, precision, and strict adherence to the rules. . . . They'd be lucky if she didn't fire Darcy and the entire LFA crew on the spot for exposing the *Bering*'s luxury clientele to such a traumatic course of events—unintentional as it'd been.

Jake handed Darcy a fleece he'd fished from his pack. "Here, you've got to be freezing."

"Thanks." Gratitude broke on her face.

Gage grimaced. He was an idiot. He'd been too preoccupied to notice the chill in his bones or the quivering of Darcy's blue lips. The slip of a thing had to be freezing. *He* was freezing. The blanket wrapped around her wasn't enough to combat hypothermia. "We need to get you out of those wet clothes."

"It's a great idea, but my pack is still submerged."

"Mine's not," Gage said, reaching for his. "I'm sure we can find something that will work."

Jake and Landon retrieved their packs as well. Once they'd pieced together an outfit for Darcy —Landon's sweats, an extra pair of Jake's boots along with Gage's Henley shirt and pair of socks—Gage set about to fish out a dry change of clothes for himself.

"Let's get a fire started and find something warm for Darcy to drink." They had to get her internal body temperature back up fast.

19

"You can use that copse of evergreen trees for privacy," Jake said, pointing to the small grouping. It wasn't large, only a handful of trees and shrubbery, but it would do.

"Thanks."

Gingerly, she got to her feet but could only wobble where she stood. Her body ached as if she'd been wrung through, but it was her soul that had taken the hardest blow.

Seeing a dead body—or what remained of it—up close had truly shaken her, bringing back images of Stacey being torn from her life, ripped away into the dark beyond.

Gage peeled off his windbreaker and pulled his sopping shirt over his head, exposing his chest.

Darcy's breath caught, her gaze drawn to the two precious baby feet tattooed above his heart.

Tucker. Her heart squeezed, tears stinging her eyes.

"You okay, Darcy?" Landon asked.

Gage's gaze flashed to hers before she could look away. He glanced down at the tattoo—resigned anguish on his handsome face—then back at her. A brief moment of unguarded emotion passed between them, and then it was gone.

She yearned to say something, to do something—to run and wrap her arms around him and not let go. But he'd want to be left alone. He always did. No doubt he'd make a joke or offer a playful smile within seconds.

He yanked on a dry shirt and cocked his head in a teasing manner. "You may want to scoot before I swap my pants." He winked, but it did nothing to diffuse the tightness in her belly or the growing depth of her feelings for him. She was coming to love the man, busted heart and all.

"Darc, I'm hardly shy," he said, reaching for his zipper.

"Right." She turned heel and darted into the shelter of the trees, her mind filled with the image of his bare chest. Forget the defined muscles. It was the tattoo—Tucker's tattoo—that had melted her heart.

Despite the wet earth and the chill permeating her very being, she dropped to her knees and prayed for the man she'd come to care for so deeply.

Father, my heart feels like it is physically cracking, shattering for Gage and the pain he still suffers. Let him know you. Let him know the healing and peace that only you can bring. Please do a great work in him, and use me in any way possible, according to your will.

She remained on her knees in silence, allowing the Holy Spirit to speak for her, to utter the cries of her heart that even she didn't understand,

156

asking, begging, for God's intercession on behalf of the man she was coming to love. *Love.* She'd felt a deep ache for him ever since she'd first seen past his playful bravado to the hurting heart underneath, but in the months since she'd last seen him, it was amazing how deep her feelings for him had rooted.

"Darcy, you okay?" Jake's voice echoed through the small copse of trees.

"Yeah." She cleared the emotion from her throat. "Fine. Why?"

"You're just taking a while. We wanted to make sure you were okay."

"Yep. Be out soon."

"We're in the wilderness, no need to impress," Gage called.

What is that supposed to mean? Any way she looked at it, the comment wasn't flattering.

She slunk off the blanket and slipped out of her frigid clothes. After pulling on Landon's sweats, she lifted Gage's Henley to her face, and despite how dreadfully cliché it was, she inhaled. The cobalt-blue shirt smelled like him—like sea air and sandalwood.

You. Are. Being. Ridiculous.

She slipped the shirt over her head, reveling in the warmth it provided, and pulled on the thick wool socks, hoping Gage was in the habit of rolling his clean socks the way she did her dirty ones. Unwilling to take the whiff test to be certain, she decided to simply appreciate the luxury of dry feet. She slipped on the oversized hiking boots Jake, having the smallest shoe size of the three men, had provided—though a men's ten compared to her ladies' six left a significant size gap.

Movement darted out of the corner of her eye and she stilled.

Nothing.

She studied the trees enveloping her, the odd feeling of being watched sinking in.

Bending, she quickly tied her laces and headed back to the others.

She emerged from the woods to a hoot of laughter.

"What?"

Gage nearly doubled over in laughter. "I'm sorry." He tried to smother his amusement. "You look like a little kid swimming in those."

She looked down, her trepidation replaced by amusement. She'd rolled Landon's gray sweats three times at her waist to keep from tripping over them, and the sleeves of Gage's cobalt Henley hung several inches beyond her fingertips. She worked to smother a chuckle of her own. "Like you said, no need to impress."

"I hadn't meant . . . it's just some women worry too much about their physical appearance, even when they're out in the wilderness like this."

She narrowed her eyes, planting her hands on her hips—though it was hard to get to them through the vast layers of fabric. "And you think I'm one of those women?"

Jake cleared his throat. "I'm going to . . . uh . . . see to that fire." He backed quickly away.

Landon was at the far end of the beach, still on the phone—no doubt with local authorities—leaving just her and a man very much on the spot.

She took a step closer to Gage. "So . . . do you?"

Gage reached for the wet clothes she carried. "Not necessarily."

She plopped them in his hand. "Care to elaborate?" It was a risk to push. She might not like what he had to say, but she wasn't the play-it-safe type. If Gage thought her vain—on top of everything else—she wanted to know.

He dumped her clothes in a plastic sack and cinched it up. "You're usually all put together."

"And that makes me vain?"

"Of course not. I'd hardly call you vain."

"Then why the comment?"

"I only meant you don't need to worry about what you look like even under the harshest of circumstances."

Her brows pinched together. "And why is that?"

He took a step toward her. "Because you're gorgeous."

Oh. She hadn't expected that, nor the butterflies suddenly somersaulting in her belly. She lifted her arms. "Yeah, I'm sure I look really gorgeous swimming in these clothes."

He stepped closer still, heat emanating from his body like steam from a grate. Warmth surged through her. He lifted a damp strand of hair clinging to her forehead and tenderly slipped it behind her ear. "Breathtakingly so."

The sensation of his skin against hers, his fingers along the curve of her neck just behind her ear was dizzying. "I . . ." His heather-gray eyes brimming with emotion sliced deeply through her.

He'd never spoken to her like that, never *looked* at her the way he was at that moment, and it nearly stole her breath away.

He dipped his head, leaning in—the movement very much like that of a man about to kiss her. Instinctually she leaned into him, her eyelids fluttering shut. His breath hovered over her lips. She parted hers and—

Someone cleared his throat.

Her eyes shot open, and she felt jolted from a dream. Had she and Gage . . . ? Had they been about to . . . *kiss?*

Gage remained a breath from her, the heat from his body making her forget the cold she'd endured all morning.

It was Landon, back at the campfire after talking on the satellite phone. "I got ahold of Chief Wyatt Mueller in Eagle Cove. He'll be out within the hour and he'll bring a couple of their SAR volunteers to assist, along with the necessary gear."

"Great," Gage said, not taking his eyes off Darcy.

"I've got the fire going," Jake said, rejoining them. "The warmer we can get you two the better."

No need there. Her entire body was on fire.

20

He stepped back from the grouping of evergreens. So that was Darcy St. James. Strange how a grown man could be frightened of such a little lass. Luckily he was in charge, and she didn't frighten him in the least. In fact, if she chose to continue her pursuit, he'd take great pleasure in teaching her a woman's rightful place. For now he'd simply focus on damage control. Fortunately the traps he'd set to ward off curious interlopers had done their job.

Phillip had claimed he was looking for a secluded spot for his morning ritual, but clearly he'd heard the boat, heard him and his men talking, but the trap had kept him from seeing anything. And nearly losing a leg would no doubt prevent future snooping. Chef Phillip was down for the count. The man should thank him, really. His hacked-up ankle would heal a lot faster than a bullet to the head.

Climbing back on his outboard, he lit a cigarette and idled away from shore. It was ridiculous the mistakes he had to cover, the people he had to punish simply because they couldn't follow basic instructions. It was time he found a new crew. His men on the *Bering* just weren't cutting it anymore.

* * *

"What was that all about?" Landon asked, his grin enormous as Gage bent to take inventory of their gear. He needed to see if anything could be of use in the retrieval.

Gage had wondered how long it would take Landon to ask. Best to keep his answer light. No need for Landon to know about the pulsating energy pinging through him. "Just trying to warm us up a bit. Nice timing by the way."

Landon smirked. "A little payback for all the interruptions when I was courting your sister."

"Brother's right. Have to give the suitor a hard time."

"Uh-huh." Landon glanced over at Darcy sitting by the fire. "Is that what you're doing here? Courting Darcy?"

"Don't read more into it than there was." He stood, having collected all the gear he could.

Landon frowned. "Meaning?"

Really? Landon was going to press. That was typically Piper's job. "It's complicated."

"Trust me," Landon chuckled. "I've been there, bro." His laughter settled. "Can I give you a piece of advice?"

Gage arched a brow. "That depends."

Landon didn't bother asking on what. He just smiled and said, "Don't fight it."

Easy for him to say. He didn't understand. Gage's feelings for Darcy had taken him from the brink of wanting to throttle her to the terror of nearly losing the woman he loved. . . .

He hung his head. Despite his stiffest measures to avoid it, he'd fallen in love with Darcy St. James, but almost acting on it had been beyond stupid. Instead of giving Landon a hard time, he ought to be thanking him for preventing him from making what would have been the dumbest mistake of his life.

"Chief's here," Jake announced.

"Great." Gage moved to greet him.

"Chief Wyatt Mueller." The slender, bowlegged man stepped forward. "Y'all can call me Wyatt."

"Gage McKenna. My company's LFA out of—"

"Yancey," Wyatt said, cutting in. "I'm told your family aided in a serious search and rescue we had about eight months back."

"That's right. The Williams boy."

"I was still up in Anchorage then, but everyone round here speaks highly of you and your family."

"That's always good to hear."

A second man stepped forward. Taller. Younger. Dark hair. "Good to see you again, Gage."

"Travis." Gage shook the man's hand.

Travis gestured to the two men coming up

behind him. "You remember Gary Wade and Hollace Kincaid?"

"Sure do. Good to see you guys again." Gary and Hollace had worked SAR with them on the Williams kid's rescue. "You all remember Jake and Landon?"

"Of course," Travis said, greeting them.

"Deputy Grainger." Wyatt stepped forward. "Thanks for the call."

"Call me Landon, please, and I wish we could have met under better circumstances."

"Such is the life of a law official." Wyatt sighed.

Travis lifted his chin. "Wyatt said you found a body?"

"Yes. Darcy's kayak flipped." He gestured toward her as she made her way over to them, holding tight to the sweats threatening to slip from her tiny frame.

Travis dipped his head. "Sorry to hear that, ma'am."

"Thanks, but I'm fine. Thanks to Gage, here, of course." Her blue eyes met his, and a wealth of passion stirred inside him. This was beyond bad.

"Can you tell me what happened then?" Wyatt asked.

"I got thrust into the sea caves. When Gage cut me loose from the kayak, I saw it."

She was trying to be brave, but Gage didn't

miss the unmistakable quiver in her jaw. She was terrified. How could he just leave her shivering like that?

With a grimace, he moved to her side, wrapping a reassuring arm about her waist. She quickly burrowed deeper into his hold. *Do not focus on how good she feels in your arms.*

A look of amusement passed between Landon and Jake, but he ignored them.

"Saw what exactly, ma'am?" Wyatt asked.

"A person. I mean a body or . . . what was left of it." A tremor shot through her, and he tightened his hold, rubbing his hand along her arm.

Wyatt turned his attention to Gage, the question clear in his weathered brown eyes.

"The remains are mostly submerged, wedged between the rocks."

Travis sighed. "That's where they usually end up."

Darcy frowned. "They?"

"The bodies."

"I don't understand. There have been other bodies found down there?"

Wyatt scratched his nose. "I'm afraid so. Not often, mind you, but we've had a couple whitewater rafting accidents where someone goes overboard and gets sucked into the wash. And then there are the ocean floaters that get tugged in."

"Ocean floaters?" she asked, her voice cracking slightly.

"Someone falls overboard from a ship or boat in the area. If not rescued or quickly retrieved, they could end up getting sucked into the wash."

"So this body . . . ?"

"Probably falls under one of those categories," Wyatt said.

"I'm guessing the remains are pretty smashed up?" Travis asked.

"Yes, but still retrievable."

"All right. We've got our gear in the boat. Let's get started."

* * *

Darcy waited on shore with Landon, Chief Mueller, and Travis while Gage, Jake, and the two local SAR men—Gary and Hollace—got to work. With safety ropes anchored to shore, Gage and Jake took lead in diving back under the water—this time fully protected from the frigid water temperatures in dry suits that local SAR had provided. Gary and Hollace braced against the boulders just out of reach of the vortex, ready to help take the body from Gage and Jake as they surfaced.

Wind slapped Darcy's face as she waited, pacing the length of the shore nearest the hole. What seemed an eternity later, Jake emerged, pulling an orange body bag behind him. Gary reached to assist, Hollace helping from behind as they heaved the body onto the boulders. Gage emerged at the tail end of the bag, and her heart settled to see him back above the water's surface.

With great care amidst the harsh surroundings, the men, working together, managed to load the body onto Wyatt's boat. Once the job was done, the men all sat back and exhaled.

Retrieval looked like hard work. Frigid water temps, unforgiving winds, lifting dead weight against a surging current, not to mention righting and retrieving her kayak along with her soaked pack—not that it would do her much good in its current state.

She was proud of Gage. Proud of the work he did with SAR. It showed his heart for helping others.

"Darcy, you ride back with Wyatt and the boys," Gage said, taking a sip of the bottled water Travis had brought for them all.

"What about the rest of you?"

"We'll kayak."

They had to be exhausted.

"We can trail them behind the boat," Wyatt said. "No sense expending any more energy today."

Gage looked at Jake and Landon, and both nodded.

"Thanks," Gage said. "We'd be much obliged."

* * *

Darcy sat quietly at the ship's stern as they headed back to Eagle Cove.

Jake kept his focus on the kayaks, making sure their equipment remained secure as they

167

maneuvered the narrow sections of the river.

Landon stood at the bow with Wyatt, the two deep in conversation.

Gage sank down on the bench beside her, watching the wind streaming through her now-dry hair. "You holding up okay?"

"Jake said the body wasn't female." Relief clung to her voice.

"Yes, it's unlikely—and it looked like the body has been in the water a long time." It was hard to tell, though. While primarily submerged in the frigid water—which helped delay decomposition —the body had been battered by the waves and surf surge washing in from the ocean. The head— above water—didn't have much left to it, which was a pretty strong indicator the remains weren't those of Darcy's friend. It took more than a few days for the bugs to get that close to bone. But he'd feel better once the M.E. made an official determination.

He leaned over, nudging her shoulder with his. "Do you want to talk about it?" She was clearly shaken.

She pulled Jake's dry fleece tighter around her. "I doubt you want to talk about what I want to talk about."

"Huh?" His brows pinched in confusion. "What is it you want to talk about?"

She bit her bottom lip and looked up at him. "The tattoo." She spoke so softly he barely heard her over the waves sloshing against the boat's hull.

The woman had nearly drowned and had discovered a badly battered corpse, and what held her attention was *his* tattoo?

He shifted, his gaze fixed on the ocean. "What about it?"

"I'm guessing they are Tucker's footprints."

He nodded, something in his heart seizing at his boy's name.

"That's precious."

He reclined, shifting his weight away from her, trying to create some distance, at least spatially. He had to. The unbridled emotions of the day finally settling, his brain was kicking back in. There was no way he could risk his heart. Not for Darcy—not after she'd held out on him. How could she go on his excursion without telling him she couldn't swim? Didn't she understand the risk that posed to everyone involved?

And what else might she be holding back? Despite his feelings for her, he knew, when it came down to it, he needed a woman he could trust—a woman who would be up-front with him no matter what. That was non-negotiable. Otherwise he was walking in blind, and he knew, from agonizing experience, that only led to disaster.

21

Gage spotted his sisters sitting on a pier bench as Travis steered the boat into an open slip in Eagle Cove's harbor. The *Bering* sat anchored on the opposite side of the marina, people littering the decks to see the commotion below.

Piper and Kayden stood at their approach and moved to greet them.

Landon hopped from the boat and tied the rope to the pylon.

Piper rushed toward him and engulfed him in a hug. "Any idea who it was?"

"According to Jake, it's not Darcy's friend," he whispered.

"What do you mean 'according to Jake'?"

Gage rubbed the back of his neck. "Jake said the remains are male, adult, and have been in the water too long for it to be Darcy's friend."

"Jake?" Kayden said. "How would he know?"

Gage shushed her as Darcy stepped from the boat. "You want her to think it's her friend?"

"Of course not, but Jake's hardly an expert. We shouldn't assign any validity to what he says on the matter." She shifted her gaze to Landon, who'd worked numerous crime scenes.

Landon shrugged. "I haven't seen the remains. Jake and Gage bagged the body before bringing it to the surface to prevent any further contamination. Chief Mueller's calling Cole in to assist me in running a full crime-scene analysis of the cave. Maybe we'll get lucky."

"I know Cole's the best," Kayden said, "but I'm here, and I've worked numerous underwater retrievals and assessments before."

"I know, but Cole runs the team, and besides, you're needed on the excursions. I wasn't even supposed to be here, remember? So my absence from the excursions won't make any difference. Yours would."

"Landon's got a point," Gage said.

Kayden sighed. "Yeah, I know."

Gage shook his head. She was disappointed because she thought she was missing out on the fun. Searching a sea cave for crime-scene evidence was hardly fun, in his opinion—it was thorough, painstaking work—but Kayden had unique interests. For him, nothing was better than sea kayaking, and he was eager to get back to it. That was, if Mullins wasn't about to fire their excursion team.

A man rolled a gurney down the gangway. He lifted his chin in greeting to Wyatt and his men and introduced himself to the rest as the town coroner, Nick Saunders. "Winters is on his way over now."

"Winters?" Landon asked.

"He's the new M.E. over on Dutch Harbor.

171

They're the closest island with a large enough medical facility to staff a permanent M.E. He took off by floatplane shortly after your call came in. Should be here soon."

Travis and Gary lifted the body onto the gurney, and Nick strapped it in place. "Who do we have here?" Nick asked.

"Not a local," Wyatt said, leaning against a pylon and popping a mint in his mouth. "I can tell you that."

"How on earth can you be certain of that?" Landon asked.

The gurney wheels squeaked as Nick maneuvered it up the gangway toward the hearse he had parked at the top.

"We had a very heated discussion regarding the fish-processing plant at the town-hall meeting last night. It affects nearly every family's livelihood, so all families on the island were accounted for last night. That's how I know it wasn't one of our locals."

"Has anyone gone missing in the last year?" Jake asked.

"No one but that Williams boy you all helped find about eight months back."

"How's he doing?" Gage asked.

"Just fine. Won't go near wells anymore, but I suppose that's a good thing." Travis chuckled.

"A very good thing," Landon said.

A well had nearly cost the boy his life.

172

"So you're thinking it's a tourist?" Jake asked, glancing back at the hearse.

"That'd be my guess."

"You get many tourists in these parts?" Landon asked.

"Mostly the adventure type and, of course, the cruise folks."

"Cruise folks . . ." Darcy murmured, tugging Gage's sleeve.

He lowered his head. "What?"

"Jake said his guess was the body had been in the water at least nine months."

"So?"

"Isn't that right about when Drake Bowen went missing?"

"Bowen?" Wyatt asked, overhearing them.

"That was before your time, Wyatt," Travis explained. "Drake Bowen was on a kayak excursion out on Kesuk. The guy snapped, killed his wife, and took off. If it is him in that body bag, then I'd say justice has finally been served."

"Okay, but if it's Bowen's body, who killed him?" Darcy asked. "Maybe Bowen was telling the truth and he didn't kill his wife after all. Maybe he took off to find her just like he'd said he was going to."

Wyatt frowned. "The wife's body was never found?"

Travis shook his head.

"Then how could they claim the man killed her?"

"She was missing and they found her blood in the couple's tent."

"Maybe Bowen wasn't killed," Landon suggested. "Maybe it was an accident. He got too close to the water while searching for his wife, fell in, got sucked into the vortex, and was dragged down into the sea caves just like Darcy was today."

Darcy paled slightly.

Gage wrapped his arm around her, despite his recent vow to keep his distance. The lady needed comforting. He couldn't ignore that. He didn't *want* to ignore that. But when this ordeal was over, he'd muster the strength to walk away and figure out how to put Darcy St. James out of his mind for good.

"Wait a minute," Kayden cut in. "Why are we all assuming that Jake is right about how long the body's been in the water? For all we know that body has only been in the water a couple days."

"Kayden," Piper said, her gaze darting to Darcy.

"I'm just saying we should wait for an expert's opinion."

"That body has been in the water for months," Jake said. He looked at Darcy. "I guarantee it."

Relief once again swept over Darcy's face at Jake's assurance.

"He's not an expert," Kayden said.

"Right." Darcy averted her eyes. "I know that."

Kayden narrowed her eyes, glancing between Darcy and Jake.

It was clear Darcy was taking Jake's ruling as final, but why? Gage didn't have Kayden's suspicious nature, but even he wondered at that. As phenomenal at tracking as Jake was, and as bizarrely helpful as he proved to be when it came to offering advice in legal and investigative matters, he surely wasn't also an expert on decomposition or forensic analysis of remains. Gage studied the man and pondered his confidence in his conclusion. Maybe Jake did know what he was talking about. But how or why?

"Winters," Wyatt said, and they all turned to find the M.E. striding toward them. Not a whole lot older than Landon—the man shared a similar rugged build and light brown hair.

Wyatt shook his hand. "Thanks for flying over."

"No problem. I took a look at the remains before Nick loaded them into the hearse." He gestured over his shoulder, and everyone glanced at the hearse slowly pulling away from the marina.

"And?"

"I'll need to do a full autopsy, but I can tell you that the remains are that of an adult male and they've been in the water at least nine months."

Kayden's shocked gaze swung to Jake.

He cleared his throat. "If I'm not needed anymore, I'm going to load the kayaks and take them to camp."

"Of course." Gage nodded, completely stunned

175

at Jake's accuracy on the matter. The man never ceased to surprise him. "Thanks for your help."

Jake nodded and glanced once at Kayden before leaving. There was something in his gaze —hurt, perhaps. Hurt that she was questioning him yet again.

Kayden released a throaty exhale once he was gone. *"Pleasssse* tell me you aren't all going to ignore Jake's unusual knowledge *again?* I mean, *how* does he know something like that?"

Darcy looked down at her feet, shuffling them against the battered planks of the pier.

Kayden pounced. "That's the second time you've done that."

Darcy looked up, startled. "Done what?"

"Looked away when I've questioned Jake's vast knowledge. You know who Jake really is, don't you?"

Landon cleared his throat. "Looks like we're garnering quite a crowd." He lifted his chin toward the *Bering*—even more passengers had amassed along the rails, staring at the activity brewing below.

Gage sighed. "Guess I better get back on board and explain to Mullins. Hopefully we'll still have our excursion contract with them come tomorrow morning."

Darcy grabbed her pack, still damp, and slung it over her shoulder. "I need to get back on the ship too. People are going to start wondering why

I'm hanging around the excursion crew and local police."

"No way." Kayden blocked her path. "Not until you explain."

"Explain what?"

"Exactly who Jake is."

22

"Please," Darcy said for the third time. "Let it go." She couldn't tell them. It wouldn't be right.

"There is no way I'm letting this go." Kayden continued to block her path.

"It's not my place."

Gage linked his arms over his chest, leaning back against a pylon. "Sounds like you already ignored your place."

He was absolutely right. This time she fully deserved the censure. She shouldn't have delved into Jake's private life, into his past, but the man proved too intriguing during her time in Yancey. The reporter in her couldn't resist snooping. She could try to claim she'd pried to protect them—that she wanted to be certain Jake wasn't a criminal, as Kayden had often insinuated, and that they weren't in any danger—but it would be a lie.

While the remote possibility had existed that Jake was hiding from a criminal past, even from the beginning Darcy knew deep down in her heart that he was a good guy. What had driven her was curiosity, plain and simple. She'd poked around a bit and found nothing, and her curiosity intensified. It became a challenge she had to master, so she'd kept on, refusing to quit until she discovered the truth, and once she had, she wished she'd never pried.

If her digging brought Jake any more pain than he'd already endured, she'd never forgive herself. She squared her shoulders. "I'm not proud of what I did—far from it—but I'm not going to make it worse by blabbing."

"Fine." Kayden cocked her head. "Then I'll call him on it myself. Tell him you know who he is."

"Please don't," Darcy said. "Leave the man be."

"Why?"

She shook her head. "You don't understand."

"Don't understand what?" Jake asked, rejoining them with a pack in hand.

All eyes shifted to him.

Darcy swallowed. "I thought you'd left."

"I grabbed Gage's pack by mistake." He eyed them all as he dropped the pack. "What's going on? Some more news on the remains?"

Emotion welled in Darcy's throat. Gage was right. Some things were meant to remain private.

"Just tell him," Kayden said, nudging her arm. "This charade has gone on long enough."

"Tell me what?" Jake asked.

"She knows who you are," Kayden said, tilting her head in Darcy's direction. "Who you *really* are."

Darcy wished she could vaporize. Swallowing, she forced herself to meet Jake's gaze. "I'm so sorry. I *never* should have pried."

"You told them?" His words came out strangled, his voice hollow.

"No." She shook her head.

"Told us what?" Kayden's tone heightened a pitch.

"Stop, Kayd," Gage said.

"You just couldn't leave it be, could you?" Jake asked Darcy, raw anguish aflame in his eyes.

Tears tumbled down her cheeks. "I'm so sorry."

Looking in the distance, Jake exhaled. "You might as well tell them. Kayden won't stop until she badgers it out of you." He slipped his pack over his shoulder and walked away.

"I need to get back to the ship," Darcy said, shame brimming within. She couldn't let this happen. Jake had earned the right to keep his pain private.

"Nuh-uh." Kayden took Darcy by the arm, pulling her onto the marina bench. "Not yet. Not until you tell me about Jake."

"I can't, Kayden. Please."

"He just said you could."

"Because he knows you won't let it go, but believe me, you don't want to know."

"So it's that bad? What did he do?"

179

Darcy frowned at Kayden. She always assumed the worst. "He didn't *do* anything."

"Look, I'm the one staying at the campground with him tonight. If Jake has some criminal ties, I deserve to know."

Storm clouds thickened overhead, the temperature dipping quickly.

"He is not and never was a criminal, and you'll have Piper and Landon with you."

"Not tonight," Landon said. "I need to remain in town until Cole arrives and we process the crime scene."

"Okay, then Piper will be with you. Not that you'd be in any danger, anyway. If anything, you'll be safer with Jake there."

Kayden narrowed her eyes. "Why's that?"

"I was planning to stay in town with Landon," Piper cut in, "since I might not see him for the rest of the excursion. We lucked out and got the last two rooms at the inn."

"Why might you not see him for the rest of the excursion?" Darcy asked, confused.

"I'm not sure how long the crime scene will take to process," Landon said. "I may be able to fly out and meet up with you all, but I can't make any promises."

"So . . ." Kayden clicked her tongue. "Just me and Jake at the campground. Super." She pinned her determined gaze on Darcy. "I deserve to know if I'm sharing it with an ex-con."

"Kayden, have you not been listening to me? He is not an ex-con." Irritation flared in Darcy's voice, in her chest.

Kayden's expression was hard, determined. "Who exactly is Jake Westin?"

Darcy squeezed her eyes shut, rubbing her temples as Kayden badgered. Jake was right. She wouldn't stop until she got answers. And she was so very wrong about the man.

"Darcy," Kayden pressed.

"He was a cop, okay!"

* * *

Kayden slumped back. "A cop?"

"A detective—one of Boston's best," Darcy said.

Gage sat down on the bench between Kayden and Darcy. He tapped Kayden's knee. "Looks like you owe Jake a big apology."

She swallowed the acid that truth brought. Kayden hated being wrong, but she *loathed* admitting it. But if he was a detective, why had she not found any information when she'd searched for him on the Internet . . . many times?

"What happened?" Landon asked, settling onto the opposite bench. "Case gone bad?"

Darcy exhaled, leaning forward. "That's one way to put it."

"Jake screwed up?" Kayden asked. Ridiculous as it was, she hoped to still salvage some semblance of pride on the matter.

"Not at all," Darcy said. "He solved the case. But . . ."

"But . . . ?" Kayden pressed as they all leaned in closer to Darcy. The eerie sensation of their having an audience lingered. Kayden glanced over her right shoulder to find numerous crew members and passengers still watching intently from the *Bering*'s decks. Clint and George included.

She shifted her attention back on Darcy as anguish filled her features. "During the case, he lost his wife." Darcy paused, looked at Gage, and when she continued, her usually strong voice was sorrowful. "And his child."

"His wife *and* child?" Gage's face twisted in agony. "How?"

Wife. Child. Jake had been a husband and a father? Kayden's heart bottomed out. She'd seen firsthand the toll losing a child took on Gage's life. No wonder Jake . . .

She squeezed her eyes shut. What a cold wretch she'd been to him.

"Jake and Rebecca had been married less than a year when the case began. Jake apparently received threats to back off the case, but his former partner said Jake refused to be bullied. He pressed on, and about a week after the threats started, his wife was killed by a hit-and-run driver."

"And his child?" Gage asked.

"Rebecca was seven months pregnant at the time."

"Are you certain?" Piper asked, tears welling in her eyes.

Kayden grimaced. Why couldn't she be openly compassionate like that?

Because if she allowed herself to feel strongly about anything, if she let her guard down to empathize, all the hurt and sorrow in the world would crush her. She was doing what she had to, to survive. But this . . . How could she block this out? How could she ignore all Jake had suffered when she'd questioned his character, his integrity, and treated him as if he didn't belong? Guilt and anguish seared like a hot knife, slicing through her guard and deep into her soul.

Forgive me, Father.

Darcy continued. "He was tough to find at first, even using my profession's resources. I found a few *Jake Westin*s, but they were clearly not him. Then I stumbled on an article about a detective named Jake Cavanagh. The article mentioned that his mother was a daughter of the Boston Westins. After reading the article I hoped, prayed, Jake Cavanagh was not our Jake Westin."

She took a long, shaky breath. "I called Detective Cavanagh's precinct and spoke with his former partner. It was quickly clear our Jake was his former partner. He was so thrilled to hear Jake was all right that he didn't hold much back during our conversation, including the unpublished information that Rebecca had been pregnant. I confirmed everything else through the papers and records."

Tears spilled from Piper's eyes, but Kayden refused to cry, at least not in front of the rest. She'd held it together for so long, she wouldn't waver now. No matter how heartbroken she suddenly felt, she'd cry alone in the dark—the way she always did.

23

Darcy followed Gage onto the *Bering*, her heart in her throat.

Gage hadn't said a word since they'd left the rest of the team, and the silence was torturous. She'd outed Jake. She completely deserved for Gage to out her with Mullins.

Even though she was on a ship with well over a thousand people, she'd never felt so alone.

"I'm sorry," she blurted, needing to apologize —not just defend her reasons or rationalize but sincerely apologize.

Gage stopped.

"I'm sorry about Jake, so sorry I didn't tell you that I couldn't kayak or swim, it's just—"

"I know, your case is more important." He

hefted her still-wet pack over his broad shoulder. For someone who was so mad at her, he was still being mighty protective of her.

"No. I mean yes . . . I mean . . ." She took a deep breath. "Look, I don't know what to do. I meant what I said—I feel awful for causing problems for you and your family." She looked down, mustering her courage. "I should have been straight with you from the start."

"Yes, you should have."

"I didn't have any time. Mullins told me I was going to have to kayak right as the vans were about to pull away. I made a snap decision. I thought I could handle it, that I had to or my cover would be blown."

"Some things are more important."

"Than someone's *life?*" Abby was missing. She understood he was mad about her prying into Jake's past—that was obvious—and even understood his frustration about her not being up-front about her fear of water and lack of swimming skills, but this was Abby's *life* they were talking about.

He lowered his voice as people shuffled past. "I understand the need to find your friend, but what makes her life more precious than anyone else's?"

"It's not like anyone died on the excursion. No one was even seriously hurt."

"How can you say that? *You* nearly died."

"I'm fine." She stepped closer, resting a hand on his chest. "And I don't think I ever properly thanked you for rescuing me."

He sighed at her touch. "You're welcome."

The memory of his lips hovering near hers took hold. She blinked, needing to think straight. They were going to have to face Mullins. "I'll tell Mullins I can't swim, that I'm the reason for the trouble."

"Maybe Mullins will let you stay on and cover things from the ship."

"Yeah, right. She's not that nice—besides, I've been thinking. . . ."

"That's dangerous."

She pursed her lips. "Seriously, what Whitney said about the Bowens got me thinking. They went missing during an excursion, and Abby was hoping I'd get the journalist gig to work the excursions with her."

"So?"

"So, what if she knew the excursions were where the story was."

"How, exactly?"

"I don't know, but if Abby's reference to the case we worked in San Diego was any indication, then drug running or smuggling of some sort is involved. Maybe it's not occurring just between ports. Maybe, whoever is involved is using the excursion points for drop-offs or pickups."

"That would be smart. It would take ship security out of the picture. But what would any of that have to do with the Bowens?"

"Maybe they saw something they shouldn't have and were killed for it."

"You think Bowen didn't kill his wife?"

"I don't know, but if someone is using the excursion points to run drugs, then we know our list of suspects."

"Ted, George, or Clint—and wasn't there another excursion member that left the cruise?"

Darcy nodded.

Mullins came barreling down the main corridor. "You both have some explaining to do. My office—now." She turned heel, and they followed.

Darcy braved a glance at Gage, who kept his attention fixed forward.

Mullins led them into her office, shut the door behind them, and settled into her desk chair. "Well, which one of you wants to explain?"

Darcy's mouth went dry, and her gaze flashed to Gage. It finally felt as if they had something to go on with the Bowen disappearance, but she couldn't let him or LFA take the fall for her.

Mullins leaned forward, her freckled arms resting on the desktop. "One of you had better explain how my luxury passengers were subjected to such unpleasantness."

Unpleasantness didn't even come close. Darcy took a deep breath and straightened. Time to come clean. She couldn't let Gage and LFA lose their contract with the *Bering*—or worse, their reputation in the industry—over her foolish actions. "It was—"

"An accident," Gage cut in.

She turned to him in surprise. What was he doing?

Mullins frowned. "An accident?"

"Yes, ma'am," Gage said.

Mullins leaned forward, no sign of understanding on her face. "The entire point of hiring a professional, of having you on board, is to prevent accidents from occurring, to ensure our passengers are safe and catered to."

"And we at LFA take every possible safety precaution, but kayaking isn't a safe sport. You can't control nature."

"So this is how *you* and your company run your business?"

"Accidents happen. But I apologize for any discomfort or inconvenience it caused the passengers."

Darcy watched pride in his company, in his safety record, fade in Gage's tone. This wasn't right. It was her fault. *All my fault.* "It wasn't Gage's fault," she said. "It wasn't anything LFA did or didn't do."

Mullins' gaze shifted to her. "Oh? So it was *yours?*"

Please, Father, give me strength to do the right

thing, even if it means risking my chance to find Abby.

She opened her mouth to confess, but Gage, once again, beat her to it.

"One of the passengers got spooked by a stick she thought was a water snake. She hollered, and it diverted everyone's attention. A few seconds is all it takes to lose focus and for the current to take hold. Darcy tried her best, but once you are caught in a vortex, there's little you can do to get out of it."

Her shoulders slumped. *Unless, of course, you're properly trained, as I should have been.* She really had endangered her and everyone else's lives. Abby's life was important, but Gage was right—so was everyone else's on that excursion, and she'd put them all in jeopardy.

"So you're saying it wasn't an error on anyone's part?" Mullins' gaze remained fixed on Darcy.

Clearly she'd heard otherwise. Darcy was placing her bet on Heath complaining.

"Mr. McKenna?" Mullins pressed. "Was it a mistake on someone's part?"

Gage's jaw clenched. "No."

Darcy's gaze flashed to Gage, her eyes wide. He'd just covered for her.

"Very well, but if any more *accidents* occur, you're fired. Understood?"

"Yes, ma'am," Gage said, his words clipped.

Darcy was overwhelmed with gratitude for

Gage's defense, and yet she felt awful for putting him in the position she had.

Mullins exhaled as she shuffled papers on her desk. "I still cannot believe my luxury passengers were exposed to a dead body."

"None of them actually saw it," Darcy said, trying to help in whatever minuscule way she could.

"It matters not. It'll be a long time before this one dies down. I've already offered all guests involved cruise vouchers, along with cabin upgrades for those who weren't already in our top suites. I can't imagine when headquarters learns . . ." She glanced up. "What are you still doing here? Go."

"Right." Darcy turned to the door, only to find Gage already walking out of it.

She shut Mullins' door behind her and hurried after him. "Gage."

He kept walking.

"Gage." She raised her voice while increasing her stride.

He turned, and she nearly bowled into him.

"I don't know what to say." There was so much she longed to tell him. "But, thank you so much."

"For what?"

"Covering for me." He'd told Mullins it wasn't a mistake on her part that caused the accident. While Whitney's scream had startled her, the fact was she had no kayak experience and no

190

right to be out there in the first place. "I'm so sorry about everything. I—"

"I understand your need to find Abby. Let's leave it at that." He turned and walked away, leaving her alone in the corridor.

"Darcy."

She turned with a start at the sound of Clint's voice. How long had he been standing there? Had he overhead any of her and Gage's conversation? Nervousness tracked through her. "I didn't see you there."

He smiled. "You were distracted."

She glanced back in the direction Gage had gone, wishing he was with her now.

"Totally understandable after the day you've had." He stepped closer, his gaze raking over her. "You poor thing. Look at you."

She slipped her matted hair behind her ear. "I suppose I look pretty atrocious." But not according to Gage—he'd said breathtakingly gorgeous.

"Nothing a hot shower and a fresh change of clothes can't cure."

"How's your arm?"

"Nothing but a scrape."

"Thanks again for trying to help."

"Anytime. I can't imagine what it must have been like to be pulled under, only to come face-to-face with a corpse."

Her chest tightened much as it had then—the

dark cold closing back in. She squeezed her eyes shut.

"I'm sorry," he said, brushing her arm. "I hadn't meant to upset you."

She stiffened. "It's fine."

"You know what you need?"

"What's that?"

"A hot shower, a warm meal, and a good massage. You take care of the first one; I've got the other two."

"That's really thoughtful of you, but I don't feel much like being around people."

"Totally get that, and I've got just the solution."

24

Knowing Clint wouldn't take no for an answer, Darcy finally relented and agreed to dinner. But a massage at the hands of a man she'd just met—even if it was his job—seemed far too personal.

Clint appeared to accept the compromise and said he'd be by her cabin in forty-five minutes to escort her to dinner.

At nine thirty, a knock rapped on her door. A part of her hoped it was Gage, but it was Clint, looking rather dapper in a fresh pair of dark blue jeans, leather loafers, and a light-blue dress shirt covered with a navy cable-knit sweater.

Clint smiled, taking in her faded jeans, black

leather boots, and a black cashmere sweater. "You look amazing."

"Thanks." She didn't much care how she looked, but she finally felt warm and relaxed from her shower, and there was a lot to be said for a fresh change of well-fitting clothes.

"You're going to need a jacket."

"Okay." Why would she need a jacket? So far she'd found the ship's restaurants to be quite warm. Without questioning, though, she simply grabbed one and slid it over her shoulders.

"Ready?" he said with a smile.

Not even close. If she was going to be spending time with anybody, she wanted it to be with Gage. But he clearly wanted his space, and who knew, maybe after sharing the ordeal they had, Clint would be more open to talking—she could keep hoping.

Clint led the way up to level seven and then, to her surprise, out onto the deck, leading her toward the bow of the ship. A small table was set for two, and one of the waiters she recognized from the ship's kitchen stood ready to serve.

"Clint, it's lovely, but you shouldn't have gone to all the trouble."

"After the day you endured, it was the least I could do." He held out her chair. She sat and he slid her in.

It felt all wrong being here. She should be looking for clues, asking questions about Abby. . . .

She studied Clint as he took his seat opposite her and smiled.

On second thought, maybe this was exactly where she was supposed to be.

"This is quite the setup," she said, taking in the linen tablecloth and perfectly arranged place setting.

Clint arched a brow as he laid his napkin across his lap. "Setup?"

"Display." That wasn't the right word either. "That came out wrong too. I just meant you went to a lot of trouble and it's beautiful."

He smiled. "You're welcome."

A cool ocean breeze wafted over the bow of the ship—the sea air fresh and crisp. She slipped her jacket over her sweater, now understanding why he'd said she'd need one.

"How's Phillip?"

"Doing fine. They stitched him up in the clinic, put him on antibiotics to fight infection, and hooked him up with some pain meds. He's resting rather comfortably."

"I'm glad to hear that. Kind of scary to think how easily something like that can happen."

"If he'd stayed within camp, it wouldn't have. People need to learn to obey the rules."

"I'm sure he just wanted some privacy."

"There's no need to go that far from camp, ever. There's a reason we say to stick close." He lifted his glass and took a sip as the waiter set their salads before them. "Thank you, Adam."

The waiter nodded. "Your entrees won't be long."

"Looks like you have some sway around here," she said as Adam slipped back inside.

"I just called in a favor."

"So that's how it works around here. Quid pro quo?"

"Isn't that how it works everywhere?" He smiled. "Go ahead. Dig in. I'm sure you must be starving."

Not having eaten since breakfast, she was ravenous.

She lowered her head and thanked the Lord for her meal, for His protection and preservation.

Clint didn't miss the gesture. He smiled when she looked up. "Now there's something you don't see every day. I'm enjoying getting to know you better, Darcy." He speared a piece of lettuce. "So, any word on the body you found?"

"Only that he was male and had been in the water awhile."

"I can't imagine they'll be able to make any sort of identification after it's been under so long."

"There's always dentals, conferring with missing-persons reports, that type of thing."

"You seem to know a lot about this."

She took a bite of her salad, stalling for the best response. "CSI fan." She smiled.

"Uh-huh."

"Plus, I overheard the excursion leaders talking while I was down there."

"Yeah, you were there awhile. With them."

Had Clint been one of the onlookers from the *Bering*'s decks?

"I suppose I was in shock—remaining with the excursion crew seemed the natural thing to do."

"Yeah, I've noticed you are quite close with them."

She shrugged. "They're easy to get to know."

Clint studied her as he took another bite of salad, clearly not buying her explanation, or at the very least, finding it thin. He was astute, and that could prove to be a very good thing for her if he chose to talk, or a serious negative if he caught on to the fact that she wasn't what she appeared.

Time to shift the direction of the conversation. "The chief of police said whoever it was wasn't local. They think he must have been a tourist."

"How could they possibly know that?" Clint asked.

She explained, poking at her salad as she did so, but watching Clint's reaction, she couldn't decide whether it was surprise on his face or something a little darker.

The moon was full and the sky clear, providing them with plenty of light along with the deck lighting and a strategically placed table candle.

She waited until Adam cleared their plates and delivered their main course—coq au vin—before leaning forward and dropping the proverbial bombshell. "They think the remains could be those of a man named Drake Bowen."

Clint coughed, choking on the bite of chicken he'd just taken. After a moment he composed himself, taking a sip of water and wiping his mouth with the cloth napkin.

"Are you okay?"

"You just startled me. Drake Bowen is a name I haven't heard in a while. How did you hear about him? I mean how did you know . . . ?"

"One of the gals on the excursion was talking about the Bowens around the campfire last night."

"Really? Who?"

"Whitney."

"Then she should have told you that Bowen killed his wife and took off. Don't see how it could be his body."

"That's just it. There was apparently some speculation that Bowen was telling the truth and when he went to look for his wife—"

"What?" Clint cut in.

Darcy set her water glass down. "I don't know. Maybe while searching for her, Bowen got too close to the water and fell in. Or maybe—"

"No. I mean what speculation? Bowen killed his wife. Her blood was found in their tent."

"Were you on that excursion?" He'd said he'd worked on the *Bering* for five years. It made sense he'd been on it.

Clint swallowed and looked down. "I was, and it was terrible. How a man can kill his own wife . . ." He shook his head. "I'll never understand."

"So you think he did it?"

"Everyone did. It was so obvious."

"Based on?"

"Didn't you see the news coverage? I thought everyone heard about the husband who killed his bride on their honeymoon."

"I vaguely remember hearing something about it."

"Tragic. Just tragic."

"Whitney said she had a friend on that cruise and that not everyone was convinced of Bowen's guilt."

"I think Whitney has her facts confused."

"But if Bowen killed his wife, how did he end up in a river?" Darcy asked.

"They don't even know if it is Bowen. And if it was, maybe he got too close to the river's edge while trying to flee and got sucked into the vortex. Either way he killed his wife."

"It must have been hard. Witnessing that. Being there."

"It was. Not too often you're exposed to something like that."

"What do you mean? Have there been other times?"

"Husbands killing their wives? Not as far as I know, at least not on any of Destiny's ships."

"What about disappearances?"

"What?" Clint cocked his head.

"I've heard some of the crew talking about Abby's disappearance."

"Abby didn't disappear. She left."

"The day after someone went overboard. Seems pretty suspicious to me."

Clint topped off his wine glass. "You're quite the amateur detective, aren't you?"

"I just find it curious. Someone goes overboard. The crew refuses to say who, and then Abby *conveniently* leaves the *Bering* without any notice."

He lowered his glass. "You're not going to stop with this until you get some answers, are you?"

"Most definitely not."

He set his napkin aside with a sigh, checked to be sure they were alone, and leaned forward. "I could get in a lot of trouble for this. Seriously, I could lose my job if anyone heard I was telling you this, so anything I say has to remain confidential. Understood?"

"Understood." She nodded, practically salivating. *Finally,* she was getting somewhere.

"I can't tell who I heard it from, but it was Abby that fell overboard."

"Fell?"

"That's what I heard. She'd been drinking too much, stumbled out onto the deck. It was slippery. She got too close to the rail and fell overboard."

"No way!" Abby didn't drink. She was allergic to alcohol. But she couldn't say that. Not without blowing her cover.

Clint held up his hands. "I'm just relaying what I heard. The lady was lucky. She was rescued and taken to the hospital on Kodiak, since we were so close to land."

"And then?"

"And then she decided not to come back. Can't say I blame her. Falling overboard has got to be terrifying."

"So, you're saying she got to the hospital and decided not to come back?"

"That's what I heard."

"From who?"

"Can't say or he could lose his job for talking."

"I don't understand. Why all the secrecy? Why not just come out and announce who fell overboard?"

"You really don't get it, do you." Clint chuckled before taking a sip of wine. "Destiny wants to erase the incident from people's minds as quickly as possible. She fell over. They rescued her. End of story."

"Then why not just say so?"

"They did."

"But they wouldn't say it was Abby."

"Of course not. They only release the name to family or, if they have any, to their traveling companions. Destiny policy. It's a kindness to Abby, really."

"How do you figure that?"

"You really think Abby would want everyone aboard the *Bering* to know she drank too much, got clumsy, and fell overboard?"

But that was *not* what happened. "Where is she now?"

Clint shrugged. "Who knows? Destiny doesn't keep track of its employees once they leave the job."

"Do you know who was part of the rescue crew that night?"

Clint paused, his fork full of chicken partway to his mouth. "Excuse me?"

"The rescue crew that pulled Abby out of the water. Do you know who they are?"

" 'Fraid I can't help you there."

"But you're a medic. Wouldn't you have been involved?"

"I'm not the only medic on board. Besides, I had a massage client at the time."

"At ten thirty at night?"

"A lot of the clients like an in-room massage before bed." He set down his fork and shoved his plate aside. "Seriously. What's up with you? Why all the questions?"

She'd said too much. Pushed too hard.

"I'm sorry. I guess I'm just all spun up from nearly drowning and then seeing a dead body or what was left of it. . . ."

Clint stood, walked around the table, and knelt at her side. "Come here." He held out his arms.

The only arms she wanted to be in were Gage's, but she didn't want to be rude. He was trying to help. And she needed to do a little damage control. She'd definitely pushed too hard.

She let Clint hug her without fully leaning into his embrace.

"What you need is a good massage. Loosen up all the knots. Make you forget about today's events."

"Thanks. That's really kind of you, but I think I better just crawl into bed and call it a night."

He released his hold and stood. "Are you sure?" He held up his hands, wiggling his fingers. "I've been told these are magic hands."

So she'd heard. She forced a smile. "Thanks, but I'm sure."

He shrugged. "Some other time, then."

She stood. "Thank you for dinner." *And a very enlightening conversation.*

"Anytime. You get some sleep."

Darcy didn't waste any time rushing to Gage's cabin and lightly rapping on the door. He answered in a pair of sweat bottoms, and her gaze once again fastened on the tiny blue footprints above his heart.

He raked a hand through his hair and glanced at the clock. "What's up?"

She stepped past him into his cabin. "We need to talk."

25

Kayden stepped from her tent to find Jake at the fire. She'd been trying to build up her courage ever since returning to camp. She had to face him, had to look him in the eye and apologize for thinking the worst of him.

The temperature had dropped another ten degrees, and despite the clear sky, the scent of rain hung in the air.

She was hopeless when it came to personal stuff. She felt affection and sorrow deeply but couldn't express them. That was Piper's strength. Kayden was best at keeping it all stuffed down deep, at being the independent one, at being strong and stalwart.

I don't even know where to begin my apology to Jake, Father. I've doubted his character, maligned his integrity, kept him at arm's length when I couldn't have been more wrong about the man he is and what he's suffered. Please, give me the words. For once let them pour from my heart. Help him to know how genuinely sorry I am for misjudging him for so long.

Jake stoked the flames as she approached, sparks flickering into the black sky.

She slid her hands into her jacket pockets—the fleece snug and warm—and took a seat on the log.

He didn't bother looking up. "She told you." It wasn't a question.

"Only after we pressed her. You were right. I wouldn't let it go."

He tossed the branch he'd been using to stoke the fire into it and stood.

She stood with him. "But I shouldn't have. I'm sorry." How could he accept a measly apology after the way she'd treated him? "I don't even know where to begin."

"It's fine."

"What?" How could he say that?

"Really. No worries. Let's leave the past in the past—where it belongs."

"But I . . ."

He didn't give her a chance to respond, just headed for his tent.

Jake kicked off his boots at the entrance and stepped inside his tent. The thick mat tarp did little to insulate his socked feet from the cold earth underneath.

He hadn't thought a heart could possibly shatter

any more than his already had, but he was wrong. *Painfully* wrong.

Kayden's eyes—always so full of strength and determination—now brimmed with pity for him. It was more than he could bear.

Losing Becca and their little girl had nearly destroyed him. It'd ended his desire to be a cop, ended his desire for much of anything. . . . And then he'd landed in Yancey and met the McKennas. Slowly he'd begun to trust again—worse yet, to *hope* again.

But now that they knew, now that Kayden knew, they'd pity him, and he couldn't stand the thought. He'd worked so long to keep the memories at bay. To erase the image of Becca dead on the road, not a block from their home, her beautiful brown eyes lifeless. But now he was Jake Cavanagh again—the Jake Westin Cavanagh he'd thought he'd left in Boston, buried with his wife and child.

* * *

Darcy tried to keep her eyes off Gage's tattoo, off his washboard stomach, off him *period*. She didn't want to make him feel uncomfortable—at least not more so than she already had.

"What are you doing here, Darcy?"

"Like I said, we need to talk."

"At midnight?"

"Yes." She stared at the still-made bed with pillows propped against the headboard and a nearly finished book lying open-faced on the seashell quilt.

Gage shut the door behind her and tugged a shirt off the back of the desk chair, sliding it over his head. "How'd your date with Clint go?"

"My . . . ?" Her eyes narrowed. "How'd you know about that?"

"Word spreads quickly among the crew."

She paused at that, wondering if he was keeping tabs on her—and she rather liked the notion. "Well, it wasn't a date—not in the traditional sense—and what's important is what I learned."

Gage leaned against the closed door. "Which is?"

"Clint confirmed it was Abby that went overboard."

He stepped from the door, moving toward her. "Really?"

"Yes." She sank on the bed, tucking a leg beneath her.

"And he knows this, how? Was he part of the rescue crew?"

"No, but like you said, word spreads among the crew."

"Okay, so what happened?"

"Clint said his source, for lack of a better word, told him Abby was taken to Kodiak Hospital, and word is she left from there."

"We knew as much."

"But Clint's the first from the crew to actually

acknowledge it was Abby that went overboard."

"And that's significant, how?"

"For one, we now *know* Abby went overboard. Whether or not she was the one who made it to the hospital three hours later is a totally different question. Clint said the rumor among the crew was that Abby was drunk, got too close to the railing, and fell overboard."

"All right."

"Not all right. Whoever said that is lying."

"And you know that, how?"

"Because Abby is allergic to alcohol."

"I've heard of that. . . . She's actually allergic?"

"Yes. Docs weren't sure what in alcohol was causing her severe allergic response. They rattled off a list of ingredients she might have been reacting to, but Abby didn't care what the cause was—two severe reactions were enough. She's avoided alcohol altogether since our senior year of college."

"Interesting." Gage sat on the bed beside her. "Did you call Clint on it?"

"How could I without exposing the fact that I knew Abby better than I claimed?"

"Right. Don't want to blow your cover."

Was that sarcasm clinging to his words? Though she could hardly blame him after the day's events. "Gage, we need to find out who was part of that rescue crew. They were the last ones to see Abby alive."

"Clint's a medic. Did you ask him?"

"Yes. He wasn't part of the rescue crew, and he doesn't know who was."

"And you don't find that odd?"

"He was giving a massage at the time."

"You don't think medics chat amongst themselves? Any of us working SAR discuss our cases in hopes that it may be of help or instruction to someone else one day."

"Either way, he said he didn't know, so we need to find another way to get that information."

"And how do you propose *we* go about that?"

"I'll talk to Clint again in the morning. See if I can't get him to ask around for me. It'll be less conspicuous that way."

Gage sat forward, his arms resting on his thighs. "Sounds like you've got it all sorted out, so if we're finished here . . ."

She rested a hand on his knee to stop him from getting up. "I am truly sorry about earlier, about putting you in that position with Mullins. It wasn't fair of me."

He exhaled. "But you're going to keep pressing forward."

"I don't have a choice."

With a sigh, he stood. "It's late, and it's been a rough couple of days. We should both get some sleep." He held his door open.

There was so much more she wanted to say, but would he even listen? If only she could go back to that moment as they stood before the fire, when his lips hovered over hers. *If only . . .*

" 'Night, Gage." She stepped out the door, and he shut it behind her.

* * *

Gage plopped back on the bed, frustration flaming through him. He'd covered for her at the risk of ruining LFA's reputation. What was wrong with him? Watching Darcy standing there so bravely, ready to admit the truth to Mullins, knowing it would cost her the excursion gig, he couldn't let her do it.

He punched the pillow beneath his back, scrunching it into place, and retrieved his Cussler novel. He had to clear his mind of Darcy St. James.

A half hour and a finished novel later, he clicked on the TV, only to find nothing—nothing but the *Bering*'s closed-circuit announcements.

Wonderful. He tossed the remote aside. And of course he hadn't brought a spare book. With a sigh, he tugged open the nightstand drawer in hopes that a previous guest had left a book behind, but found only a brown leather-bound Gideon Bible.

Figures. Die of boredom or read the Bible.

He grabbed the book and kicked back on the bed, flipping to the first chapter of the first book—Genesis 1. *"In the beginning, God created the heavens and the earth."* The verse tugged at his heart. He recalled it from his youth spent in church, but that was before everything fell apart.

He considered tossing the book aside, but glancing at the clock and finding it barely past one and himself wide awake, he decided anything was better than staring at the ceiling. Maybe it would even put him to sleep.

Gage flipped the page, shocked to find himself at the end of Genesis and surprised that so much of it had seemed familiar. How had it held his attention so? He looked at the clock. Nearly half past three.

He tucked the Bible back in the drawer and reclined on the pillow. Whoever wrote Genesis sure knew how to tell a story. A talking serpent, a birthright sold over a bowl of stew, adultery, and a man falsely imprisoned . . .

It was definitely intriguing, but it couldn't possibly hold the answers he so desperately needed or the healing he craved.

26

The next morning, rain lashed against the windows, effectively corralling everyone aboard the *Bering* inside. A day at sea with all exterior decks drenched in a downpour meant a hot, stifling interior. Darcy had yet to locate Gage. She'd headed to his cabin first thing, yearning to see him, but there'd been no answer. She knew he had a training class at one, and if she couldn't locate him before then, she'd wait outside the meeting room for him to arrive. She hated how they'd left things last night, and she wouldn't be able to focus until she'd spoken with him.

Oddly enough, the undercurrent of unrest pulsing through her seemed to be pulsing through the entire ship. Everyone was antsy, anxious to reach Dutch Harbor, ready to explore—but they were stuck, the torrential rain boxing them inside like caged animals. She had no idea what her role would be in the next excursion or if she'd have one at all.

With her lack of applicable skills and non-existent swimming ability, Gage could rightly refuse her continuing on the excursions. He hadn't said anything in Mullins' office yesterday, but come tomorrow morning's excursion . . . who knew? Gage and LFA's motto was "Safety First." He could hardly allow her to continue and still hold true to their principle.

She stepped on the elevator and pushed the button for Deck 9, hoping to find Gage in the activities room.

The elevator paused at Deck 5, and her heart skipped a beat until the doors slid open. Two women stepped on, both in their early twenties with long dark hair, one about three inches taller than the other. Darcy glanced over to greet them and froze. Her gaze fastened on the taller woman's neck—more precisely, on the distinctive shell necklace nestled in the swell of her collarbone. The shell, purple in gradient shades, rested in a sterling silver mold following the natural outline of the shell itself. It was unique, one of a kind. It was Abby's.

"That necklace," she said, finding her voice. "Where did you get it?"

The woman flipped her long hair over her shoulder. "It was a gift."

Darcy stepped closer, thankful the elevator doors had shut and the woman was trapped, at least until the next stop. "A gift from whom?"

The woman squared her shoulders. "What's it to you?"

"It belongs to my friend."

"I don't think so, lady." She turned her back on Darcy, resuming her conversation with her friend.

"Look on the back," Darcy interrupted, resisting the urge to grab the woman's shoulder and spin her back around. "You'll see the initials *A. T.* followed by *Proverbs 17:17.*"

The woman's gaze shifted down, but she didn't touch the pendant.

"Look, lady," the other woman said, "you've obviously got Celia's necklace mixed up with your friend's. It's not like it's one of a kind or anything."

The elevator beeped, and the doors started to

open. Darcy panicked, hitting the Emergency Stop button. "Actually, it *is* one of a kind."

"Are you loco?" The woman reached for the button as the emergency alarm sounded.

Darcy shielded it with her body. "I know it's one of a kind, because I made it for my friend. Please just look on the back—you'll see her initials."

"Just do it, Celia"—the woman sighed—"so we can get away from this crazy broad."

"Brandi . . ." Celia protested.

"Just do it and prove her wrong."

"Fine." Celia huffed and flipped the pendant over. Her eyes widened as her mouth slackened.

Darcy smiled. *Another clue, Abbs.* "Where'd you get it?"

"It was a gift. I didn't steal it from nobody."

"I'm not suggesting you did, Celia. But who gave it to you?"

Celia looked down, nibbling her bottom lip coated thick with red gloss.

"Someone on the ship?" Darcy guessed.

Celia looked down, embarrassment flushing her cheeks. "I didn't know he stole it."

"He, who?"

"Ted."

"Ted Norris? Does he work excursions?" Darcy tried to hide the shock in her voice, not wanting to upset Celia any more than she already had.

"Yeah . . ."

Brandi shook her head. "Mmm, Cee, I told you

the guy was a loser." She planted her hands on her hips. "He gave you some other chick's jewelry. He's just trying to get in your pants . . . or worse."

"What do you mean worse?" Darcy asked.

"Brandi's watched one too many of those cop shows." Celia slipped off the necklace. "Here . . ." She dropped it in Darcy's hand. "You can give it back to your friend."

"I wish I could. She went missing off this ship a few days ago."

The shrill emergency alarm ceased, and a voice crackled over the intercom. "Don't panic. We are working to get you out as fast as we can."

Darcy stepped away from the control panel.

"What do you mean missing?" Brandi asked.

"I mean, she was working on the ship, and supposedly she's the person who went overboard. The cruise line says they took her to the hospital on Kodiak after the rescue, but from there she vanished."

Celia's eyes narrowed. "What are you? Some sort of cop?"

"Or spy?" Brandi's eyes widened.

Celia cocked her head. "A spy? Girl, you've got to be kidding. She ain't no spy."

Brandi eyed Darcy up and down. "Then what are you?"

"I'm just looking for my friend."

The doors opened, and they were greeted by the

same man who had rescued Darcy her first night on board.

"You again?" He arched a brow before checking on the other two ladies. "Everyone all right?"

"Just fine," Celia said.

"Stupid alarm just went off," Brandi said, glancing in Darcy's direction with a smile.

Darcy mouthed *thank you* as she clutched Abby's necklace tight, willing the tears not to fall.

She needed to find Ted. Had he been part of the rescue crew that night? Had he pulled the necklace from Abby's neck? Abby never took it off. Period. Not in all the years since Darcy had given it to her back in their freshman year of college.

Fear tingled through Darcy's fingertips. What had happened to Abby after she went in the water?

"Lady."

Darcy turned to find Brandi bustling down the corridor toward her.

She reached Darcy's side a bit winded. "We need to talk."

Darcy followed Brandi down the hall and into the stairwell. Brandi leaned over the rail, looking up and down before speaking, just as Darcy had done with Gage her first day on board.

"Do you know something about Abby?" she asked, praying she'd finally found someone truly willing to talk.

"Your friend. No. Sorry, girl."

It took a moment for the pain of that disappointment to subside. "Then . . . ?"

"Last spring, right about when I started working on the *Bering*, another gal fell overboard."

"Off the *Bering*?"

"That's right."

"Were they able to rescue her?"

"Uh-uh."

A door shut above, and Brandi stopped talking. Voices and footsteps descended a flight, and then another door shut.

Brandi leaned back over the rail and peered up to be sure they were alone again. "That's the strange part," she finally whispered.

Darcy's brows pinched together, the excitement of a possible lead coursing through her. "Strange?"

"The girl was vacationing with her family. She was out on the balcony reading when her family went to bed for the night. Next morning her book is on the balcony floor, but she's nowhere to be found."

"What?"

"Everyone assumed she fell overboard."

"And that was it?"

"Far as I know. Coast Guard did a search, but nothing turned up. Her parents were upset and carried on for a while, but it simply died down. There was nothing to do."

So within the past year a female passenger was

presumed to have fallen overboard but no body was ever found, then Mrs. Bowen disappeared or was murdered and *her* body was never recovered, and now Abby.

Could they all be related?

* * *

Where is he? Darcy banged on Gage's cabin door one more time in frustration. She'd searched the activities center—the entire ship, actually—and ended up back here. His meeting didn't start for hours, and she was dying to share what she'd learned. She *needed* to share and wanted it to be with him. The *Bering*'s past was revealing a history of missing women.

"Hey, Darcy."

She turned to find Ted strolling down the corridor. At least she'd found one of the men she was looking for.

"Just the man I was hoping to see."

Ted smiled. "Oh yeah. Why's that?"

She pulled the necklace from her shirt pocket and let it dangle from her hand. "Care to explain?"

"Explain what?" His smile held.

"How you came across this necklace?" She held it up, anger for Abby fueling her.

"What are you talking about?" He looked at her as if she were crazy.

"You gave it to Celia. . . ."

"Celia? Oh right." He snapped. "The hottie from the gift shop. What about her?"

"Where'd you get it?"

"Get what?"

"The necklace. Where did you get it?"

"Why are you getting so worked up?" He stepped closer. "Disappointed I haven't shown you any favors?"

Was the guy insane?

"It's only because I thought you and Clint had a thing going," he continued.

"Clint and I don't have anything going."

"Cool." He smiled, inching closer still.

Her skin crawled with each step he took. "This necklace"—she shoved it in his face—"belonged to Abby Walsh."

He frowned. "The chef?"

"Yes."

He shook his head. "I don't think so."

"This is Abby's necklace."

He cocked his head slightly. "You know, for a woman you only met once, you seem to know an awful lot about her."

"I saw her wearing this the day I boarded." *She always wore it.*

"Those shell necklaces are a dime a dozen."

"Not with Abby's initials on the back." She flipped the pendant over.

He squinted. "A. T.? Correct me if I'm wrong, but I thought Abby's name is Walsh. You just said so."

How did she cover that one? Misdirection. "The point is, I saw Abby wearing this necklace the day I boarded, and Celia said you gave it to her, so the question is . . . where did you get it?"

He remained silent a moment, then sighed. "Look, I'm not proud of it, all right, but . . ."

"But?"

"I found it."

Darcy crossed her arms. "You found it?"

"Yeah, out on one of the decks."

"Which one?"

"I don't remember. People are dropping stuff all the time. After a day passed and no one claimed it, I figured it was fair game."

"When did you find it?"

"A couple days ago."

"But Abby was wearing it the morning I boarded the *Bering*."

"She must have lost it shortly after."

"How would she lose it if it was around her neck?"

"Things fall . . ." He narrowed his eyes. "Wait a minute. Why all the questions about Abby? You know, you are starting to act just like her."

"What do you mean?"

"She was always asking questions."

"What kind of questions?"

He smiled, but there wasn't any warmth in it. "There you go again. Another question."

"What can I say? I'm a curious journalist."

"I think *nosy* and *misdirected* describe you better." He glanced at his watch. "Now, if you'll excuse me, I've got someplace I need to be."

27

Darcy knocked on Abby's cabin door, praying she'd find Abby's roommate, Pam, in a more amicable mood than the last time they spoke. In an effort to help that mood along, she'd come armed with a piping hot mocha—extra whipped cream and chocolate shavings.

Her encounter with Ted had reminded her that she still had the rest of Abby's belongings to go through. The night of Abby's disappearance, she'd only been able to grab Abby's purse—which was now missing.

While she doubted Abby would have intentionally left anything incriminating in her own cabin—anything that could show the truth of who she was—perhaps Darcy would find some clue. And if nothing else, she wanted to make sure Abby's things remained safe, that Abby's roommate didn't decide they were fair game.

She knocked a second time, and the door opened. Pam leaned against the doorframe, looking no less tired than she had the morning they'd met.

"Yeah?"

If it were possible, she looked even less pleased to see Darcy than before.

"Hi."

Pam stared at her blankly.

"I'm Darcy. We met the other night."

"Oh, right. The journalist with all the questions." She looped her belt across her fluffy pink robe and knotted it.

Darcy held up the peace offering. "I brought you a mocha. Thought you could use it. I'm sure you had another long night."

Pam eyed her cautiously but took the drink. "Thanks."

"I'm sure it's hard working such late shifts."

Pam shrugged and walked back into the room, leaving the door open. If that wasn't an invitation, Darcy didn't know what was. She darted inside before Pam could change her mind and shut the door behind her.

The room was much as it had been the other morning: Abby's bed made, her side of the cabin neat—Pam's half rumpled and tossed with clothes.

"What do you want?" Pam asked, lounging back on her bed and removing the lid of her drink. Steam escaped in a swirl, but Pam's eyes lit at the generous dollop of whipped cream.

Darcy sat in the only chair that wasn't filled with clothes and contemplated how she could claim Abby's things without making Pam suspicious. "When I spoke to Abby my first day on board, she indicated she had some excursion notes to show me." Actually, they were case notes, but Pam didn't need to know that.

"Notes?" Pam took a tentative sip, whipped cream clinging to her upper lip.

"Like a travel journal of sorts."

"To help with your assignment, your story?"

"That's my hope." Though, again, she doubted Abby would leave anything too incriminating in her room, amongst her personal belongings. She'd have found another place on the ship to stash her notes. Someplace where no one could tie them back to her. But with the ship being so enormous, it seemed easiest to start with her cabin and move out from there.

Besides, protecting the rest of Abby's belongings suddenly felt important. What if Pam decided they were up for grabs? What if she started wearing Abby's things or, worse yet, selling them off to crew members? "Mullins has been breathing down my neck to get the right feel for my stories, and I thought maybe looking through an excursion crew member's travel journal could give me great insight."

Pam lifted a nail file and started with her right hand. "I get what you're saying about Mullins. She can be a real pain in the neck, but I imagine she has to be with the crew she's got."

"What do you mean?" Darcy's gaze roamed over Abby's nightstand, which was clear on top, and then to her bed—*Is that a book?*—before quickly shifting her attention back to Pam.

Pam set the nail file aside, taking another sip of

mocha, then retrieved the file and set back to work. "How would you like to be in charge of some four hundred employees? She has to stay on top of them all. I don't know how she keeps everyone straight."

Mullins. Of course. Being employee liaison, she'd have access to everyone's files, access to their personal information and employment history. Darcy grimaced. She'd clearly been out of the game too long—she should have started with Mullins.

"Toss in a high turnaround rate and snooty passengers," Pam continued, switching the file from her right hand to her left. "I wouldn't want her job for the world."

"Yeah, doesn't sound like much fun." No wonder Mullins was stern—she probably had to be to get the job done.

"I think her only pleasure comes in firing people." Pam blew across her nails.

"That's sad." Darcy stood and stepped toward Abby's bed. The book looked like a Gideon Bible. It was highly unlikely it had anything to do with Abby—she avoided Bibles at all costs.

"That's Mullins. Takes pleasure in people's pain." Pam took another sip of mocha and grabbed a red bottle of nail polish from her nightstand.

Darcy sank on the edge of Abby's bed, hoping she wasn't being too obvious, praying Pam wouldn't ask her to go just yet. "I get the feeling

Mullins wasn't particularly fond of Abby."

Pam knocked the bottle of polish against her palm, shaking it up. "That's for sure."

Darcy scooted forward, resting her elbows on her knees. "Any idea why?"

"Things were fine before, but she seems steamed that Abby took off without notice."

"I imagine it's pretty hard finding replacements when you're out at sea."

"Yeah. You'd think." Pam took a Q-tip and corrected a spot she'd polished onto her skin. "But Mullins has a surprising ability to find new people."

"Really?"

"Yeah." Pam resumed polishing, switching to her left hand. "None of us are sure how she does it, but when someone leaves unexpectedly, Mullins quickly reorganizes the shifts so we all pick up the slack—but fortunately for us, that never lasts long. There's always someone new waiting in the next port or, at the very least, in time for the next cruise."

It couldn't be easy always finding replacements on such short notice, but she had mentioned something in the meeting about their usual provider working on finding a permanent replacement for Abby. "That's impressive."

"Resourceful is probably a better word for it."

Interesting. "You seem to know exactly how stuff works around here."

"I should." Pam dropped the applicator brush back in the bottle of polish. "I've been on the *Bering* for five years."

"Five years?" She looked *young*.

"Started when I was sixteen," Pam said, blowing on her freshly polished nails.

"Is that even legal?" *Good, Darcy, call her on the legality of her profession. That'll help. Sheesh.* Where was her head?

"It's legal to work at sixteen. Besides, the ship is registered in the Bahamas—totally different set of rules."

"Why is an Alaskan cruise line registered in the Bahamas?"

"Because that's where the cruise line originated." Pam carefully retrieved her mocha, holding it so as not to mess up her polish job. She took a sip and then continued, "Destiny still has ships in the Bahamas. It's only been running the *Bering* in Alaska for the past five years."

"Interesting combination—Bahamas and Alaska."

"The ships go where there's an interest in cruising."

"Right." The perfect setup for smuggling between the U.S. and foreign markets. She'd read about drug busts on Caribbean ships. Was it possible someone had decided to work the same scheme between Alaska and Russia? But what had scared Abby so? They'd investigated drug runners before.

Pam stood. "Thanks for the drink, but I better get ready for my shift."

"Oh. Sure." Darcy got to her feet. "I'll just look through Abby's things for that journal and be on my way."

"Ain't going to happen."

But she'd thought they'd been making so much progress. "Why's that?"

Pam moved to the closet, gingerly fingering through her garments, careful not to get any polish on them. "Her stuff isn't here."

"Not here? What happened to it?"

"It was collected after she left the ship."

"Collected? By whom?"

"Mullins."

Mullins. There was no doubt about the next person she needed to speak with.

"Oh, okay." Darcy took a deep breath and made a show of looking around the room. She ended by picking up the Bible from Abby's bed. "What about this?"

"Don't know. It's been there since Abby left, but I don't know why she would have taken it out of the drawer. We didn't see each other very often —because of our schedules and all that—but I never saw her reading it."

It must have been underneath Abby's purse when Darcy grabbed it that first morning—that might make it significant. "Hmm, I've always wondered about these." She opened the Bible and flipped through the pages. No obvious clue struck her, but maybe a closer examination would reveal a message from Abby.

She held up the Bible. "Mind if I take this with me?"

Pam was still focused on drying her nails. "Sure, nobody ever reads those goofy things, anyway."

Darcy tucked it in her purse and thanked Pam for her time. As she left the room, she was tempted to stop to more carefully search the Bible, but she decided the search for clues was better accomplished in the privacy of her cabin—or maybe she would stop by Gage's room.

More than likely the Gidcon Bible would come to nothing, but with a lighter heart than she'd felt in days, she headed for the elevator. Rounding a corner she heard a rustle and turned to—

28

Gage rushed to the ship's clinic the second word of Darcy's accident reached him.

Please let her be okay.

Thankfully, Whitney had sought him out after witnessing Darcy being wheeled past her in the hall on a gurney.

He reached the clinic and Clint caught him by the arm. "Whoa, there. Doc's still examining her."

Gage glared at Clint's hand on his arm, and Clint released his hold.

"What happened?"

"Don't know. One of the maids heard a sound out in the hall, went to investigate, and found Darcy blacked out. She called the clinic."

"Blacked out?"

"That's what I was told. I was late to the party."

Gage arched his brows at Clint's choice of words.

Clint lifted his hands. "Hey, man, I didn't mean anything by it, just saying I wasn't there."

"Who was?"

"Other than the maid that found her? No one that I'm aware of."

The ship's resident doc stepped from the exam room. He had a southern gentleman's gait to his walk.

Gage rushed to him. "Is she okay?"

"She took a pretty hard knock to the back of the head when she fell, but otherwise, she's right as rain."

"Fell?" Gage said.

"Can't remember much. Says everything just went black. Probably low blood sugar or a dizzy spell. It happens."

Gage wasn't buying it. "Can I see her?"

"Sure." The doctor gestured toward the exam room.

Gage knocked on the door, more anxious to see

her than he'd been to see anybody in a *very* long time.

"Come in." At least her voice sounded strong.

He cracked the door and peered in.

Darcy stood at the foot of the exam table, rubbing her head.

"You okay?"

"Yeah. Just feel a bit woozy."

Gage stepped fully inside and closed the door behind him, catching a fleeting glimpse of Clint's arm wrapped around Doc Greene's shoulder as the two conversed. *Odd.*

Darcy took a wobbly step forward.

"Whoa." He lunged to her side, supporting her. "Why don't you sit back down for a moment?"

She nodded, then winced, clearly regretting the motion.

He helped ease her up on the exam table, the white paper rustling beneath her.

Gently sweeping the hair from her brow, he studied her beautiful face, concern and protective-ness welling inside. "What happened?"

"I don't know."

Her breathless vulnerability nearly broke his heart. He never wanted her to feel scared or alone again. Whatever he had to do to make her feel loved and protected, he yearned to do. The rush of emotion, of love crashing through him nearly knocked the breath from his lungs. Where had that come from? Better yet, when had he fallen so desperately in love with Darcy St. James?

He scrambled for words, for sanity, for anything solid to grasp onto.

Her case. Focus on her case. "Can you remember anything before you blacked out? What was the last thing you did?"

"I was talking with Pam."

"Pam?"

"Abby's roommate."

"Okay. Do you remember what you were talking about?"

"Yeah." She explained finding Celia wearing Abby's necklace, confronting Ted about it, talking to Pam and learning Mullins had collected Abby's belongings. "So nothing of hers was there. But"—she patted her purse—"I grabbed a Gideon Bible I found on her bed. And then I left. . . ."

"Okay . . . so then you were heading . . . ?"

"I headed for the elevator and . . ."

"And?"

She squeezed her eyes shut. "I heard some-thing."

"Describe *something*."

"I don't know. Just a noise behind me, then everything went black."

"Can I take a look at your head? The doc said you took a pretty good knock." Working SAR, he and his family were all first-responder trained.

"Sure."

With great care and tenderness, he spread his

fingers through her hair, gently feeling the lump on the backside of her head. "It's definitely swollen. The doc thinks you got the knock when you fell." He brought his hands to his side.

"But you don't?"

He sighed. "I don't know. What do you think? Any chance the sound you heard was someone conking you over the head?"

"It could have been, but if it was, then it means someone knows I'm not exactly who I say I am."

"Or they aren't happy with the questions you're asking."

* * *

Darcy led Gage back to the corridor where her accident had occurred. She began at Pam's door and walked toward the elevator.

"I was about here." She paused in front of the maintenance closet.

Gage opened the door and glanced inside.

Darcy peered in behind him at the mops and brooms lining the near wall.

"Plenty of things to hit someone over the head with," Gage remarked.

They stepped back into the corridor.

"The only other explanation is you hit the back of your head on this"—Gage grasped the wall rail—"on your way down. Were you feeling dizzy?"

"No. I was fine."

"And now?"

"I've got a killer headache, but the doc gave me some ibuprofen, so hopefully it'll settle soon."

"Did he test you for a concussion?"

"Yes. No blurred vision, no sensitivity to light, no nausea or dilated pupils."

"Good, but just for precaution, I want you sticking by my side today."

She didn't argue. Being by Gage's side was never something to complain about, but if someone really was on to her, she'd feel a ton better having someone she trusted with her.

* * *

Darcy tapped on the doorframe of Mullins' office, glancing back at Gage seated on the sofa in the reception area. He smiled and she turned her attention back to the task at hand.

Mullins glanced up from her computer, irritation on her ruddy complexion.

"Don't tell me. Another problem?"

"No." Darcy stepped into the woman's office, noting the distinct temperature drop. Mullins liked a cool work environment.

"I heard about your accident."

Word traveled fast.

Mullins shuffled papers. "You really ought to be more careful."

"Right." What had she heard, *exactly?* "Who knew halls could be so dangerous." She smiled, trying to ease Mullins' tension.

"Are you suggesting your fall was the cruise line's fault?"

"No. Not at all." This was not a good start. She needed something from Mullins, which meant any inference of Destiny's fault in her accident would only put the woman on the defensive. Besides, it wasn't a puddle on the floor or a cord she'd tripped over that had caused her fall. If anything, someone had hit her over the head, but suggesting that possibility would only draw more attention to the fact she was digging for answers on Abby's disappearance. "Actually I was hoping you could help me with something."

Mullins arched a brow.

"Ms. Walsh . . ." Darcy was determined to avoid the perception of a personal tie to Abby, though she'd failed horribly by pressing about Abby's whereabouts in such a persistent manner her first day on board. Which was precisely why reporters never worked an undercover case with personal ties. It compromised one's ability to investigate without bias.

Mullins cleared her throat. "Are you going to continue your sentence, or is that the extent of your request?"

Darcy smiled. *So not a fan of this woman.* "The morning I boarded the *Bering*, Ms. Walsh indicated that she had kept a travel journal of her experience on the excursions and offered to let me read it—as a resource for my articles. I asked her roommate about it, and she said you'd collected her things."

Mullins rolled back from her computer with a huff. Propping her elbows on her chair arms, she steepled her fingers. "When an employee leaves without taking their belongings, we remove them from their cabin. It's standard protocol."

"Do employees do that often?"

"Do what?"

"Leave suddenly without taking their things?"

Mullins sighed. "You'd be surprised. Some people are so eager to abandon their commitments, they will leave everything behind."

Hmm. This could be her chance to get into Mullins' good graces. "That's terrible."

"Don't take a job if you aren't willing to stick with it—that's what I always say."

Darcy sank into the chair facing Mullins' desk, wondering just how many employees had been reamed out while sitting in it. "Perfectly reasonable."

Mullins eyed her like a hawk eyeing a mouse. "Was there something you wanted?"

Either Mullins hadn't been listening or she was avoiding the subject. "I was hoping you'd let me look through Ms. Walsh's belongings."

Mullins gaped at her.

"To find her travel journal. It could be a great resource for my blog posts. A day in the life of an excursion chef . . ."

Mullins rolled back to her computer. "I'm afraid that's not possible. While we were docked at Eagle Cove, I had Ms. Walsh's belongings shipped to the address she supplied on her application."

Interesting, and surprisingly thoughtful on Mullins' part. "That must have cost a lot."

"We deducted it from her paycheck."

"Of course. Well, in that case, may I have Ms. Walsh's contact information?"

Mullins' head snapped up from the monitor, and she stared at Darcy as if she had three heads.

Darcy leaned forward, praying she appeared far more composed than she felt. "I could still interview her over the phone. I want my coverage of the *Bering*'s adventure excursions to be complete."

"While I appreciate your dedication, Ms. St. James," she said dryly, "I'm afraid all information in an employee's file is strictly confidential—contact information included. Nevertheless, I'm confident your coverage will be perfectly complete without having to interview every crew member who has ever worked the *Bering* excursions."

"Of course." Darcy eyed the line of file cabinets flanking the left wall and stood. "You're right. I'm sure I have plenty to work with right here."

"Glad to hear it." Mullins waved her hand in dismissal, then reached for her phone.

Darcy smiled—she knew when she wasn't

wanted. If Mullins wouldn't give her access to what she needed, she'd simply come back after hours and take a look for herself.

* * *

Gage stood to leave as Darcy exited Mullins' office, but she stayed by the door and leaned close, as if listening. He had less than ten minutes to make his excursion meeting, but he wasn't heading there without her. He was about to ask what she was doing, tell her to get moving, but she finally turned and approached with a twinkle in her eye. And that meant only one thing—trouble.

"What were you doing?"

"She made a call as I left, and I was trying to hear the conversation."

Yes, he was right—trouble. "And . . ."

"Couldn't hear a word, but she sounded upset."

"Darc, we need to get going. I'm going to be late for the meeting."

She nodded and strode ahead of him into the hallway.

"So did she give the go-ahead to look through Abby's things?"

"No, she—"

"Darcy."

They turned as Clint approached.

Of course.

"How are you feeling?" Clint asked, wedging himself between Gage and Darcy.

"Much better."

"Glad to hear it. Hey, Mullins just called and said you wanted to focus on the excursion crew's perspective."

Darcy's eyes widened a bit. Mullins must have been talking to Clint.

She glanced back over her shoulder at Mullins' office. "Mullins called you?"

"Yeah. Said you'd just been to see her, and when we had time, she thought it'd be helpful if George, Ted, and I sat down with you."

"Wow, that was fast."

"Well, I think it's a great idea to get not only the passengers' perspectives but the excursion crew's as well. And it just so happens we're all available for the next half hour." He held out his arm. "So, shall we?"

She cast her gaze at Gage.

"Darcy was just about to accompany me to the excursion meeting," he said.

Clint wrapped his arm around Darcy's shoulder. "I'm sure you can catch her up on the details later."

Gage took a step toward Clint. "And I'm sure there'll be another time for Darcy to meet with you all."

"Mullins said *now*. If you want to go hash this out with her"—he gestured toward her office—"feel free."

"It's fine," Darcy said, her gaze fastening on Gage. "Apparently Mullins thinks this is more important right now. I'll catch up with you after the meeting. Okay?"

Gage gritted his teeth. No, it was not okay. He didn't like it one bit. "Are you sure?"

"Positive." Her eyes pleaded with him.

If he caused a scene, it'd only draw more attention to her—and that was the last thing she wanted.

"All right. Where will you be? I'll come find you after the excursion meeting."

"I told Ted and George to meet us in the Kodiak Café," Clint said.

"Great." A public place. Lots of people. That made him feel a little better. "I'll see you there."

She nodded. "See you there."

His hands balled into fists as he watched Clint lead her away.

29

Kayden shifted restlessly on the express ferry carrying her and Jake, along with the excursion gear, from Eagle Cove to Dutch Harbor. They'd left the marina before dawn and weren't due to arrive in Dutch Harbor until five tomorrow morning—just ahead of the *Bering*. Piper had opted to stay another night in Eagle Cove with Landon and would be traveling by floatplane early tomorrow to meet up with them in Dutch

Harbor when the *Bering* docked. While it was understand-able that Piper wanted to be with Landon, it had left Kayden alone with Jake, *again*.

What had been an uncomfortable situation before now felt nearly unbearable for completely different reasons. There was so much she wanted to say, wanted to ask, but she had no right. Not after how horribly she'd treated him—how she'd doubted and assumed the worst. She felt like a heel, and she had no one to blame but herself.

Why couldn't she have been trusting like Piper? Like *any* of her siblings?

She shifted on the crate she was using as a stool and watched Jake standing at the stern. The waves were turbulent in the ferry's wake, spitting white foam. The dying rays of the sun emblazoned in rose hues across the twilight sky silhouetted his strong shoulders.

He wore his sorrow like a cloak. All these years she'd missed it, mistaken his anguish for hiding something shady. He'd been hiding something, but it was not even close to what she'd suspected.

His sorrow pierced her heart—a sensation she hadn't experienced in years, not since the death of her mom. She'd hardly thought it still possible to feel such deep heartache, and the fact that it was because of Jake blew her mind.

The stirring in her heart, in her soul, nudged her to go to him—to say something to try to ease his pain—but the stirring had it dead wrong, so wrong it was almost laughable.

Me provide comfort? Ha! She wasn't the comforting type. That was Piper's thing. Kayden was the one her family called on when they needed strength, logic, or straightforwardness.

Straightforwardness.

She glanced up at the heavens with a shake of her head.

I see what you're doing, but I'm not the one to help heal him. I'm a big part of what has hurt him.

I AM Jehovah Rophi. The-Lord-Who-Heals.

She balled her fists tight. *When you* want *to be.*

She hopped down from the crate, the squawk of seabirds finally settling in the crisp coming-night air. She'd slip quietly away, leaving Jake to his peace—or more likely, his pain.

What would you have me do, Lord?

"Praise be to the God and Father of our Lord Jesus Christ, the Father of compassion and the God of all comfort, who comforts us in all our troubles, so that we can comfort those in any trouble with the comfort we ourselves receive from God."

You want me to comfort him . . . ? Me?

She felt Jake's gaze shift to her—she'd always been able to sense when he was watching. How could she possibly explain? How could he possibly understand why she was the way she was? And after she'd treated him so cruelly, why would he even care?

* * *

He excused himself, stepped into the back office, and answered the cell. "Yes?"

"The journalist found one of the gift-shop girls wearing the reporter's necklace."

"And?"

"She was told people lose and find things on the ship all the time."

"Did she buy it?"

Silence.

He balled his fists, resisting the urge to strike something. "If everything I've built crumbles because of some trinket . . ."

"It won't."

"You're right there."

"I gave her a warning, like you said."

"I think we're far past warnings."

"What do you want me to do?"

"What do you think?"

"Won't we be calling too much attention to ourselves if another one goes missing so soon?"

He fought to hide his rage. It would do no good to lose it with a promising client seated in the next room. "It wouldn't be too soon if you'd taken care of the reporter as I instructed the first time around." He inhaled and released it slowly. "Trust me, a little attention is nothing compared to what will happen if we don't meet our quota. Do you understand?"

"Yes."

"Good, then get it done." He ended the call.

Imbeciles. Every one of them. First they'd nearly botched silencing the reporter, but in the end, it'd played to his advantage. That's exactly what needed to happen now—his team needed to step up and see that things went to their advantage, or it'd be all their heads, *literally*.

He delivered. He *always* delivered. He'd worked too long and too hard to build his network. No nosy broad or weak underling was going to destroy it. Even if it meant he needed to get his hands dirty on this one.

* * *

Gage paced restlessly in his cabin. *Where is she?*

He'd told her he'd find her at the Kodiak Café as soon as his meeting was finished, but had she waited for him? No, of course not. The waitress he'd frantically questioned upon not finding her there said she'd seen Darcy leave shortly after Clint and the other men had, but where she'd headed no one seemed to know.

He tried between his scheduled onboard activities to track her down without drawing massive attention to the urgency boiling inside.

The gift shop cashier said Darcy had dropped in to chat a bit, and one of the maids had passed her in the corridor not long before Gage had entered, but he'd been unable to put eyes on her. Finally he decided it was best to do what he'd instruct anyone else in his situation to do—go to where the person can find you.

So he'd returned to his cabin at eight o'clock and decided to give her until ten. If she didn't seek him out by then, he was sounding the alarm, come what may. Darcy's safety was too important for him to ignore her absence.

What if someone was on to her? What if the same person who had gotten rid of Abby had done something to Darcy?

He glanced at the clock—nine o'clock. It had been the longest hour of his life. Could he really wait another hour? Was that even the right thing to do?

A light knock rapped on his door, and the death grip in his chest slackened. *Darcy's knock.*

He flung open the door, and a swell of relief swept through him. He yanked her inside and into his arms, kicking the door shut behind them.

"Hi," she said, her voice muffled by his embrace. "My kind of welcome."

As incredible as she felt, and as reluctant as he was to ever let her go, he did, alarmed frustration brimming to the surface. "What happened? You said you'd wait for me."

"I know, and I'm so sorry. The guys only had a half hour before Clint had a massage scheduled, and Ted and George needed to help the stage crew with some structural issues they were having. I thought I'd just come to you, so I headed for your meeting, but Pam caught me in the corridor, asking about my fall. We started talking, and she started opening up, and I thought . . ."

"You might get another lead."

"Yeah, and by then your meeting was over and I saw on the activities schedule you were pretty much booked the rest of the afternoon and evening, so I paid Celia another visit."

"And did you learn anything more?"

"No."

Everything she was saying, everything she'd done, was logical, but didn't she realize how worried he'd been? Or didn't she care?

"I wish you'd at least stopped by the activities center and told me everything was fine—or left a message on my voice mail." How pathetic did he sound? He hated everything about this situation, hated the danger she'd put herself in, hated her lack of concern for her own safety even more.

"You're right, I should have. I just . . ."

"You were thinking of the case."

Her shoulders fell. "I just thought . . ."

"Don't worry about it. You're fine. So it all worked out."

"Gage, I . . ." She stepped to him, taking his hand. "I hope you know how much I appreciate your help and concern."

But the case came first. No doubt a story always

would. He grabbed his soda and plunked down in a chair. "No sweat. So what did Mullins have to say about your looking through Abby's stuff?"

Darcy hesitated before sitting.

Just answer the question, Darcy. Don't make a big deal out of this. They were obviously at different places, as usual.

"She said I couldn't because she'd already shipped them off."

"Wow, that was efficient. So no opportunity there. Learn anything from Clint and the gang?"

"No. They pretty much gave me the party line—painted a grand picture of adventure for future passengers, but I did sense some tension between Clint and Ted."

"Over what?"

"Nothing that I could pinpoint. Just an underlying current." She shifted. "I don't know, Gage. It seems like that's how everything has been going—I catch on to the hint of a clue and then it all breaks apart. Maybe this is all in my mind. Could I be imagining that Abby is in danger?"

"I don't know, Darc. As unconvinced as I was earlier, I think you are on to something here." He wished he could think of something to give her hope. "So, did Abby's roommate say if there was anything strange in how Abby was acting before she disappeared?"

"No, she didn't notice anything out of the ordinary. But I guess they rarely saw each other.

She said—" Her eyes widened and she started pawing at her purse.

"Darcy, what's wrong?"

"I can't believe I forgot about it." She pulled out a Gideon Bible. "It's probably nothing, but I should have remembered to check."

She slowly fanned the pages, and about half-way in, she stopped and pulled out a folded square of white paper.

"Abby uses these index cards for taking notes." She unfolded the paper—"this is her writing"—and scanned the card. "But this makes no sense."

"Can I see it?" Taking the paper from her out-stretched hand, he read, *"Head cheerleader at Baylor plus Bio I lab partner."*

Darcy finished paging through the Bible and rubbed her eyes. "Is it a message or just some random scribble?"

"Does it mean anything to you?"

"Well, the head cheerleader for most of our time at Baylor was Jessica Hardy—I'll never forget her. And Abby didn't take biology, so maybe she means my Bio I lab partner, who was Brad Matthews. But I don't have any idea what they would have to do with Abby's disappearance or smuggling."

She shrugged, put the note and Bible back in her purse, and asked, "So how did your meeting go?"

"Fine." Apparently she was on to the next

topic. "A new couple joined tomorrow's excursion. The Benjamins. They participated in a couple excursions earlier in the cruise. They're on board for the full twenty-day cruise option from Seattle to Russia."

"So they were on excursions with Abby?"

"Yes. Two, including Abby's last."

"The day Abby was supposed to explain everything to me."

"Right, and according to the Benjamins, Abby didn't seem herself."

"See! I told you something was bothering her before she left. What did they say?"

"They said she was distracted, and Mrs. Benjamin thought she appeared somewhat frightened."

"Did she say of whom or what?"

Gage shook his head. "No, but it unsettled Mrs. Benjamin, and when she heard Abby had left the *Bering*, it spooked her for a bit. Her husband said he was finally able to talk her into trying one more excursion."

"So they'll be along tomorrow?"

"Yes."

"And will I be on that excursion?"

He sighed. "I won't blow your cover."

She leaned forward. "You won't?"

"No. I thought about it. If Piper or Kayden were missing, I'd do anything to find them. I may not agree with your approach, but I understand your heart." The way he'd felt while unable to locate her for a few measly hours provided him a tiny glimpse of the terror she must feel for her friend.

"Thank you." Emotion swelled in her voice.

"You may not want to thank me just yet." He couldn't in good conscience overlook her safety.

Her brows dipped. "Why not?"

"You can come on the excursion, but you have to ride on the transport boat."

"But Mullins—"

"Will understand. You just took a significant blow to the head. I'm sure for one excursion it won't be a big deal. Besides, say you're just following her idea of covering the crew. Joining Ted on the transport vessel will give you some more behind-the-scenes coverage."

"Say she buys it, what about the next excursion?"

"You're in luck. The third and final LFA excursion is an overnight hiking and rock-climbing excursion—no kayaks involved."

She smiled. "I like the sound of no kayaks."

"Riding over in the boat will get you there faster, so you'll have more time to poke around the island while Ted is setting up."

"The boat." She sprang to her feet.

"What about it?"

Her countenance brightened. "The *rescue* boat."

"Yeah?"

"If someone wanted Abby dead, if they pushed her overboard, why lower a rescue boat?"

He pondered that a moment. "Someone else must have seen her go over."

Darcy smiled. "And they sounded the man-overboard alarm."

"So . . ." Gage ran with the scenario. "Whoever pushed Abby overboard regrouped, knowing they had to be the ones to pull her from the water. They couldn't risk letting someone else reach her first."

"They?"

Gage shook his head. "No way it could be a one-man job."

"Okay. So *they* launch the rescue boat, pull her from the water, and then . . . ?"

"Supposedly take her to Kodiak Hospital."

"Yeah, that's what they claim." Darcy paced just as he had until she'd knocked on his door. The worry was finally easing from his bones. "Landon said the woman claiming to be Abby didn't show until three hours after she went overboard."

"It would never have taken that long to reach the hospital if they were close enough to shore to make the call to take her in the first place."

"That's what Landon said."

"So . . . what? They got some other woman similar in appearance to Abby, sent her in only to have her leave before she could be properly registered or assessed?"

"Right . . . That way if anyone followed up, the story of Abby being taken to the hospital and then leaving of her own accord would hold true."

"But if it wasn't Abby they took to the hospital, what did they do with her?"

Darcy's hands balled at her sides. "I don't know."

Gage stood, intercepting her path. He rested his hands on her shoulders, gently keeping her in place. Dipping his head, he looked her straight in the eye. "I know it's difficult, but I think at this point you have to consider the possibility . . ."

She shook her head. "Don't say it."

His heart melted at the fierce determination in her eyes and the quivering of her bottom lip. "Darcy . . ."

"She's not dead."

"Then where is she? It's been four days." He didn't want to hurt her, to crush her hope, but he feared Abby was dead, and the sooner Darcy came to grips with the possibility, the better.

"I don't know, but when we get to the bottom of this and find out exactly who's involved, we'll find her. I just know it." There was so much resolve clinging to her voice, mixed with such fragile hope, he didn't have the heart to break it.

"I hope you're right." He truly did, but it didn't seem realistic.

She gave a weak smile. "I thought you didn't believe in hope."

He cupped her face so she couldn't look away. "I believe in your tenacious ability to find your friend if she's still alive."

"Don't say *if*." Her voice cracked on the last word.

"Darcy . . ." His fingers lightly caressed her jaw. He needed her to feel what he was feeling if only for the briefest of moments.

He lowered his mouth to hers, ignoring every warning signal shooting off in his brain. Kissing might not be the smartest move, but it felt *beyond* right.

Her lips parted, her sweet breath mingling with his.

What was he *doing?*

Her hands slid up his neck, her fingers threading through his hair.

He worked to rein in his quickly evaporating self-control. Despite everything, he'd fallen for her *hard,* and if he wasn't careful . . .

Careful was the exact opposite of what he was being, of what he was doing.

Mustering massive restraint, he pulled back.

Her eyes fluttered open. She yanked her hands to her sides, staring up at him.

He swallowed, the taste of her watermelon lip gloss still on his lips. "You . . ."

"Should go," she said, stepping away.

"What? Go where?"

"I need to break into Mullins' office, and now is the perfect time."

"You need to do *what?*"

251

30

Darcy ignored the stirring in her heart, the jabbing at her mind, moving for Gage's cabin door, refusing to think about their kiss, and more importantly—unreasonable as it might be—refusing to even entertain the possibility Abby was dead. She couldn't give up on Abby—not yet. Not knowing . . .

Please, Father, let her still be alive. Don't let it be too late for me to reach her. To save her. Not again, Father. I can't let another friend down.

She grabbed the door handle, and Gage lightly tugged her arm, turning her to face him. "Are you insane? You can't break into Mullins' office."

"I have to."

"Why, exactly?"

"Because I need to get a look at Abby's records."

"Why? You know it's all fake information to match her cover."

She tried to keep her gaze from fastening on Gage's lips—lips that had just been wonderfully pressed to hers. Her mind, her emotions, were spinning in a thousand directions, and she had to stop—stop and focus on Abby.

"I know, but I want to see what address Mullins supposedly sent Abby's stuff to so I can follow up." She slipped on her sweater, knowing Mullins kept her office cool.

"What do you mean, *supposedly?* You don't believe Mullins mailed off Abby's things as she said?"

"Please." She pulled her hair out from under the sweater. "Do you really think Mullins would go out of her way to ship an employee's belongings home after they'd supposedly just up and left without any warning?"

"It doesn't seem likely, but maybe Mullins isn't as glacial as she appears."

Darcy arched a skeptical brow. "She said she took the postage out of Abby's last paycheck, but the cost of shipping all of Abby's things from Eagle Cove had to be outrageous." Darcy opened the door, ready to head out.

"Wait." Gage shut it, resting his hand on the door, blocking her way. "Did you say Eagle Cove?"

"Yeah, why?"

"Mullins said she shipped Abby's stuff from Eagle Cove?"

"Yes." Was this some sort of stall tactic to keep her from breaking into Mullins' office? If so, it wasn't going to work.

Gage rubbed his chin, his finger gliding over his adorable chin dimple. "That's interesting."

Her curiosity was piqued at his tone. "How so?"

"There is no post office at Eagle Cove."

"What?" Her eyes widened.

"There's no post office at Eagle Cove—no shipping company of any kind."

"Then how do folks mail stuff?"

"It goes through the ferry system."

"So maybe Mullins sent Abby's things to the ferry station."

Gage leaned against the door. "Maybe, but unless things have changed in the last few months, mail only ships on the ferry from Eagle Cove once a week."

"Are you sure?"

"We get orders for gear from Eagle Cove, and of course, we track all our deliveries, so we know exactly how long it takes for packages to ship there. And in addition to me leading kayak excursions there, Cole has led a number of diving excursions off the coast. Trust me, you quickly learn how convenient daily postal service is when you've forgotten something and know it'll be at least a week before what you need arrives."

"Any idea what day it runs?" Maybe Abby's belongings were still sitting at the ferry station.

Gage shook his head. "I'm not sure, but I'll shoot Cole an e-mail from the Internet lounge. He'll remember."

"But Jake said the computers are monitored."

"So what? I highly doubt me asking my brother about mailing something is going to raise any red flags."

Darcy glanced at her watch. "I'm not so sure

we should take the chance." And it was high time she headed to Mullins' office.

"Okay. I'll get in touch with him when we dock in Dutch Harbor tomorrow. I should have plenty of time before we head out on excursion —that way he'll have time to personally check with the ferry station, see if Abby's stuff went out or if it's possibly still there."

"Awesome. Now I've got an office to break into."

"Not alone, you don't." He grabbed his sweatshirt off the back of his chair.

"What?" He didn't possibly think . . . ?

"I'm coming with you." He slipped on the hooded sweatshirt, the dark navy bringing out the faint specks of blue in his heather-gray eyes.

"I can handle this."

"Of that I have no doubt, but this way I can be sure you're safe."

"Your concern is sweet." But how could she possibly concentrate in his presence? Not after that kiss she couldn't.

"I'm coming."

She opened her mouth to protest, but he cut in too quickly.

"I go or I blow the whistle."

She narrowed her eyes. "You wouldn't."

"Rather than risk your safety?" He smiled. "Try me."

She wasn't sure whether to smile or grunt at the man. "Fine, but if you louse this up . . ."

"So far I'm two for saves, zero for lousing."

She planted her hands on her hips. "How do you figure two?"

He held up one finger. "I saved your hide in that cave." He held up a second finger. "And I covered for you when Mullins asked where the blame should rest for the 'excursion fiasco,' as she put it."

Darcy exhaled. "Fine, but stay close and be quiet."

Gage swiped his thumb and pointer finger across his lips, showing they were zipped.

His lips . . . so soft and . . . *You will not swoon, Darcy St. James. You are a professional, and you will remain focused.*

Gage followed quickly behind as they moved down the corridor leading to Mullins' office, his steps so close he nearly nipped the back of her heels a couple times. At least he was taking her instructions to heart.

"I can't believe you are going through with this," he said as she knelt before Mullins' door and pulled out her lock-picking kit.

She glanced up at him standing like a sentinel beside her, keeping watch on the corridor while shielding her from view. What part of quiet hadn't he understood? She set to work on the lock, trying to ignore him. Like that was possible.

"I'm not even going to ask how you know to do that," he murmured.

A few more clicks and the lock popped open.

Gage offered a hand, helping Darcy to her feet, and the two slipped inside Mullins' reception area and closed the door. Darcy clicked on her flashlight and tried Mullins' door—unlocked. She opened it and quietly shut it behind them.

She moved straight for Mullins' desk, switching on the small lamp. It would give them enough light to work by but wouldn't draw nearly the attention the overhead fluorescent lighting would if someone entered the outer office.

"You find Ted's file while I locate Abby's."

Gage nodded, and each moved to the appropriate filing cabinet based on the first letter of the last name. "While we're here, it wouldn't hurt to pull Clint's record too."

She glanced over at him in the dim light. "Why Clint's?"

"Something doesn't sit right with me about the guy. Besides, he was on the Bowen excursion and he worked with Abby."

"Are you sure it's not just jealousy fueling that request?" She was only teasing, but it was clear Gage wasn't a fan of Clint's. He hadn't been since she and Clint had casually flirted over the potato skins that first night on Kesuk.

"Don't flatter yourself." He winked.

Ignoring the jab. "Fine, then while we're at it, we should grab George's too."

"I can, but seeing it's his first stint with the *Bering*, I doubt he's our guy."

"What do you mean first stint?"

"Don't you remember? When Mullins introduced him, she said it was his first cruise with the *Bering*, just like it's mine."

"That's right. So who did he replace?"

Gage shrugged. "You can always ask Clint. I'm sure he'll be more than happy to share."

She worked to smother her smile. The man *was* jealous. She fingered through the *W* files, searching for Abby's, and her frustration flared on her second pass through. "It's not here."

"What's not?"

"Abby's file."

He pulled Ted's file and shut the drawer. "Maybe Mullins refiled it somewhere, like in a past-employees file."

"Good idea." She searched while he pulled Clint's file. She found the previous-employees cabinet and searched through, but still no Abby.

"No luck?"

She shook her head and got to her feet, brushing off her hands. "It's got to be here somewhere. Mullins said she pulled Abby's contact information off her application."

"Maybe the newer employee files are on the computer. A lot of companies are making the switch to paperless."

"Makes sense." Darcy clicked on Mullins' computer and waited for it to boot. Once fully loaded, an *Employees Files* icon appeared on the desktop. She double-clicked and a series of folders opened—*New Employees, Employees, Past Employees.*

"Click on *New Employees*. Let's see what we can find out about George."

Darcy did so, and they scanned the information. "Looks like he was sent over from Alaskan Adventure and Travel Employment Agency."

"Alaskan Adventure? Isn't that who Mullins said was their usual excursion liaison, the company that provided the ship's excursions staff and auxiliary personnel?"

"Yeah."

"Any criminal record listed?"

Darcy scanned the screen. "Nope."

"Okay. Let's move on to past employees. See if we can search by termination date."

Darcy clicked the file and entered the date of Abby's disappearance. "Nothing."

"Try the next day. The day George and I boarded in Yancey."

She typed in the date. "Two hits. Abby and a Jeremy Harnett."

"Let's jot his social security number down along with those of everyone working excursions. We'll have Landon run them, just in case Alaskan Adventure missed something."

"Good idea." She wrote down Jeremy's and George's, while Gage took care of Clint's and Ted's. Then she clicked on Abby's file. Her heart

259

lurched at Abby's personnel photo, her excited smile. There was nothing Abby loved more than an investigation.

That's where they differed. Darcy loved God more, her family more. She glanced over at Gage. . . . Heaven help her—she loved Gage more. But this wasn't just any investigation—this was her friend's life. She'd already let one friend slip from her hand; she refused to let another.

Gage squeezed her shoulder. "Do you recognize the address Abby listed?"

"Yeah. . . ." She recomposed her thoughts. "It's one of the fakes we've used in the past. If Mullins sent Abby's things there and Cole doesn't intercept them before they leave Eagle Cove, I'll call my old boss and ask him to collect them. Kevin will go through them, see if anything of interest pops."

"It'll take a while. He probably won't even get them until we're done with this cruise."

"Then I might have to stay on for another."

"But I'm currently only contracted for this cruise."

The thought of being on the *Bering* without Gage filled her with trepidation, but what choice did she have? She couldn't leave until she got to the bottom of things. "I have to stay until I find Abby."

"What if staying makes no difference?"

"It has to. Abby was on to something—something that scared her enough to beg me to come back in after three years away. She wouldn't have done that unless she was desperate." Abby completely understood her stance. While she didn't share Darcy's aversion to the job, she understood that Darcy's feelings on the matter were strong.

"Desperate, how?"

"She's worked dozens of undercover investigations since I left. For some reason she felt this one was serious enough that she needed my help."

"And then she vanished."

Darcy nodded.

Gage leaned down, resting his palm on Mullins' desk not an inch from hers. "How do you know the same won't happen to you?"

Darcy was about to respond when light flashed through the transom above the door into the waiting area. Her breath caught, and she looked to Gage as he switched off the desk lamp. They scooted to the ground, their backs against Mullins' desk.

Darcy peered around the edge, listening to the rustling in the other room.

Was it a janitor? If it was Mullins, surely she would have come straight into her office.

Whoever it was, they didn't stay long, and moments after the light turned off, Darcy switched on the flashlight and Gage signaled for them to move. They dashed out of Mullins' office and through the waiting area. Once in the corridor, Gage grabbed her hand and they raced back toward the stairwell and on to his cabin.

* * *

Another bloody investigative reporter. Unbelievable. Darcy St. James had hidden her past well. It'd taken some serious digging and more than one bribe, but he'd gotten to the bottom of her investigative history—a history she shared with Abigail Tritt, aka Abby Walsh. No wonder she'd been poking around about Abby's absence, asking so many questions. She was on board to find her friend. Well, if she missed her friend so much, he'd be sure to reunite them.

31

Kayden stepped off the ferry to find Piper waiting. She was huddled under a red umbrella, puddles pooling at her feet. "Did Landon get ahold of Abby's family?" With more than seventy-two hours passed and no sign of Abby, they'd all agreed it was necessary to inform her folks.

Piper nodded. "He made the call last night. It was horrible. They are talking to the FBI."

"That's good," Jake said, zipping up his windbreaker against the slashing rain, "but I don't think they'll be of much help."

"Why not?" Piper frowned.

"Because the *Bering* is registered through the Bahamas and sails under their flag."

Kayden's brows arched.

Jake shrugged. "I did a little investigating of my own while you all were . . . busy."

She cringed. He meant while they were all talking about him.

"So what does the country a ship is registered in have to do with the FBI being of help?" Piper asked.

"It makes things complicated. Since Abby is a U.S. citizen and she went missing on U.S. soil—supposedly in Kodiak—the FBI has jurisdiction, but as far as the *Bering*'s involvement . . ." He raked a hand through his hair. "It sounds like the evidence indicates Abby was last seen leaving Kodiak Hospital, which has nothing to do with the ship."

Kayden shifted her gaze to Piper. "Did you and Landon learn anything yesterday?"

"Yeah, and it's not good." She went on to explain how Landon had set her up at the police station while he and Cole got to work on the crime scene. With Deputy Travis McCormick's help, she'd done quite a bit of digging on the *Bering* and missing women. Piper surveyed the street and pointed toward a restaurant. "How about we get out of the rain and discuss this over breakfast?"

It seemed everyone else had the same notion—

the Dutch Harbor Ferry Station Café was packed to near capacity. Kayden wondered if the rain would let up before the *Bering* started off-loading passengers for the day. At least they'd have time to fill up on a warm, hearty breakfast before heading out on excursion.

"So what did you learn?" she asked as the three crowded into a small booth.

Piper took a sip of her freshly poured coffee before answering. "It looks like roughly twenty people—mostly women—have gone missing off cruises in the last year."

"From the *Bering*?" Jake asked, nearly choking on his coffee in the process.

"No. Worldwide. But . . . counting the Bowens and Darcy's friend, four have gone missing off the *Bering*."

"Who's the fourth?" Jake asked.

"A gal by the name of Jessica Matthews." Piper slid the missing-person flyer she'd pulled from the computer across the table to Jake. "Parents said good night to her out on their private balcony where she was reading. In the morning, the book was there and their daughter was gone."

"Let me guess . . ." Jake sat back. "The cruise line insisted she must have fallen overboard during the night?"

"Yeah." Piper's brows pinched together. "How'd you know?"

"That's always the excuse."

Kayden shifted to face him. "What do you mean *always?* This has happened before?"

"Unfortunately, yes. We didn't work a lot of cruise cases in Boston, of course. The only cruises you have in that area are the New England fall tours, but we had a couple of women from Boston go missing off cruises and, in both cases, falling off their balconies during the night was the official party line. Their parents came to us when they got back home, asking for us to investigate, but there was little we or the FBI could do. There was no evidence to suggest foul play other than the vanishings themselves."

Kayden shook her head. "That's insane."

"But sadly, true."

"What do you think really happened?" she asked.

Piper gaped at her.

Yes, she'd just asked Jake's opinion on something, genuinely asked. It would help if her sister would stop staring. *"What?"*

Piper shook her head, reaching for a sugar packet. "Nothing."

She turned back to Jake. "So, what do you think?"

He cleared his throat. "I . . . I think at least some of the women are being trafficked."

Piper's brown eyes widened with horror. "Trafficked? As in . . . ?"

"The sex-slave trade," Jake said, sorrow heavy in his voice.

Piper leaned forward, her expression aghast. "Why hasn't anyone dug deeper? How can the cruise ships just get away with something like that? Do you think that's what's happening on the *Bering*?"

Jake took a deep breath, rubbing the back of his neck. "If I were a betting man . . ."

"But three women over the course of a year hardly seems like a serious trafficking network," Kayden said.

"Kayden! It doesn't matter if it's only one. It's still horrid," Piper said.

"I'm not disagreeing. I'm simply saying it seems unlikely that three women a year are enough to sustain a human trafficking network."

"She's right," Jake said, lifting his mug. "There's got to be more to it."

* * *

Darcy followed Gage down the gangplank, relieved to find the rain had finally stopped, but even more relieved that she'd be riding in the transport boat. Mullins had taken Gage's suggestion, and Darcy was more than pleased to avoid climbing into another kayak. Unfortunately, Ted would be piloting the boat, and she was growing less and less keen on the guy every day.

Seeing the McKennas clustered at the end of the pier, she moved toward them, zeroing in on Piper. "I've got a favor to ask you."

"Anything." Piper smiled.

"Can you call Landon before we head out?" She explained about Abby's belongings supposedly being shipped from Eagle Cove.

"Sure. I'll tell him to head over to the ferry station when he gets a chance. I think the mail only runs on the ferry on Fridays, so we still have a chance. Maybe we'll luck out and her things will still be there."

"Awesome, thanks."

Piper rubbed Darcy's arm. "How you holding up?"

"Okay."

"I see Gage has you on the supply boat today."

"Yes." She smiled.

"Have you learned anything new?"

"Quite a bit."

"Landon and I did as well. We'll have to catch up tonight at the campground."

Darcy nodded as Ted stepped to her side. "Ready?"

"Yep. Let's do this."

Ted helped her into the boat and steered out of the marina, the cold spray of the sea sprinkling Darcy's face as he increased his speed.

Apparently he was in a hurry. Probably about as thrilled as she was at the prospect of being stuck together for the better part of the day.

"After your kayak incident, I figured you wouldn't be too eager to get back in the water," Ted said, glancing back from the helm.

He had that right.

He shook his head. "Crazy, finding a body like that."

Crazy was one word for it.

"Gets a person thinking, though." He gazed out across the water.

"About?"

"How many bodies the sea must be hiding. I bet the oceans are littered with them."

She glanced at the dark blue water, the crystalline surface like glass in the distance, the churning, frothy waves surrounding their craft. "What a horrid thought."

Ted shrugged with an odd smile. "Just saying . . ."

Great. Now she had even more reason to dislike the sea. She'd lost one dear friend to it; she just prayed she hadn't lost another.

Ted remained silent the rest of the ride, leaving her to her troubled thoughts.

Please, Lord, take this anxiety from me. Lift this burden from my chest. You are in control. Help me to remember it.

She'd spent the last five days thinking she was the only one who could save Abby, and though God may have very well placed her in this position to help, she had to remember He was in control.

Remind me of your unfailing love, of your provision. Remind me that you are greater than the seas threatening to swallow me.

A couple hours later, they reached the uninhabited island where they'd be spending the night. The rest of the team would be hours behind. Darcy climbed from the boat. *Super*. Just her and Ted, on their own for hours.

She unloaded the food supplies while Ted began setting up camp. At least, on the bright side, everything would be in place when the rest of the team arrived, which meant more time sitting around the campfire catching up with Jake and Piper. She was dying to know what they'd learned and couldn't wait to share what she had—including the fact that Ted gave her the creeps.

32

Five tense hours later, the first blue tip of a kayak came into view. Darcy approached Gage the minute he pulled his craft onto shore. He glanced up the slope at Ted whittling wood. "Everything okay?"

"Yeah." She rubbed her arms. "The guy totally creeps me out." *Like with that bizarre ocean comment.* "But he kept pretty much to himself. How did kayaking go?"

"Awesome," Heath said, striding past her up to camp. "Hope you got the grub ready. I'm starving."

269

"Isn't he just charming," his fiancée, Amber, snorted, following Heath up toward the picnic tables and campfire.

"Wow. They're a cheery couple," Darcy said.

Gage lifted his pack from his kayak and slung it over his shoulder. "Maybe they deserve each other." He smirked.

* * *

Darcy stared at the fish before her. Actual fish. Packed on ice in all their natural glory, transported from the *Bering* in a cooler.

Since Phillip would no longer be part of the excursions, Mullins had efficiently split up the task of cooking among the remaining excursion crew, including her. Tonight's dinner was her assignment. Mullins thought it would be a great addition to her coverage and instructed Darcy to not only blog about it when she returned to the *Bering* but to make sure plenty of pictures were taken.

When she'd learned the main course was salmon steaks, Darcy hadn't flinched—she grilled fish all the time. But the fish piled in the cooler were nothing like the prepared cuts of fresh fish she picked up in the seafood department of her local grocery store.

No, what sat in front of her were five huge salmon—scales still in place, heads still on, eyeballs staring up at her. What on earth was she going to do with them?

After several attempts to grasp the slippery, slimy beasts, she decided she would have to sacrifice her gloves. Maybe she could clean them enough to be of use later, but right now she needed to get those fish prepared.

After donning her gloves, she pulled the first fish out by the tail.

"Darcy!"

She looked up in time for Gage to snap what had to be a charming shot of her and her first salmon victim. He was going to enjoy his meal-prep-photographer role way too well.

With a grimace she laid the fish on the tray she'd placed on the picnic table and grabbed a knife. *First, chop off the head.* That way he couldn't keep staring up at her. Taking a deep breath—and conscious of avoiding any photo-worthy grimaces—she lifted the knife and chopped down in an axlike movement, whacking the head clean off. She screamed as it shot from the tray, and Gage ducked to avoid being hit by it as he snapped another picture.

"Easy there. The task is to fillet them, not butcher them."

"I've never worked with whole fish before."

"That's obvious."

"Okay, I think we have enough pictures." She reached out to take the camera, and he stepped back, grimacing at her slimy gloves.

"Ahh, I'll just leave it here." He placed it on the

table. "I need to help get the crew tents set up anyway." After a few steps he turned with a smirk. "If you need any help, just give us a yell."

Tempted to retrieve the fish head and do her best to throw it at his retreating back, she instead returned her attention to the beheaded fish before her. Her stomach surged slightly at the smell.

"Would you like some help?"

She flinched and turned to find Clint leaning against a tree.

"That would be great. Thanks so much." Stepping back, she let Clint have the workspace. She peeled off the nasty gloves and tossed them aside, then moved around to sit on the opposite side of the picnic table.

Clint worked with precision—cutting the fish into perfect grilling-size portions.

"Wow! You've got some mad knife skills."

"The combo of spending a lot of time in the wilderness and medic training."

Here was her opening. "Speaking of being a medic . . ."

He gave her a sideways glance. "Why do I feel another interrogation coming on?"

She smiled. "Any chance you could find out who was part of the rescue crew the night Abby went overboard?" He'd been told by a fellow crew member that it had been Abby who went overboard, so surely that person had some firsthand knowledge. It stood to reason that either they were part of the crew or had spoken to someone who had been.

Clint finished the last fish and set the tray of salmon, ready for grilling, in front of her. "I think you can handle it from here. I'll dump the remains off the shore. It'll give the waterfowl some good eating tonight."

"And my request?"

"Explain why you want to know and I'll consider it."

She swallowed. How much should she say? How much could she really trust Clint? "I don't understand why it's such a big secret. You'd think those who were part of the rescue crew would be happy for people to know they're heroes."

"Heroes?" Clint lifted the bag of fish waste.

"They rescued a woman from drowning."

"I suppose that does make them heroes."

"So why all the secrecy?"

"It's not a secret. It's just not public knowledge."

"Because?"

He shrugged. "Protocol."

"What protocol?"

"You don't have a clue about how the cruise-ship world works, do you?"

"Cruise-ship *world?*"

"It's its own entity."

"How so?" He had her curious.

"Out on the open water, the ship is its own city, its own world."

"How do you figure that?" The *Bering* consisted primarily of U.S. crew and passengers. The ship was a means of vocation and vacation, not an escape to another world.

"It's self-sustaining, set apart, and operates under its own set of rules and agendas."

"Such as?"

"Protocol takes priority. Now if you'll excuse me, I've got some waste to get rid of."

"What was that all about?" Gage asked, striding up.

"I don't know. I asked him if he could find out who was part of the rescue crew the night Abby went overboard, and he gave me some weird lecture about a ship's autonomy and the most important rule being protocol."

"Okay . . . so was that his way of saying no?"

"I don't know. The entire conversation was strange. Sometimes I think he's just struggling with it."

"With what?" Gage picked up a carrot stick and popped it in his mouth.

"Wanting to be helpful but wanting to protect his ship, his livelihood, by strict adherence to protocol as he's been taught."

"Well, you've clearly got him wavering."

"You think?"

"I see the way he looks at you."

"Oh, really, and how is that?"

"Like he wants you for himself."

The thought sent a shiver up her spine—and not the good kind.

33

After cleaning up from the meal, Darcy wasted no time in sidling up to Kayden and Jake around the campfire. She'd been trying to talk to them alone ever since their kayaks pulled up to shore, but until then the opportunity hadn't presented itself. Everyone was content on a full stomach and all were preoccupied with their own conversations spread out about the camp.

A full moon hung in the sky, illuminating the treetops. A strong wind rustled through the upper limbs, but they were sheltered by the strategic camp layout, nestled among the backdrop of trees.

Darcy wrapped her hands around the warm cup of cider. Her gloves—washed and rinsed with fresh water and sprayed with sanitizer—lay on a nearby rock. She hoped the fire would dry them before they had to put it out for the night.

Jake relayed what Piper had learned while in Eagle Cove and explained what he was afraid was happening. Fear gripped Darcy as the words flowed from his lips. *Sex trafficking*. She'd never even considered that possibility, though it would explain Abby's fear.

The thought of Abby, of any woman, being subjected to such horrific slavery twisted her stomach in knots. She was in way over her head. This was something for the police—not a single reporter who had been out of the undercover game for nearly three years.

But Jake had already explained that local cops had no jurisdiction on a cruise ship registered and sailing under a foreign flag. And clearly, the *Bering*'s poor excuse for a security force wasn't going to be of any help. Just as Clint had said only a few short hours ago—the cruise ship was its own world and operated under its own set of rules.

You'd think they'd want to get criminals off their ship, but it seemed that protecting their family-friendly image was what mattered most to them—not protecting innocent lives. It prodded Darcy all the more to push forward, to bring whoever was responsible for these women's disappearances to justice.

She shifted, her mind scrambling to wrap around the depth of evil they were facing. "What are we going to do?"

The whir of a plane's engine circled overhead.

"Floatplane," Kayden said without bothering to look up.

"Who'd be flying into here?" she asked. Maybe it was a drop shipment. She scanned the crowd.

All the women were accounted for. Was it drugs? Was it someone completely unrelated to their excursion landing to camp for the night?

"I'll check it out." Jake stood, and from across the camp Gage followed, the two disappearing into the woods.

Clint walked over from where he'd been checking the kayaks to join Kayden and Darcy at the fire. "Wonder who that is."

"Does that happen often?" Darcy asked.

"A floatplane landing during one of our excursions?"

She nodded.

"A time or two, but it's rather dangerous to be landing at night without any lights—other than the moon."

Darcy scanned the campground for Ted but didn't see him. "Have you seen Ted?"

Clint took a bite of an apple. "Can't say that I have."

"Or George?" she asked, not seeing him either.

"Nope." He took another bite.

Maybe George and Ted were making a pickup or drop-off of some kind. How would they react if Gage and Jake interrupted them? What were the chances either were armed? "Excuse us a moment."

"Sure."

She tugged Kayden off to the side. "Any chance Jake is armed?"

"About one hundred percent. Why?"

"Gage and I were speculating that whoever is smuggling or trafficking is probably using these excursion points for drop-offs and pickups. If that floatplane is a courier and Gage and Jake go barging through the trees . . ."

"I got you. Let's go." She yanked Darcy into a run.

Without asking what they were going to do, or how on earth they could be of help, she let Kayden lead her through the woods, her heart thumping in her chest.

Twigs crunched beneath her boots, branches pulling at her hair. What were they about to encounter?

They broke through the copse and found the floatplane resting on the water's dark surface, its lights bouncing off the outgoing tide. Darcy's gaze flashed in horror to the men gathered round, and then she frowned. "Landon?" she asked, squinting. "Is that you?"

"Hey, Darcy." He waved.

"What are you doing here?" Did he have urgent news? Had he found Abby? Hope flared in her chest, quickly followed by dread. Had he found her dead?

"Cole hitched a plane back to Yancey, so I figured I'd hitch one out here."

"Oh." She tried not to sound too disappointed. She was happy to see Landon, but she'd hoped . . .

"Now, that's commitment," Kayden said. "Hope when I get engaged my fiancé is half as committed."

Everyone turned to Kayden, shock evident on their faces.

"What?" She shrugged. "I could get engaged one day."

Gage held up his hands. "Just never thought I'd hear the words *my fiancé* coming out of *your* mouth."

"Moving on to the matter at hand . . ." Darcy pointed her flashlight at Landon. "Did you bring any news with you?"

"I'm afraid so."

34

"What's going on?"

Darcy startled as Clint broke through the trees, flashlight in hand, followed closely by Piper.

Piper stopped abruptly and smiled. "Landon . . . what are you doing here?"

Landon opened his arms to embrace her. "What can I say? Can't stay away from my girl."

"You're so sweet."

Kayden rolled her eyes at Darcy. "Committed, but sickening."

"I think it's precious." Darcy smiled. She adored Piper and Landon and prayed she would be invited to join in the celebration of their August wedding.

"You've caused quite a stir in camp," Clint said.

"Why's that?" Landon asked.

"First a plane lands, and then people go disappearing into the woods." Clint chucked an apple core into the trees behind them.

"Well, it looks like I'm not the only visitor," Landon said.

"What?" Darcy asked as Clint quickly echoed the question.

"As we made our approach, I saw a boat on the west side of the island."

"You mean the east side," Darcy said. "That's where Ted anchored the supply boat when we arrived."

"No. It was definitely on the western shore. I had the pilot circle around to be sure. Caught my attention because it had its running lights on."

Darcy looked at Gage, and without a word, they took off for the western shore.

"Where's everyone going now?" Clint asked, his voice trailing through the trees.

The answer seemed quite obvious. It had to be Ted. She hadn't seen him at the campsite, and now Landon had spotted a boat on the western shore. What were they dropping off or picking up? It had to be drugs. Surely all the women . . .

She stopped short. "Gage."

He halted, turning to face her in the dim woods.

Footsteps were rapidly approaching from the east. "What?"

"The women on our excursion . . . were they all in camp?" She tried to picture everyone who had been sitting around the campsite. "What if . . . ?"

He grabbed her hand. "Hurry." He ran at a speed she found difficult to keep up with, her legs being so much shorter than his.

They reached the western shore and scanned the beach. *Nothing?*

"I don't understand." She hunched to catch her breath, her hands at her waist.

"Look at the water." Gage pointed his flashlight to the left, at the ripples evident of a boat's wake.

"Anything?" Landon asked, stepping onto the beach—followed by Clint, Jake, Piper, and Ted.

Ted? How had he . . . ? "Were you meeting someone, Ted?" she asked.

"What?" Ted frowned. "Why would I be meeting someone out here?"

"Landon said he saw a boat here when he circled overhead."

"A boat?" Ted looked sincerely confused, which confused Darcy all the more. Did he really have no idea what she was talking about, or was he just that good of an actor? "We anchored on the east side," Ted said, appearing to question her sanity. "You were there."

"I know. Landon said it was another boat. Its running lights were on."

"So?"

"So don't you find that strange?"

"The only thing I find strange is your behavior. What is up with you? Are you one of those conspiracy nuts or something?"

"We were just trying to keep track of the excursion crew," Gage said.

"You and George weren't around earlier, and . . ." Darcy began.

"And?" Ted squared his shoulders.

"We were trying to locate you," Gage said.

"Thanks, but I'm a big boy. I can take care of myself in the woods. Now if you'll both excuse me, I'm going to hit the hay." He pushed past them into the woods, headed back for camp.

Darcy looked at Gage but refrained from commenting in front of Clint. And they still didn't know where George was.

"We ought to follow Ted's lead and head back to camp," Jake said. "Nothing to see here."

Darcy hung at Gage's side as they trekked back to camp. Clint remained surprisingly silent on the evening's turn of events. She couldn't figure out if he shared Ted's attitude toward her, or if he was simply going along with the flow.

Their earlier conversation had ended awkwardly without any kind of clear response from Clint on her request. She felt it vital that things remained smooth between them. She needed Clint—needed his insight and knowledge of the crew, of the excursions, and of the members of the rescue crew the night of Abby's disappearance. Surely, Clint had to wonder at Ted's abrasive nature too.

She'd talk to him once back at camp, to make sure they remained on good terms, that the connection she'd been trying to build hadn't been fully severed.

Gage wouldn't like it—wouldn't like her bonding with Clint to gain information, wouldn't like her bonding with Clint *period*—but she had to do it. Clint held knowledge she needed, knowledge pivotal to the case. She just knew it.

* * *

Gage watched with irritation as Darcy approached Clint with two cups of cocoa. She smiled as he suggested she take a seat beside him on the log.

The firelight danced off her blond hair, bathing her in a golden glow. She was so beautiful. *And dangerous.* Very dangerous when it came to his heart.

Landon cleared his throat. "We need to talk."

Gage followed him into Jake's tent, where Jake was waiting. "What's up?"

"While the girls are keeping the rest of the crew and passengers occupied, we thought it would be a good time to talk."

"Okay." Gage sat on the open cot with apprehension.

"I relayed my latest findings to Piper and Jake as we made our way back to camp. And Jake shared his insights with me." Landon sat on the matted ground, his back braced against his cot. "Piper can fill Darcy in tonight when they bunk up. And Jake"—Landon glanced at him, still standing near the entrance, keeping an eye out to be sure no one approached—"can fill Kayden in during the next transport."

Gage shifted uncomfortably on the cot. How bad was this about to get?

"First things first. I checked the ferry station for Abby's belongings."

"And?"

"Nothing was delivered from the *Bering*," Landon said.

"So either Mullins is lying, or whoever she told to make the delivery decided not to," he said.

"Probably figured it wasn't worth the trouble," Jake added.

"Or he decided to sell or give away Abby's things. Darcy found one of the gift-shop workers wearing Abby's necklace," Gage said.

"Makes sense." Landon nodded. "Tell Darcy to keep an eye out for anything else that looks like it could have belonged to Abby."

"Trust me, with her tenacity, I'm sure Darcy's been combing the ship for the slightest glimpse of anything that could be Abby's."

"She is determined," Jake said. "I'll give her that."

Gage couldn't miss the weariness of Jake's

brow. What Darcy did—digging into his past, exposing private details of his life—wasn't right. "I'm sorry, man."

Jake held up a hand. "We've got more important matters on our plate."

"Which brings me to the body Darcy found," Landon said.

"What about it?" Gage asked.

"The remains have been positively identified as Drake Bowen's."

Gage rocked forward. "What?"

"Confirmed dentals today. Everything's done over the computer. Seems Drake's family had insisted on keeping his missing-person file open and up-to-date. They had his dentals ready should a body be found. According to Travis, who spoke routinely with Drake's sister Anna, after Drake went missing on Kesuk, the family—including his wife's parents—never doubted his innocence. They didn't believe he would run. Not like that. They knew foul play had come to him."

Jake slid his hands in his pockets. "Looks like they were right."

Landon crossed his arms over his chest. "Cause of death was a gunshot wound to the back of the head—execution style."

"Not to be grotesque, but how could the M.E. make that determination with the amount of decomp?" Gage asked, having seen firsthand what little remained.

"Bullet hole in the skull. Killer used a .45."

"So it stands to reason Bowen didn't kill his wife," Jake said.

Landon nodded. "I agree."

"There's no way it could have been suicide?" Gage asked, just wanting to be sure they considered every possible angle. "Remorse over killing his bride."

Landon shook his head. "Impossible at the angle the bullet hole was found, but it's good to ask those questions."

"Suicides are almost always to the temple or in the mouth," Jake said.

Gage processed that for a moment, realizing Jake had an entire history he'd never known about until the last couple days.

"So . . ." Landon said, shifting to sit on the cot, "I think it's fair to assume that whoever killed Bowen's wife killed Drake Bowen too."

"Maybe Mrs. Bowen wasn't killed," Jake said.

Landon arched his brows. "What are you thinking?"

"Mrs. Bowen's body was never found. The only clue was a small amount of blood in their tent that could have resulted from a cut finger or a bloody nose—just enough to plant doubt in people's minds about Drake Bowen. Gage, you said you heard they were drinking that night?"

"Yeah, Whitney said one of the men on the

excursion told her friend there was a lot of drinking going on."

"Okay, so whoever is involved in this waits until the Bowens pass out for the night; maybe they even slip a little something extra in the Bowens' drinks to ensure they'll be out. They go in, take Mrs. Bowen. Perhaps she wakens and struggles. She gets knocked out and her nose bleeds, or they slice a finger and allow her blood to drip along her sleeping bag as they carry her out. The husband wakes up, finds his wife missing, and freaks."

Landon jumped in. "Everyone starts looking for her, and then someone sees the blood in their tent and the suspicion shifts to Drake."

"The guy insists he's innocent," Jake said, continuing with their rolling theory. "And he takes off, determined to find her. The men responsible fear he'll make too much noise or come across something. It's too risky to leave him be, so one of them follows Drake, shoots him execution style, and dumps his body in the river."

"Okay, but what did they do with Mrs. Bowen?" Gage asked.

Jake exhaled. "The same thing I fear they did with Jessica Matthews and Darcy's friend Abby. Sold them into slavery."

Gage looked at Landon.

Landon shook his head. "I hate to say it, but I think Jake's right."

"Doesn't that usually work the other way around?" Gage asked. "I mean, you hear about poor women from other countries being trafficked into the U.S., but American women trafficked out . . . ?"

"Can you imagine the price some buyers would pay for an American sex slave?" Landon said to Jake.

Jake nodded. "The question is how. Kayden made an excellent point at breakfast today when I shared my suspicions of human trafficking. . . ."

"Which was?" Landon asked.

"Our investigations have found three women who have disappeared from the *Bering* in the last year. That's horrible, but it doesn't make for a very viable trafficking network."

"Darcy assumed they were trafficking drugs when Abby called her in," Gage said. "Maybe that's their prime trafficking focus, but they deliver an occasional sex-slave victim when they receive a request."

"I'd agree, except for what I found earlier today." Landon grabbed a file from his bag and spread the paperwork and images on the tent floor.

"When Cole and I finished up with the crime scene, I checked in with Travis at the station, and he shared what Piper had learned about the girl who disappeared from her family's balcony. I started digging and discovered that, in addition to the three missing women off the *Bering*, four other women have gone missing under mysterious circumstances on Alaskan cruises this past year —and that's just the beginning."

"What do you mean?"

"I still have Travis, Wyatt, and the boys back in Yancey tracking things down, but it looks like this missing-women pattern has been showing up for nearly five years."

"Missing-women *pattern?*" Gage's gut clenched at the thought of such depravity and the horrors those poor women suffered. He wanted Darcy away from the *Bering* as soon as possible.

"Young women," Landon said. "As young as sixteen all the way up to late twenties. Most traveling alone, but clearly not all."

"That's a lot of women disappearing from Alaskan cruises," Jake said. "You'd think someone would have put it all together by now."

"The cruise lines work hard to keep these things quiet. It's only because of the families' persistence—when there is family to persist—and efforts of watchdog agencies like the International Cruise Victims that there's anyone making noise and any sort of record of the disappearances."

"Surely the disappearances make the news or the papers," Gage said.

"Only if there's family to make noise to the papers, or more often if a reporter catches wind of the occurrence while a ship is docked in a nearby port. The women go missing off the larger cruise ships like the *Bering* and off of the smaller yacht-style cruises too. But they aren't just disappearing off cruise ships. I've got a lot more investigating to do, but over the years women have gone missing on various adventure excursions unrelated to cruises—when hiking or camping in small groups or on their own, and even from several of the lodges."

"So we're talking a vast criminal network," Jake said.

Landon nodded. "Looks that way."

Jake sighed. "It's very smart. Spreading it out. Makes the disappearances seem completely unrelated. Someone very savvy and obviously diabolical is running the operation."

Landon nodded. "I agree."

"So where do we go from here?" Jake asked.

"I know one thing," Gage said. "I'm not letting Darcy back on that ship."

"You can't do that," Landon said.

"What? Are you crazy?"

"Landon's right," Jake said.

"You're both crazy."

"Darcy's getting close."

"Exactly. It won't be long before whoever is involved figures out Darcy's connection to Abby—if he hasn't already."

"Just hear me out," Landon said. "If we can pinpoint at least one player in the network—

which I believe Darcy is very close to doing—then we may be able to use him to trace back to whoever is running the whole thing."

"I'm not willing to sacrifice Darcy's safety."

"She's not going to walk away, and we both know it," Jake said. "Not without her friend."

"Her friend is most likely dead. She learned what was happening, got too close to fingering those involved, and they killed her. Darcy just doesn't want to admit it."

"Based on what we've figured out," Jake said, "a completely different prospect exists."

"You don't think . . . ?" *Abby sold into the sex-slave trade?* His stomach flipped. Jake was right—Darcy would never run from this fight. "What do you think we should do?"

"Darcy said you two decided that Abby had brought her in to work excursions because she believed someone on them was involved."

"Yeah . . ." Gage raked a hand through his hair. *This is insane.* "But that was when we thought they were using the excursion points to run drugs, not people." What kind of monsters were they dealing with?

"If someone on the excursions is involved," Gage said, "our suspect list is short. Darcy's bet is on Ted, but I'm not a fan of Clint."

A look passed between Landon and Jake.

"What?"

"You're not a fan because of the attention he

pays Darcy or because you really think he may be involved?" Jake asked straight out.

Gage seriously weighed that. "Both," he answered truthfully.

"What about George?" Jake asked.

"He's new. Brought on the same day as me."

"We need to find out who he replaced," Landon said. "The timing is too convenient. I mean, Abby goes overboard, and the next day someone on the excursion team leaves."

"Already suspected that. Darcy and I got a look at the employee liaison's files."

Landon arched a brow. "Not going to ask how."

"Better if you don't. But the man George replaced was Jeremy Harnett. Darcy and I jotted down all their socials for you." He handed Landon the slip of paper. "We thought you could run them. See if anything pops."

"Anything in their files that suggested a history of trouble?"

"No."

"I'll still run them, just to be thorough."

"Darcy will appreciate it."

Landon smiled.

"What?"

"Nothing." His smile grew.

35

"Thanks for the cocoa," Clint said, finishing it off.

"You're welcome." She'd been very careful not to press on anything—her earlier request, his strange *cruise-ship world* comments, or even what had happened in the woods. This time spent with Clint was damage control. She'd inquire about the rescue crew again, but not tonight.

"So what was all that out there?" Clint gestured to the woods as he set his empty cup aside.

"What do you mean?" She took a sip of her lukewarm cocoa.

"I mean, you and Gage racing all over the woods, searching for planes, boats, and crew members. Are you really some conspiracy nut like Ted believes?"

"No. Definitely not. We were just curious about the plane."

"And the boat," he added.

"Right." She smiled. "And then Gage noticed some of the crew were missing . . ."

"I didn't realize we were all supposed to remain under lock and key."

"It's not like that. Gage just wants to be sure everyone's safe."

Clint gave a knowing smile. "Especially you."

She thought it best just to let the comment slide.

"If I didn't know better, I'd think you two were an item."

"Gage and I aren't an item." She couldn't even go there—delving into her feelings for him, her love. Not while Abby was still missing. Her focus had to remain on the case, but she still found both her head and her heart filled with Gage, filled with the memory of their kiss and the questions left unanswered.

"Come on." Clint stood and extended his hand. "There's something I want to show you."

"Now?" It was late and dark.

"I was going to show you earlier, but you and Gage went racing off."

She shifted uncomfortably on the log, glancing back at Jake's tent, where Gage still was. He'd throttle her if he found out she'd gone off alone with Clint.

"Don't you trust me?" Clint asked.

If she said no, if she declined, it could very easily mean the end to his cooperation—limited as it had been thus far. "Of course." She smiled. He wasn't the one who worried her. Ted was the one she'd never venture into the woods alone with.

"Come on, then."

She stood and placed her hand in his. No warmth passed through her, as it did whenever she held Gage's hand. There was no sense of security or protection.

"Where are we going?" she asked, trepidation filling her the farther they moved from camp. She looked back, the campfire no longer visible.

"You'll see."

"I'm not really a surprise kind of gal."

He turned back with a peculiar smile. "Yet you keep surprising me."

* * *

Gage exited Jake's tent, adrenaline burning through his veins. Women being trafficked, sold into the sex-slave trade, and they were most likely working side by side with the men responsible.

He glanced around the fire. Ted had already turned in as soon as they got back to camp. George was back and conversing with the newlyweds at the fire. When had he returned, and more importantly, where had he been?

He scanned what remained of the group for Clint but came up empty, and then it hit him—Darcy wasn't there either. Had she already turned in? He hoped that was the case, but in his gut he knew better. He was going to throttle her. He stepped toward Whitney. "Have you seen Darcy?"

"Yeah, she took off with Clint."

He knew it.

"Any idea which way they went?"

Whitney pointed toward the far side of camp.

"Any idea how long they've been gone?"

"I'd say fifteen minutes, maybe?"

Great. Was she completely insane? "Thanks." He grabbed a flashlight.

"You want some company?" Whitney asked, standing.

"I thought you never left the group."

She smiled. "I think you're trustworthy."

"I appreciate that, but I'll feel better knowing you're safe here."

Her smile wavered. "Are you worried something is happening? I mean, I thought it was stupid of her to go off with Clint like that but figured they just wanted some privacy."

The thought left him ill, but he knew it wasn't the truth. Didn't he? "Nothing's wrong. I just want everyone staying in camp. You go wandering through unfamiliar woods at night, you could easily stumble and break a leg."

"Right." Whitney smiled, clearly not buying his explanation.

"I'll see you in a bit."

She nodded as he headed for the opposite end of camp.

"Where are you going?" Jake asked as he passed.

"To get Darcy."

"You want help?"

"Nah." He held up a hand, not slowing his pace. "I'm good."

Truth was, he was far from it. Darcy had gotten

under his skin, in the good way, in the very good, *very* dangerous way. He hadn't been able to shake her from his mind since she'd left Yancey last December, but now she'd burrowed her way past his guard, deep into his heart. He cared for her. . . . Who was he kidding? He loved her—strongly, passionately.

He'd been reading the Bible each night since he'd first pulled it from that nightstand drawer. It was so different from his memory of the Bible from his youth.

He'd started at the beginning with Genesis and read through Exodus, and then his attention had been drawn to Psalms—the cries of David's heart were more real than anything he'd thought he'd ever encounter in the Bible. David had lost a son just as he had, and yet David still chose to praise God, to see God as good and sovereign.

His mind flashed back to that day in the hospital, to holding his precious, fragile child in the NICU. The mask and robe on, his hands scrubbed—the only part of his skin able to touch his son's. He'd prayed, cradling Tucker gently to his chest, prayed when the doctors had given up hope, prayed like he'd never prayed before, but God didn't answer. God took his son.

Could he ever praise God again like David had? Could he release the anger and bitterness that had been suffocating him for so long? Could he embrace his Father and breathe the fresh air of grace again? It seemed too good to be true, and yet his soul was stirring with hope.

After ten minutes of stomping through the woods, his flashlight glinted off the ground ahead, sweeping across two pairs of shoes. He lifted it and found Darcy's and Clint's startled eyes.

Darcy blinked, lifting a hand to shield the glare from her face. "Gage, is that you?"

"Of course it is." Clint sighed.

"What are you doing out here?" Darcy asked.

"Out for a stroll."

"Uh-huh," Clint said. "Sure you weren't keeping tabs on us?"

"Why would I need to keep tabs on you?"

"I have no idea. I was just showing Darcy the view from Magellan's Rock."

"You seem to have a knack for finding those types of spots."

"I like to explore the islands I visit."

"I'm sure you do." *Searching out the best places for drop-offs and pickups.*

"We were just heading back," Darcy said.

"I suppose you're about to do the same?" Clint asked.

Gage smiled. "How'd you guess?"

"Just lucky, I suppose," Clint said through gritted teeth.

"What was that all about?" Darcy asked once Clint had said good night and Gage had her to himself at the edge of camp.

"What were you thinking?"

"I didn't realize going for a walk was such a big deal. I did it our first excursion out and you didn't react like this."

"Because I didn't know then what I know now."

"Which is?"

"Women are being trafficked."

"I know. Jake told me."

When would she learn? Was she afraid of nothing? "And you still went off with our chief suspect into the woods on an unfamiliar island at night. Are you always this reckless?"

"Since when did Clint become our chief suspect? If you recall, he was with us when that boat was on the western shore earlier, so it stands to reason that he's not the one involved—Ted is."

"We can't rule anybody out. Not yet." He told her what he, Landon, and Jake had discussed while she'd been off gallivanting through the woods with Clint.

"It *was* Drake Bowen's body?" she said, clearly jarred.

"Yes." His gaze dropped to her bare hands. "Where are your gloves?"

"Drying by the fire."

"That was stupid." He pressed her hands between

his, rubbing to warm them. They were cold as ice.

"They reeked like fish."

"Oh, and frostbite is so much better."

"I kept them in my pockets most of the time."

He wasn't even going to ask where they'd been the rest of the time. The thought of Clint touching her hand, let alone holding it . . . Possessiveness mixed with genuine concern fueled him. "I want you to do something for me."

"Okay," she said slowly, clearly apprehensive.

"Promise me you won't go off with Clint or any of the *Bering*'s crew members until this is solved."

"But, I—"

"I couldn't take it if anything happened to you."

She tilted her head, her expression shifting from one of preparing to argue to I-didn't-see-that-coming. "You couldn't?"

He stepped closer, clutching her hands tighter. "No."

She shifted her stance, leaning in to him. "Because?"

He smiled. Leave it to Darcy to press. He took a deep breath. "Because insane as it is, I've somehow managed to fall quite madly in love with you."

Shock broke on her face. "You have?"

"I'm afraid so."

"Try not to sound so excited about it." Her jaw tightened.

"I didn't mean for it to come out that way. It's just . . ."

"Just?"

He'd never anticipated this happening, didn't want it to be happening, and now that it had, he had no idea how to proceed, other than to ensure Darcy's safety. Once they were off the ship and he knew she was safe, maybe then they could sort through it all. "I need you to promise me you won't go off with Clint alone again."

"What if he holds the answers I need to find Abby?"

"What if he's the one who killed Abby?"

"Don't say that." She pulled back, shoving her hands in her pockets.

He didn't want to hurt her, didn't want to be mean or blunt, but if that's what it took to make her realize the severity of the situation, if that's what it took to protect her, then so be it. She could hate him as long as she was safe.

"Abby's not dead. She can't be."

"Can't be? What do you think? That whoever dumped her overboard wasn't up to the task of killing her off after pulling her from the water?"

"No. It's not that." She turned away from him.

"Then what?"

She didn't answer.

"Darcy, these are cold-blooded killers, drug smugglers, human traffickers. These aren't nice men. They don't have consciences. If they

301

thought Abby was on to them, if they dumped her overboard to get rid of her, I highly doubt they'd hesitate to—"

"Stop. Please." She turned around, tears streaming from her eyes.

"Oh, honey." He hadn't meant to make her cry. He tugged her into his arms. "I'm sorry. I was only trying to emphasize how dangerous these men are."

"I know. It's just that she can't be dead. Not yet."

He pulled back slightly and tipped her chin up. "What do you mean not *yet?*"

Her shoulders dropped. "Abby's not saved."

"I know . . . But as bad as it looks, there still is some hope."

"No." She shook her head and sniffed. "She doesn't know Jesus. I've tried, but she never . . ."

"You're worried about Abby's salvation?"

"If she died not believing in Christ . . ." She shook her head, determination fixed on her brow. "I failed Stacey. I can't fail Abby too."

"Stacey? Who's Stacey?"

"She was my best friend when I was little. When we were seven, we got pulled into a rip current at our local beach. I was the stronger swimmer. I grabbed hold of Stacey's hand as we were dragged under, but I couldn't hold tight enough." Darcy squeezed her eyes shut. "It ripped her away. I can still see the terror in her eyes as the sea tore her from me." Tears streamed down Darcy's cheeks.

Gage clutched her close, cradling her head against his chest as her sobs broke loose.

"I was rescued, but Stacey . . ." She swallowed. "Her body was never recovered. I let go, and she died. I refuse to let go of Abby."

"Honey." He stroked her hair. "You were just a little girl. It wasn't your job to save Stacey. You did everything you could."

"I won't let go of Abby. I can't."

Gage escorted Darcy to her tent, his arm still around her.

"What's wrong?" Piper asked when she saw them approaching.

"I'd better let her explain when she's ready," Gage said.

Piper took her from his arms, and he stepped away. Though he hated leaving, hated not having her in his arms, she was safe and would be well taken care of.

36

Darcy emerged from her tent to find breakfast served, the scent of bacon hovering in the crisp morning air.

Piper smiled as she approached the coffee thermos.

"What's going on?"

"It was Gage's turn to make breakfast." Piper handed her a steaming cup of French roast.

"Ah." Gage was quite the cook. It was clear why he'd planned upon high school graduation to attend culinary school. But that was before he lost Tucker, before his girlfriend, Meredith, took off for Anchorage, abandoning him and the future they'd planned together.

"Morning," Clint said, pulling his fleece over his head. "Looks like a gorgeous day."

The sun was bright, the sky clear.

"I hear you ladies are missing out on the trip back." He popped a biscuit in his mouth and headed for the kayaks lined along the shore.

Darcy looked at Piper. "Ladies?"

"Yup. Looks like I'm riding back with you on the boat."

"Let me guess . . . Gage's doing?"

"He didn't want you alone with Ted."

Well, at least his safety precautions went across the board and didn't focus solely on Clint.

"How did you explain the change to Ted?"

"I just said I had a sore shoulder and wouldn't mind sitting this one out, and he was totally cool with it."

"Well, I'll be glad for the company." The less time she spent alone with Ted, the better.

* * *

Piper cleverly kept Ted talking the entire ride. She had such a sweet, unassuming nature that people naturally opened up to her—even muleheaded, testosterone-loaded Ted. By the time they reached the Bering, he'd provided several places to dig into his background—his family, his hometown, places he'd traveled after high school.

Landon and Gage were right—Piper had a gift.

Darcy thought she'd had a gift too—until the Sanchez case, the last case she'd worked with Abby. It had started like any other case, with rumors of corruption among the border patrol officers down along the San Diego–Tijuana border. They'd infiltrated the situation by getting waitress positions at a local border patrol hangout.

Week after week they worked to form friendships with the men they suspected of drug running and the people in their lives—girlfriends, softball buddies, colleagues. They got attached to their families, got invited to parties. One border patrol agent, Robert Sanchez, took a particularly strong liking to Darcy, and his friend Pat to Abby. Up until that case, Darcy had always been able to keep herself at arm's length, but something shifted with the Sanchez case. She and Abby were in too deep. They were living lives that weren't theirs anymore, and it came with a price.

When Darcy refused Robert's advances after months of friendship, he became suspicious. Abby said they'd come too far to walk away, that they were too close to give up. She told Darcy she didn't have to sleep with the guy, just show him some affection. But for Darcy it was a line she couldn't cross. She called her boss, Kevin, who also happened to be her boyfriend, and to her great disappointment, he told her the same.

Making up the excuse of a sick relative who needed help, Darcy left. She knew her leaving could compromise Abby's cover, but staying would have meant compromising her character.

Abby remained undercover and eventually broke the story—which reached far deeper than either of them had realized, including a corrupt DEA official as well as a state senator. It was the type of story a reporter lived to break, but in the end it fractured her friendship with Abby and ended her two-year relationship with Kevin.

The Sanchez case tainted her love of investigative reporting and prompted her to find different stories to cover. As much as she enjoyed the thrill of the hunt, it wasn't worth her soul, and that's what she had feared it would eventually come to. One little compromise led easily to another, and before she knew it, she feared she'd be willing to show affection to a source just for a piece of information. She'd had no choice but to leave.

Now that they had uncovered what they were chasing, she understood why Abby called her back. It wasn't for a story—it was about women's lives, about their dignity, about rescuing them from slavery. This was about so much more than just Abby's life. Who knew how many lives were at stake? She couldn't quit now, but how did she proceed? What was the next step? She needed to talk with whoever pulled Abby out of the water that night. If Clint wouldn't help her discover their identity, she'd have to find another way.

Father, I'm out of my league. So many lives may be at stake. Please help me to know what to do. Please guide me and protect me.

Once the supplies had been off-loaded from the transport vessel, Darcy took the few free hours she had before the rest of the excursion group returned and headed with Piper to a coffee shop in downtown Dutch Harbor.

Piper studied Darcy over the rim of her mug. "You look like you have the weight of the world on your shoulders."

Darcy pushed at the potato hash with her fork. "I feel like I do."

"You want to talk about it?"

Piper had been so kind to just let her rest last night—not pushing, simply being there for her in the silence.

Darcy considered a moment, then set her fork down and shoved her plate aside. "Have you ever been in love with someone who wasn't a believer?"

Piper smiled.

Not the reaction she'd been expecting.

"You're in love with my brother?"

Darcy nodded.

"I knew it!" Piper smothered her grin. "Sorry. That's not the point."

"It's fine."

Piper loved playing matchmaker and detective nearly as much as she loved her family.

"The answer to your question is yes," she said.

"Really?" Darcy leaned forward. "Who was he—somebody in high school?"

"My fiancé."

"Landon? I'm confused. I thought he went to your church, helped Cole with youth group. . . ."

"He did, but participating in church activities doesn't make a person a believer."

"Of course not, but . . . ?"

"Landon knew all about God, but he didn't have a relationship with Him. Not until last winter."

"Last winter?"

Piper nodded. "Everything that happened, everything we went through, God used to bring Landon into a saving relationship with Him."

"But Gage . . ."

"I believe Jesus can reach even the most broken of hearts and make them whole again, and I believe with all my heart that He'll break through to Gage. But all I can do, all you can do, is to continue to pray for him and to share Christ's love with him. Only God can convert the soul."

Darcy bit her bottom lip. "Abby's not a believer.

I've tried sharing Jesus with her over and over again, but she's never wanted to listen. What if . . . What if I'm too late?"

Piper reached her hand across the table and clasped hold of Darcy's hand. "Would you like to pray?"

Darcy nodded, too choked up to speak.

Piper closed her eyes and began, "Father, we bring Abby to you in prayer. You know where she is and what's happening to her. We pray if she is still alive that you will reveal yourself to her. As long as she's alive, it's never too late. I pray that wherever Abby is right now, she will make that genuine repentance of sins and accept of the free gift of your grace."

Piper's hand tightened on Darcy's. "And I pray that if Abby has already left this world without accepting you as her Savior, you will free Darcy from the bondage of believing it was up to her to save her friend. Amen."

Darcy opened her tear-filled eyes to find Piper's tearing up as well.

"It's your job to tell others about Jesus, about what He's done in your life and what He can do in theirs, but you can never make someone believe, no matter how strong or pure your intentions. Salvation is between that person and God," Piper said.

Piper was right, but it didn't make accepting the truth any easier.

The utter vacuum of hurt consuming Darcy from the inside out filled her as she and Piper made their way back to the *Bering*.

She caught sight of Gage helping passengers off-load their packs. The sun glistened off the flecks of blond running through his brown hair, and her heart emptied out to the Lord on behalf of the man she loved.

37

"Okay," Landon said as Gage and Darcy prepared to reboard the *Bering*. "I'll dig where I can, but it wouldn't hurt if you two could get another look at those employee files—see if there are any similarities, any connections we may have over-looked."

Darcy exhaled. "Maybe Gage has been right all along. What if we just go to Mullins? I think we have enough evidence to at least warrant further investigation by the cruise line. Maybe she'll let us look at the files."

Gage looked over at her with surprise.

"Things are far worse than I imagined," she said. "What's important is getting to the bottom of this. Maybe it's time we lay our cards on the table."

Jake rubbed the back of his neck. "I really wouldn't recommend it."

"Why not?"

"From what you've described, Mullins is a serious team player. She's looking to protect her ship and her livelihood. I don't think she'll just hand over those files."

"But surely when we explain that women are being trafficked, she'll want to get to the bottom of it—like any decent human being would."

"We can hope, but if the extent of the situation goes public, the *Bering*'s reputation—as well as that of the entire cruise line—will be damaged."

"So you think she'd be willing to overlook criminal activity to protect her company's reputation?"

"It's possible. The way I see it, you have two choices—go to Mullins and hope she'll do the decent thing, or get another look at those files yourselves."

"If I go to her and she says no . . ."

"Your cover will be blown and you'll never see those files," Jake said.

* * *

Darcy paced Gage's cabin while they waited until it was late enough to break into Mullins' office for a second, and hopefully equally successful, time. "I can't believe this is happening."

"No wonder Abby believed she needed your help."

"I can't imagine how terrified she must have been when she realized the type of trafficking she'd uncovered." Darcy sank down on the edge of the bed.

"Do you think she knew they were on to her?"

"I'm pretty sure I saw terror in her eyes the day I boarded the *Bering*. And when she insisted I wait in my cabin for her, I think she was trying to protect me until she could explain, until she could warn me of the danger."

Gage sat down on the bed beside her and wrapped his arm around her shoulders.

"She must have been so scared."

"What you said the other night about your friend Stacey, about Abby . . ."

"Yes?" She looked up at him, yearning for support.

"You did what you could to save Stacey. You were just a little girl. You didn't fail her."

"I was the stronger swimmer."

"But you were still a kid. You can't blame yourself."

She looked down. "And Abby?"

He lifted her chin with his finger, looking her straight in the eye. "You're doing everything you can to save her too."

Her jaw quivered. "And if I'm too late?"

He pulled her into his embrace. "Then you know and I know that you did all you could. Sometimes there is nothing you can do, no matter how earnestly you ache to. Not even if you're willing to give your life in place of theirs."

She sat back, wiping the tears from her eyes. Was Gage saying . . . ? Was he talking about . . . ? "Are you talking about Tucker?"

He cleared his throat and gazed across the room. "I'm just saying I know how it feels to be helpless, to want to save someone so badly you'd die to do so and it still doesn't make a difference."

She cupped his face, and to her surprise he didn't pull back. He was so beautiful—inside and out. "I can't fathom the pain of losing a child."

"I didn't lose him. God took him." The edge was back in his voice when he spoke of the Lord. "You know what I don't get?" he quickly continued. "Why did God even bother creating Tucker if it was only so he could die?"

Her heart physically ached, her chest tightening at the hurt and anguish in his soulful eyes. "God didn't create Tucker to die. He created him for eternity."

He looked at her with such longing, her breath caught. "Gage, Tucker's time on earth was short, heartbreakingly so, but his life didn't end in the NICU. He's alive for eternity."

A hint of moisture glistened in his eyes, his words coming out choked. "You really believe my boy is alive?"

"With all my being."

"How can you sound so sure, be so certain?"

"Because of God's Word. He's never reneged on a promise, so I know He'll keep His promise of eternal life for the innocent as well as those who choose to accept the redemptive death of His son. And I know your son and your family and I—all of us who love you—want to spend eternity with you."

He exhaled, his eyes moist with tears. "But after how I've treated God . . . He can't possibly . . ."

"Salvation is not earned—it's a gift, it's grace. All you have to do is accept Him as your Savior. Ask Him into your life. He's waiting. He's always been waiting."

Gage's shoulders dropped. "You make it sound so easy."

"For us it is. Christ is the one who paid the cost."

"You really believe I can see my boy again?"

"I believe you can spend eternity with him because Jesus loved you so much He died on a cross to bring you Home."

* * *

How on earth was he supposed to focus on the task at hand after that conversation?

Gage stood half numb beside Darcy as she once again picked the lock to Mullins' office.

Eternity spent with his son? Eternity, *period*. He'd read about it as a child, heard his siblings quoting and discussing Scripture after their Bible studies on the subject. One verse in particular flooded his mind.

"For God so loved the world, that he gave his

only begotten Son, that whosoever believeth in him should not perish, but have everlasting life."

"Gage, you with me?" Darcy asked from across the waiting area, with Mullins' door ajar.

"Yeah." He followed her inside, shutting the outer door and the office door behind them.

"I'll print out Abby's and Jeremy's files from the past employees database, along with George's from the new employee one. You grab Ted's and Clint's files from the cabinets and start copying."

"Roger that." He set to work as Darcy turned on Mullins' computer. It took little time to grab the files, and then he headed for the copier. "I hope it's not too loud." Like the one they had at LFA that rattled the walls every time it shot out a copy.

He flipped it on, waiting for it to boot up, and then started copying. Luckily it was a newer model that made little more than a low hum as it copied and spit out the sheets.

"Got them," Darcy said, pulling the paper from the printer tray as Gage finished and shut off the copier.

She fanned the pages out, laying the files side by side. "That's interesting. . . ."

"What's that?" He glanced over her shoulder.

"They were all sent over from the Alaskan Adventure and Travel Employment Agency."

"Really?"

"Abby's roommate said that Mullins had a remarkable way of always filling empty spots quickly."

"And Mullins said they were her usual excursion provider."

"Did they hire you?" she asked.

"No. Headquarters did."

"Me too."

"Mullins said something in the meeting to that effect—how headquarters had personally brought us in, but Alaskan Adventure, their usual excursion liaison and provider, would still be staffing and running the photo excursions, as well as supplying our auxiliary personnel."

He studied her; something was definitely changing. "What are you thinking?"

"That—"

Gage clamped a hand over her mouth, his gaze fastening on the door.

She squirmed but followed the direction of his gaze.

The distinct sound of approaching footsteps and jangling keys.

"Kill the computer while I kill the light," he whispered.

Once they finished, they dove under the desk as the office door opened.

Darcy stared up at Gage wide-eyed as the overhead light switched on.

He lifted a finger to his lips, peering under the

desk slit. *Mullins*. He'd recognize those functional shoes anywhere.

"Mullins." A man rushed in.

Is that Ted's voice?

"We've got a situation."

"What now?"

"You better come with me."

"You'd think I could have one night without a crisis to deal with, but no," she grumbled, flipping off the lights and following him out the door. "What is it this . . ."

When they no longer heard voices, Darcy exhaled. "That was close."

Gage helped her to her feet. "Too close."

"We should follow them."

"What?"

"I'd like to know what situation Ted was referring to, especially at this time of night."

It took a little searching, but they eventually located Ted, Mullins, and Clint at the ship's clinic. Apparently there had been some sort of medical emergency.

"I guess Clint wasn't busy with a massage client during this emergency," Gage said, not bothering to hide his sarcasm.

"Guess not."

"Looks like they're going to be there awhile. Do we need anything more from Mullins' office?"

"No, but . . ."

He cringed. "Why don't I like the sound of that?"

"Come on." She grabbed his hand, leading him down the corridor at a fast clip.

"Where are we going?"

"To break into Ted and Clint's cabin."

38

"This is a really bad idea," Gage said under his breath as Darcy worked the lock. Electronic key card locks were trickier to break into but not impossible. Fortunately, she'd had her fair share of experience. Under a minute and they were in.

"What are we looking for, exactly?" Gage asked, glancing about the room.

"Anything that ties Ted to Abby. If nothing else, he might have some of her things stashed here. He's probably the one Mullins asked to mail Abby's belongings from Eagle Cove. Instead, he kept them and is no doubt doling them out as favors. You search the dresser and I'll take the closet."

Ten minutes later, Darcy shut the closet door in frustration.

Gage looked up from the bottom dresser drawer. "You might want to be a tad quieter."

"Right." She bit her bottom lip. "Sorry." She stalked across the cabin. "I just can't believe we're coming up empty. I thought for sure we'd find Abby's things here."

"If Ted is involved, he'd have been smart to have dumped them. Leave no ties."

"Then why keep the necklace and give it to Celia?"

"Who knows? Maybe he thought Celia would like it and he was into her. He probably figured no one would recognize it as Abby's or trace it back to him."

Gage looked at the clock. "Let's quickly check Clint's stuff while we're here, but then we need to move."

"You take the bathroom and I'll go through the rest," Darcy said.

A few minutes later, Gage called, "Hey, Darc."

"Yeah?" She stood, hitting her head on the top bunk. She rubbed it. That'd leave a bump.

"Come take a look."

She found Gage standing on the commode, holding a black lockbox, the ceiling tile overhead shifted to the side. "How on earth did you even think to look up there?"

"I noticed a tile was askew."

"Good eye."

She set the lockbox on the lower bunk and picked the lock.

Gage paced. "We need to hurry. We're pushing our luck."

Darcy pulled out a handful of pictures—women aboard the ship, lounging around the pool.

319

"These look more like surveillance photos than consensual images."

"Any of Abby?"

She thumbed through them. "No."

He cracked the door and peered into the hall. "I've got a bad feeling we're about out of time."

"Wait." She fished out a plastic bag, and underneath she found a black leather notebook. She opened the bag. "Syringes, vials, and pills." She held the bag up to the light. "You think they used this to drug Abby?"

"Time's up." Gage stepped from the room, shutting the door behind him.

What on earth? She slipped the black notebook in her pocket and shoved the rest of the contents back in the box as the fire alarm went off.

Brilliant man.

She put the lockbox back in place, slid the tile over, and shut off the lights. Stepping into the corridor, she quickly blended in with the stream of people pouring down the hall.

A hand reached out and grabbed hers. *Gage.* When they hit an intersecting hallway, they broke off from the crowd and rushed for the opposite stairwell. Now moving with a new mass of people headed for Deck 9—the designated emergency floor—she held tight to Gage's hand, moving with him to Deck 3 and then slipping out of the stairwell behind him.

They hurried to his cabin, slid inside, and locked the door.

"You don't think they'll miss us?" she asked.

"They'll be so relieved when they figure out it was a false alarm, I highly doubt they'll notice the new excursion leader and adventure journalist missing."

"That was brilliant," she said.

"I heard Clint's voice as the elevator doors opened and knew I had to do something. Saw the red switch not five feet from their cabin door and yanked it."

"And, of course, Ted and Clint would follow protocol and report to their duty stations."

"Exactly."

"Duty stations," she said.

"What about them?"

She loved that he knew her well enough to know she was on to something simply by how she phrased a statement or question. "Even if Clint was giving a massage when Abby went overboard, once the alarm was tripped . . ."

Gage smiled. "He'd have to report to his emergency protocol station."

"So even if he wasn't part of the rescue crew, he probably had word of who went out. But he's so bent on protocol, protecting the cruise line . . . I doubt he'll spill."

"Maybe he's trying to protect a friend or roommate," Gage suggested.

"Ted? You think Clint is worried Ted's involved? The two have bunked together for years."

"Maybe there are some answers in that black book you snagged."

"How'd you know I took it?"

He gave her a sideways glance with a smile. "Because you're you."

"I'm not sure if that's a compliment or an insult."

"What do you think Ted's going to do when he realizes it's gone?"

"I'm hoping we'll have enough evidence to bust him before that happens."

He reclined into one of the chairs. "Guess we better look at that book."

Darcy sat, leaning forward, flipping through the pages. "It lists descriptions of women and notations about their cabins and various locations throughout the day."

"We need to see if we can match those descriptions to the women we know have gone missing off the *Bering*."

"Know?"

"There could be more. You heard what Jake said—the only time noise is raised is when the victim has family to advocate for them."

"So there could be more than Mrs. Bowen, Abby, and the woman that fell off the balcony?"

"That reminds me . . ." Gage stood and strode to his closet.

"Me too."

"Huh?" He retrieved his windbreaker, reached inside the pocket, and pulled out a folded-up piece of paper.

"Everyone keeps insisting that *Bering* employees leaving suddenly, like Abby did, isn't out of the norm. Maybe other crew members have vanished like Abby, only they weren't quitting . . ."

"They were being kidnapped," Gage finished her thought. "That's a really frightening possibility."

"We're going to need another look at those photos—show them to crew members, see if anyone recognizes the women as former crew members. See if we can't match their descriptions to ones in this book."

Gage unfolded the paper he'd taken from his windbreaker and handed it to her. "Did you see her in any of the pictures?"

Darcy studied the photo on the missing-person flyer. "Where'd you get this?"

"Landon gave it to me last night in his tent."

Her eyes scanned the information, freezing on the name. "Jessica Matthews?"

"Yeah." He shifted closer. "Is that name significant to you?"

She shook her head. "Well, it explains the note we found in the Gideon Bible."

"I still don't get it."

Darcy clutched the missing-person flyer. "The

head cheerleader was *Jessica* Hardy. My Bio I lab partner's name was Brad *Matthews*."

"Jessica Matthews," Gage said.

"Abby was trying to point to one of the victims she'd uncovered."

"Smart lady," Gage said.

"Great reporter." She held the flyer. "I'm pretty sure she was in one of the photos, toward the bottom of the pile."

"Are you sure?" Gage said, knowing the time pressure she'd been under when she'd found the lockbox.

"I can't be positive, but I'm pretty confident Jessica's picture was in there. I have a knack for faces."

"That could be the solid evidence we need to tie Ted to the missing women." He shifted. "What about the book? Is there a description fitting Jessica Matthews, now that we know what she looks like?"

Darcy thumbed through the entries. There were ten descriptions of women, but more than fifty location and date notations, though a vast number of the locations were duplicates. "White, fair, redhead, 100G. 5.4 Drop N57/W165."

"Jessica was white, fair, slim, and redheaded. I'd say it's a probable match."

"And the 100G?"

"The price someone was willing to pay . . . ?" The thought made her sick. "And the rest?"

"The rest have got to be coordinates."

"But it's incomplete. It's only showing degrees, not minutes or seconds."

He took the book from her, studying the notations. "Maybe they are familiar drop spots so they don't need all the coordinates, just a marker to know which one."

Darcy ran her hands through her hair, fighting the gnawing headache pulsating through her temples.

"You need to eat."

"What?"

"You need to eat something. You look like you're about to pass out."

"How can I think of food at a time like this?"

"You're no good to anyone if you're too weak to think, let alone fight."

"Fine. I'll grab something."

"I'll order room service." He stood and strode to the phone. "What sounds good?"

"Nothing."

"Then we'll go with a fail-safe option." He pressed the room-service button and ordered two cheeseburgers, medium well with the works, and two sides of fries.

"Thanks."

He smiled. "Someone's got to look out for you while you're trying to save the world."

"Save the world, huh? That's a far cry from how you typically describe my profession."

He sank in the chair beside her. "Not all reporters are the same—and you're definitely not as bad as most of the lawyers I know."

She scooted forward. "Oh?"

"I owe you an apology."

"You do?"

"Most definitely." He reached over and clasped her hand. "You're not Meredith—nothing like her—and I'm so sorry for making you out to be."

"I know what she did was—"

"It doesn't matter. She doesn't matter. Not anymore. What matters is you." He clasped her hand tighter, meeting her gaze straight on, his soulful eyes brimming with emotion. "I love you, Darcy."

"I love you too."

He smiled, lowering his warm mouth to hers.

When he pulled back, she sank into his arms. "You weren't entirely wrong, though."

He stroked her hair. "I wasn't?"

"No. I'm not cut out for being an undercover reporter."

"But Abby, the women . . ."

"Don't get me wrong. I'm going to see this through to the end. Those men have to be exposed and their crimes brought to justice, but this is absolutely my last undercover case."

He threaded his fingers through hers. "Why's that?"

"Because I know God is calling me to something different. I knew it when I first walked away, but after leaving Yancey and you, I started to doubt that. I felt restless, empty."

"And you thought returning to a case with Abby would fix that?" he asked without any trace of judgment.

"Yes, but I was wrong. It wasn't Abby and undercover reporting He was pulling me back to."

"No?"

"No."

"Then what was it?" He brushed the hair from her face, cradling her cheek in his calloused hand.

She leaned in, hovering her lips over his. "You." She couldn't explain it, but she knew in her soul that God was at work in Gage's life, that God was drawing him to a saving relationship with Him. She could practically see the Spirit quickening inside him. If she was wrong, she'd just told a man she could never be with that she loved him. But she did love him and he loved her, and she trusted the soft, still voice telling her Gage was turning to the Lord.

* * *

Room service arrived and Gage set the food before them. "So what's our next step?"

She loved the sound of *our*. "It all goes back to that first night, the night Abby went overboard. Whoever pulled her from the water has answers." She popped a fry in her mouth. "There has to be a record of the rescue crew that night."

"Of course there is."

"It wasn't in Mullins' office." She'd looked both times they'd broken in.

"That's not where they'd keep it."

"Okay then, where *would* they keep it?"

"We keep our SAR logs at the fire station. Aboard ship, the most likely spot is the medical clinic."

"Of course." Why hadn't she thought of that? "Well, there's no breaking in there tonight. Not with everyone out and about with the medical emergency and then the fire alarm."

"Maybe we don't have to break in to get a look."

"What do you mean?"

"I've got an idea." He smiled, popping a fry in his mouth—the mouth that had just been lusciously pressed to hers.

* * *

Convincing Darcy to return to her room and get some rest while there was nothing more to be done wasn't easy, but he'd finally managed to escort her back to her cabin, and now he returned to his. Silence surrounded him, but Darcy's words still churned deep in his soul.

He pulled out the Bible he'd been reading, opened to Romans, and started at the beginning, working his way through and pausing on verse nine of chapter ten. *"If you declare with your mouth, 'Jesus is Lord,' and believe in your heart that God raised him from the dead, you will be saved."*

This is insane. So long he'd walked away. So long he'd raised his fists in anger.

How is it possible I can feel you reaching out to me after all these years of turning away from you? I know what Darcy said, and I've read it in your Word, but is it true, Lord? Will you forgive me?

"I have loved you with an everlasting love. . . ."

The air left Gage's lungs in a whoosh as God spoke to his heart. He dropped to his knees, a mixture of awe and revelation spiriting through him. *I'm so sorry, God. Please forgive me for my anger. For turning away. For refusing to believe what I knew was true. I want to spend eternity with you, with Tucker. Please come into my life and be my Savior.*

* * *

Gage picked Darcy up at her cabin sharply at eight the next morning, as he'd promised. He was eager to share his news but decided to wait for the right time.

"So what's this grand plan of yours?"

"You'll see."

He led her to the ship's clinic, tugging her to a halt just outside. "Wait for my signal, okay?"

"What?" She glanced in at the nurse, then back at Gage. "What's your plan, to flirt her into giving you access?"

"No, but I like that you acknowledge I possess that magnitude of charm."

"Please." She blew the bangs fringing her eyes.

"I'll distract her, get her into the exam room, and you do your thing at the front desk. I can buy you ten minutes max, so focus."

Her eyes narrowed. "What exactly are you doing to do?"

He winked. "Watch and learn."

Stepping into the clinic, he greeted the nurse. She was young, midtwenties, with long amber hair.

"Morning," she said without looking up. She was busy typing some notes into the computer.

"Is the doc in?"

"Not until nine." A smile curled on her lips as she glanced up and made eye contact. "Is there something I can help you with?"

"Well, I sure hope so." He leaned on the corner of her desk with a wide smile. "I'm Gage, the new excursion leader."

"Roxanne."

"Like the Police song?"

She laughed. "Yeah, but you can call me Roxi. So"—she leaned forward—"what can I do for you?"

"My throat." He cleared it.

"It hurts?" She pouted.

"Something like that. Do you think you could take a look?"

"I'd be happy to check you out." She stood and moved around the desk. "Follow me."

Before following the nurse, he signaled Darcy to enter behind him. She gave him a disgusted "I can't believe you stooped to that cheesy level of flirting" look, but it had worked. They'd get the information they needed.

"Take a seat on the exam table," Roxi said.

He hopped up, positioning himself so he could keep an eye on the front room and Darcy, effectively putting Roxi's back to the door.

"Are you hot?" she asked.

He grinned. "I like to think so."

She shook her head as she slipped a sleeve on the digital thermometer. "I meant, do you feel like you have a fever?"

"No."

"Let's check just to be safe."

Gage opened his mouth and she slipped the thermometer in. She grabbed a tongue depressor while the numbers rose.

Gage glanced at Darcy, clicking away at the computer station. She didn't look happy.

The thermometer chirped, and Roxi checked it. "Ninety-eight point four. Practically perfect."

He smiled. "Yeah, I get that a lot."

"You're really something." She chuckled.

"You have no idea." He winked.

She held up the tongue depressor. "Open wide." She glanced down his throat. "Say *ah*."

"Ahhh."

She tossed the depressor in the trash. "Looks

331

fine. You're probably just adjusting to the sea air."

He'd grown up surrounded by sea air, but no sense bringing that up. He caught sight of movement out of the corner of his eye. Had the doctor arrived early? Had he caught Darcy on the computer?

Voices carried into the exam room.

"Take a seat and I'll be with you shortly," Roxi called without glancing over to the waiting area. "Looks like it's going to be a busy one."

"Do you get a lot of patients?"

"You'd be surprised."

"That many people get sick?"

"It's not all sickness."

"What else? People falling overboard?" He laughed as if making a joke.

"Actually, that happens more often than you'd expect."

"You're kidding."

"Afraid not." She relayed the story of Jessica Matthews that they already knew.

"That's terrible."

"I know, right? Glad my cabin doesn't have a balcony. If you know what I'm saying."

"Now that you mention it, I heard something about a crew member going overboard the night before I boarded in Yancey."

"Yeah. Such a shame. Rumor was she drank too much and got too close to the rail."

"I heard she was rescued."

"Yeah. She was lucky someone saw her go over."

"Did you treat her when they brought her back on board?"

"Nah. We were close to land, so she was taken to the nearest hospital."

"Who took her?"

"I don't know. Whoever fished her out of the water, I suppose."

"Excuse me, nurse."

Gage turned to find an older gentleman in the doorway.

"My wife's got a terrible migraine. The longer we delay treatment, the worse it will get."

Roxi nodded. "We're just about finished here, and she'll be next."

With a squint of frustration and a grumble about a poorly run office, he stepped back into the minuscule waiting area.

"Richies always expect you to drop everything where they're concerned."

"I'll let you take care of them." Gage hopped off the table, eager to see what had become of Darcy. "Thanks, Roxi."

"You can thank me over a drink sometime."

He waved as he exited the room and glanced up and down the corridor. He spotted Darcy at the south end of the hall.

She gestured for him, and he quickly strode to

her side, anxious to know what she'd found. "What happened?"

"I moved toward the door as soon as I heard someone coming and just left as they entered."

"What if the man says something to Roxi about you being there?"

"So what if he does? For all they know, I was looking for the doc, saw he wasn't in, and decided to come back later."

"True."

"Nice flirting back there," she said with sarcasm that rivaled Kayden's.

"It worked, didn't it?"

"Sadly, yes." She smirked.

He grinned. "Did you find anything?"

"I discovered there were two rescue crews launched that night."

"Two?"

"The report says the second crew, which included Ted, launched but that the first rescue crew had already pulled the woman from the water and was in the process of transporting her to Kodiak Hospital, so they turned back."

"Okay, so if Ted wasn't part of the crew that pulled Abby from the water, who was?"

"The first rescue crew consisted of Jeremy Harnett—"

"The guy who left the *Bering* the day after Abby went overboard?"

She nodded. "And Clint."

39

"Whoa. Hold up. Did you just say Clint was part of the rescue crew?"

She nodded. "He lied to me."

"So he and Jeremy are the ones involved?"

"And probably George, now that Jeremy's gone."

"What about Ted?"

"He still might have a role in it, or at the very least, he's turning a blind eye."

"So what's our next step?"

Darcy looked at her watch. "We're supposed to head out for excursion in an hour. Can we get in touch with local police and have Clint and George arrested when they step off the ship?"

"These are the Pribilof Islands. There is no police force. We're talking a population well under one thousand for all four islands—only two of which are inhabited."

"But from here it is right on to Petropavlovsk, Russia. There's no way we can have them arrested on foreign soil." Darcy shook her head. "We have to go to Mullins and explain what is going on. Surely, as a woman, she'll empathize. We can have Clint and George detained until the FBI arrives."

"Why don't we just head to ship security?"

"Because Mullins is the one that can pull the files we need, their employee files . . ."

"We have copies of those."

"You really want to waltz into Security with copies of files that we got by breaking into Mullins' office?"

"Good point."

"Besides, Mullins has all the excursion files. All of our reports go directly to her."

Gage exhaled. "Mullins it is."

* * *

Mullins sat back. "Are you certain?"

"Positive."

Darcy went back through all the facts, leaving out only the little tidbit of having broken into her office.

"I can hardly believe that any of my employees would be involved in something so heinous as sex trafficking."

"A member of our excursion team is law enforcement," Darcy said.

Mullins arched a brow.

"He's about to be my brother-in-law," Gage explained. "He came along to be with my sister."

"When the gangplank lowers, we thought we could bring him on to assist your security team until the FBI arrives."

Mullins looked at the clock. "We've got less than an hour—they are supposed to head off on your excursion. Let me pull the necessary records, and I'll go to Security. In the meantime, I'll need you two to go on the excursion as planned."

"What? No," Darcy said. "We need to stay here. To question Clint. He's the only one who knows what happened to Abby."

"Abby? They took her to Kodiak Hospital. How would anyone on this ship know what happened to her after that?"

"That's just what he told you so no one would go looking for her."

"What do you think he did with her?"

Darcy bit her bottom lip. "I don't know. That's why I have to talk to Clint." She needed to get the truth out of him.

"Ms. St. James." Mullins frowned. "I have a dozen of the *Bering*'s elite passengers expecting one last excursion before we dock in Russia the day after tomorrow, and they are going to get it as planned or *your* company"—she pinned her gaze on Gage—"will be in breach of contract. I will have Clint and George detained and pull one of our auxiliary activities engineers and another medic to escort you, but this excursion will go on as planned."

* * *

Gage headed down the gangplank knowing he had little time to brief his family and get Landon on board before the excursion set off. Darcy had remained in Mullins' office, anxiously awaiting the woman's return with word that Clint and George had been detained. Getting her to stay put had been a fierce battle, but she'd promised him she wouldn't leave Mullins' office until Clint and George were secure. The thought of Clint or George intercepting her before Security reached them . . . Gage cringed at the thought.

His family waited at the edge of the pier. His heart raced as he approached them, and his protective nature kicked in full force. The thought of someone enslaving his sisters was horrifying. They needed to get the men running the entire organization—not just a few of the players. Otherwise, all they'd managed to do was interrupt one of the tentacles of the operation.

Landon had said nearly a dozen women had been taken from Alaska over the last year alone— a dozen women subjected to sexual slavery, but sadly that number wasn't even a blip on the screen of women enslaved in the sex trade worldwide. His and Darcy's Internet search had indicated estimates as high as two million worldwide— mostly poor women and children from Asia and Latin America, promised a new life and decent jobs in America or other countries, only to be forced into the sex-slave trade and drugged to be kept in line. It had to be a hellish existence— the mere thought of it made him ill.

"What's changed?" Jake asked the minute he spotted Gage's face.

Darcy paced Mullins' office. How long would it take? Surely Mullins had reached Security and they were detaining Clint and George by now.

Mullins had promised to return the moment they were detained. Darcy had to speak with Clint. She couldn't wait until the FBI arrived. She needed answers, and she needed them now.

The door opened and Mullins stepped through.

Darcy brightened, but then her heart seized as Clint and George followed, rolling in a large cooler. "What's going on?"

She looked past them for a security guard.

"You're going to have to move quickly," Mullins said, shutting the door behind them.

Clint stalked toward Darcy, a syringe in hand.

"What's going on?"

He grabbed her neck, and she opened her mouth to scream, but George's hand clamped down over it as he held her in a viselike grip.

"Now," George said.

Clint stabbed her in the neck with the needle. Fire burned through her veins, her vision rapidly deteriorating.

George slackened his hold, and she fell into him as everything went black.

* * *

"We went to Mullins," Gage said.

"Why Mullins?" Jake asked.

"Because she has access, *legal* access to the

files we need to prove Clint and Jeremy Harnett, the man George replaced, were the rescue crew that supposedly took Abby to Kodiak Hospital that night."

"Clint?" Piper blinked. "But I thought Ted . . . ?"

"He might still be involved, but we know he wasn't part of the rescue crew that pulled Abby from the water," Gage said.

"So what's happening?" Jake asked, concern marring his brow.

"Mullins is pulling the necessary paperwork to prove Clint, Jeremy, and Ted worked the excursion where Mrs. Bowen went missing, and that Clint and Jeremy were the rescue crew that pulled Abby from the water."

"And George?" Kayden asked.

"I feel confident whoever is in charge of this trafficking ring replaced Jeremy with George when things went south with Abby," Gage said.

"You don't think Clint's in charge?" Kayden asked.

Jake shook his head before Gage could answer. They were on the same page—whoever was in charge, the network reached far wider than a single ship.

"That's the next step. Right now Mullins is taking the information we asked her to pull to ship security and the captain, requesting they search Clint and Ted's cabin—where we hinted they might find something of worth hidden amongst the ceiling tiles."

Jake and Landon arched their brows and Gage explained.

"You left the lockbox there?" Jake said, not bothering to hide his shock.

"Darcy made a quick decision. Clint and Ted were returning to the room. I triggered the fire alarm—"

"Where is Darcy?" Piper asked, anxiously surveying the passengers off-loading from the ship.

"Secure in Mullins' office, but as you can see"—he gestured to the excursion passengers grouping up at the designated spot—"we've got a situation. Mullins insists we continue with the excursion."

"Is she crazy?" Piper said.

"She's thinking of the *Bering* and the group of elite passengers expecting an excursion."

"The last thing she's going to want to do," Jake cut in, "is highlight the criminal situation taking place."

"Right." While he understood Mullins was committed to protecting her ship, who was protecting the poor women being trafficked? He wanted everything halted until they could be found and the trafficking ring busted up, but sadly he knew it wouldn't work that way. Business would go on as usual, though he doubted Destiny

Cruise Line would be able to salvage its reputation after the news broke.

"What's going to happen next?" Kayden asked.

"Mullins said she'd have *Bering*'s security call in the authorities."

"Who knows how long it'll take them to arrive?" Piper said, gazing about their secluded setting. "How are we supposed to just head off on an excursion in the meantime? This is huge. We can't pretend like nothing's happening."

Gage rubbed the back of his neck. "I don't know. Mullins said we'd be in breach of contract if we refused to continue on as planned, but maybe this is one of those times when it's better to face a breach of contract in order to do what we know is right."

"The rest of us can go," Kayden offered. "You and Darcy can stay here."

"Mullins insists I go, but she's agreed to let Landon come on board."

"Really?" Landon asked, not bothering to hide his surprise.

"Mullins agreed we could bring you on to confer with ship security until the FBI arrives."

"That's going to take some time," Landon said, "as far out in the Aleutians as we are. I know Abby's folks called them after we spoke, but they are focusing their investigation in Kodiak, since that's the last place Abby was seen. I'll give them a call and update them regarding the situation, if ship security hasn't already."

"At least the *Bering* will be docked overnight," Jake said. "That may give them time to arrive if they're on Kodiak."

"True, but they are going to have to move fast, because once the *Bering* leaves here, they're headed straight for Russia, which makes this entire situation very precarious." Gage clamped a hand on Landon's shoulder. "At least knowing you're on board will make me feel better about Darcy staying."

"All right." Landon nodded. "Let's get on board and see what the status is."

Gage approached the check-in point and handed his card to the guard. "This is Deputy Landon Grainger. Mullins has requested his assistance with a situation."

"I'm afraid I can't allow him on without Mullins' or the head of security's specific order."

"Mullins said she would call it in when I left her office"—Gage glanced at his watch—"nearly a half hour ago."

"I'm sorry, but I've received no such orders."

"Then you need to check with your superior. Obviously the order wasn't properly relayed."

The man looked over at his fellow guard, gesturing for him to take over while he checked into Gage's claims. He stepped off to the side and conferred with someone over his radio.

Minutes later, another man—no doubt his superior—arrived. "I just spoke with Mullins, and she gave the go-ahead. You can let them through," he instructed the check-in guard.

"Thank you," Gage said as they stepped through.

"Mullins said to tell you she's waiting in her office."

Gage entered Mullins' office expecting to find Darcy waiting and Security most likely present, but he found only Mullins.

She sat behind her desk, glancing over a file in hand.

"Where's Darcy?" Had she already gone to Security to speak with the detained men?

"I have no idea. I returned to my office and she was gone."

Gage tried to ignore the horrible sinking feeling in his gut. "But the men have been detained."

"I'm afraid not."

"Why not?" Landon asked before Gage could.

Mullins arched a brow. "The deputy sheriff, I'm assuming?"

Landon stepped forward, his hand extended. "Deputy Landon Grainger."

She didn't bother standing. "Thank you for coming."

Gage raked a shaky hand through his hair, trying to ward off the fear nipping at him. "I don't understand. When I left, you said you were going to Security, Darcy said she'd wait here, and—"

"I cannot vouch for Ms. St. James' actions, but I pulled the employment files you asked me to and took them to Security."

Gage swallowed. "Did you have them search Clint and Ted's cabin?"

"Yes, and they found nothing."

"They checked the ceiling tiles?"

"Yes, and there was no lockbox."

"Where are Ted, Clint, and George now?"

"I have no idea. They weren't in their cabin. We paged them, but none of them showed up to Security as requested."

"You announced over the loudspeaker they were to report to Security?" Gage asked, incredulous.

She'd given them warning to jump ship, whether she'd intended to or not.

"But you have their employment files?" Landon asked.

Mullins lifted the stack of files in her hands. "Right here, but I see nothing of concern in them."

"Other than the fact Clint, Ted, and Jeremy Harnett all worked the Bowen excursion," Gage said.

"How are you aware of Jeremy? He left before you joined the *Bering*."

"We've been talking to people. And what about the clinic records relating to the rescue crew that was deployed for Abby Walsh?"

"There are no records of that rescue."

"What? How can that be?"

"Looks like they've been erased."

"Erased?"

Mullins typed on her screen, linking into the clinic's records, and showed the record empty for the date in question.

"Do any of them have authority to access that report?" Landon asked.

Mullins sighed. "I'll ask IT to take a look, see if they can figure out if the records have been tampered with."

"They were tampered with," Gage insisted, his concern mounting. If the men hadn't been located and Darcy was missing . . . He turned to Landon. "We need to find Darcy. Now!"

* * *

"Something's wrong," Piper said, pacing the pier, the sun rising in the sky.

Jake studied the restless excursion passengers huddled up at the meet-up spot. "It shouldn't be taking this long. I agree with Piper—something's not right."

Heath stepped from the group and moved toward them. "What's the deal? We were supposed to have left by now, and we're all getting sick and tired of waiting around."

Piper addressed him. "Sorry for the holdup. We need to wait for Gage before we head out."

"Why?"

"Because he's the leader."

"Well, the supply crew obviously didn't feel like they had to wait on Gage, so I don't see why we do."

Jake stepped to him, his stomach sinking. "What?"

"Clint and George left with the supply ship while you were all jabbering over there with Gage."

"Are you certain?"

"Positive. I chatted with them as they loaded the last cooler on. They took off from the south side of the ship."

Piper's eyes widened. "We need to let Gage and Landon know."

"Now," Jake said, rushing for the gangplank.

40

Darcy came to and tried to move, but she was confined. It was dark except for a small shaft of light sneaking through a crack above her. Where was she? And worse yet, what had gone wrong?

Mullins was involved—that's what had gone wrong. How could she have missed that? *Easily.* Mullins was a woman, and the thought of a woman selling another woman into sexual slavery was abominable. *How could she?*

They'd handed her everything. Everything except the black book she'd stashed in her pocket, though her pocket was feeling disappointingly empty. She squeezed her eyes shut on an exhale.

They'd trusted the wrong person. She only prayed Gage figured it out before it was too late.

* * *

"Let's go to Security," Landon said as they rushed from Mullins' office. "We need more hands to search for Darcy and the men."

"You head there while I check Darcy's cabin." Though he knew she wouldn't be there.

Lance Wilkinson, head of *Bering*'s security, was conversing with someone at the end of the hall. *Perfect.*

He looked up as they approached. "Seems you have more people trying to come aboard."

"What?"

"Raul just radioed. He's got another man claiming to be a friend of yours trying to board. Says he has urgent information for you."

Gage looked at Landon. "Jake."

They rushed down to the check-in point with Lance fast on their heels. Jake was frantically pacing at the other end of the metal detector.

"They're gone," he said when he caught sight of them.

"What?" Gage's mouth went dry.

"Heath saw Clint and George loading a large cooler into the supply ship and taking off while you were still out on the pier with us."

Gage swallowed. "A large cooler?"

"Heath presumed it was supplies for the excursion. Please tell me Darcy is with you."

Gage shook his head as his world threatened to crumble.

* * *

They crowded into Security's video booth as Lance Wilkinson ordered the footage of the crew checkpoints to be played, starting from the *Bering*'s anchoring in Pribilof.

"There," Landon said, pointing to the black-and-white footage.

Clint and George wheeling a large white cooler out through the supply checkpoint.

"Where's Ted?" Gage asked. "He's not in the footage."

"Heath never mentioned Ted," Jake said.

After personally confirming Landon's credentials and realizing the severity of the situation, Lance introduced them to the captain—who was more than eager to get to the bottom of the matter.

Considering the remote location, and the unknown extent of the danger, the captain officially suspended all further excursions until the cruise ended in Russia—which wouldn't be until the day after tomorrow.

The *Bering* was secured with all guests inside for the duration of their anchoring time in Pribilof, but it did little to ease the fear coursing through Gage. There was no trace of Darcy. . . .

Clint and George had her. He had no doubt.

They must have intercepted her in Mullins' office before Mullins returned.

"Looks like Ted was left behind," Lance said, reentering the room after taking a radio call.

They all followed Lance to the clinic, where they found Ted, half alert on the examination table.

Gage lunged for his throat. "Where is she?"

Jake and Landon wrestled to pull him off.

"Where is she?"

"Where is wh-wh-who?" Ted said between choking breaths.

Gage slackened his hold at Ted's genuine confusion. "Darcy."

"Why would I know?"

"Because you're part of it."

"Part of what?"

"The trafficking network."

"Whoa! No. I had no part in that."

Landon rested a hand on the edge of the table. "No part in *what?*"

Ted swallowed.

41

The lid lifted off the container Darcy was crammed into. Bright daylight assaulted her eyes. She tried to lift a hand to shield them, but found her hands bound.

Clint bent, gazing down at her.

"You creep." She kicked, her foot colliding with his jaw.

His head swung back with the impact, and he swore.

George chuckled from somewhere nearby. She could hear his voice, just couldn't see his face. "I told you she was trouble."

Clint wiped the blood dripping from his mouth. "Well, she's not our problem any longer. Help me get her out."

Darcy readied to kick again but stilled at the sight of George's gun aiming down at her.

"Why don't we just finish her off now?" he asked.

"Because"—Clint reached in a bit more apprehensively, wrapped his arms around her, and lifted her out—"we have a quota to meet."

George leaned against a wooden post, the sort you'd hitch a horse to, the gun still aimed at her. "We would have already met our quota if she hadn't messed it up. The boss is pretty upset that we've delayed the shipment for so long."

What were they talking about?

"No matter." Clint set her on the ground at the base of the post and adjusted her bonds, securing her to it. "One blond-haired, blue-eyed American completes the list, so they can sail tomorrow. Doesn't matter if her name is Whitney or Darcy."

George chuckled, kneeling to look her in the

eye. "Yeah, where you're going, no one cares about names, sweetheart."

She fought the urge to kick again. If they were taking her where Abby was being held, there was still a chance she could find her friend.

George stepped into the boat and started the motor. "Let's go. We can call the boss about picking her up once we're on our way."

"Sorry it had to go down this way," Clint said. "I really liked you. You should have minded your business like I said, and then all of this unpleasantness could have been avoided."

"Unpleasantness? You're selling human beings into slavery."

"I'm not. The boss is. All I do is make the drops."

"And that keeps your conscience clear?" Was he insane?

"That, and the money helps." He laughed and joined George in the boat. They pulled away, leaving her stranded.

* * *

"So, you're seriously claiming you had nothing to do with smuggling women or drugs between America and Russia?" Gage pressed.

"No, man, I swear." Ted held up his hands. "If I did, do you think they'd leave me here?"

"Someone slammed you over the head with a metal pole. I don't think they were trying to leave you behind; I think they were trying to kill you," Gage said.

Ted looked down.

"You know more about what's happening than you're letting on." Landon leaned on Ted. "We *are* going to get to the bottom of this. So the way I see it, you have two choices. You tell us what you know and aid in the rescue of a kidnapped woman, or you hold out and we tell the Feds when they arrive that you were uncooperative."

"I don't know how it works. Seriously. I just know Clint and Jeremy"— he shook his head as if trying to clear it—"Clint and George now, work the ring."

"Ring?" Jake asked from the doorway.

"That's just what I call it. Look, I know what they're into is no good, but I've made it my business to not make it my business. I do my job and—"

"And ignore the fact they are kidnapping women and selling them into the sex-slave trade," Gage said. *Real nice guy.*

"I didn't know anything about that. I thought they were just dealing drugs."

"Oh, come on," Gage roared. "You can't be that dumb."

Ted's jaw tightened and he shifted uncomfortably. "Until that chef lady came around asking questions about missing women, I thought it was just drugs."

"And then?"

"And then she went overboard."

"So now . . . ?"

"I still don't know."

Gage slammed his hand on the table beside him. "That's not helpful, Ted. They've got Darcy out there somewhere. Where? Where would they have taken her? There were a bunch of coordinates in the black book we found in your room. Where do they lead to?"

"Black book?"

"Yes. It had descriptions of women, location points, and other numbers we hadn't figured out."

"I've never seen any black book."

Gage inhaled, fighting the fear threatening to overtake him. They were losing precious time. "Did Clint or Jeremy ever leave the excursion islands at this port stop to your knowledge?"

"Yeah. A time or two."

"Any idea where they went?"

"I figured to one of the outer islands."

"Outer islands?"

"There's a whole series scattered around here, heading up toward the Bering Sea."

"These trips. How long would they be gone?"

Ted pressed the heel of his hand to his forehead. "An hour, maybe."

Gage looked at Jake. "That gives us a place to start."

* * *

He stepped into the courtyard to take the call. Clint better be calling to say they were set to

354

go with the blond woman's drop tonight. "Yes?"

"Change of plans," Clint said.

"Excuse me?"

"The reporter went to Mullins."

"And?"

"Mullins played the good soldier. She called us in and helped us get rid of the evidence. We took the reporter to the drop spot."

"She's there now?"

"Yes."

"Good. You and George wait for me there."

"I don't think so. We're blown. We're taking the backup plan and heading out."

"That contingency exists when I say it exists."

"Seeing as how you're not the one *Bering*'s security and the reporter's cop friend are after, it's no longer your call. We kept you out of it. Now we're leaving."

His jaw tightened. Who did the vermin think he was? "And Ted?"

"We took care of him before we left the ship."

"You're certain?"

"Yeah, George took care of it. Besides, it's not like he actually knows anything."

"He's seen me. And you said he's figured out quite a bit about our operation over the years. That's enough to bust us all."

"He's too stupid to even go there, and besides, it's a moot point. The guy is dead. George whacked him good."

The line went dead.

He gripped the phone so tightly, the plastic casing cracked. He called his men to him. "You." He lifted his chin at Jason. "George and Clint think they're flying the coop. Meet them at the locker." They'd no doubt go there for the new IDs and cash he'd promised would be stashed there if anything went wrong. "Take them out."

The man nodded.

"And you . . ." He pointed to his brother, Steve. "Go get the girl."

42

Gage and Jake jumped into the first of the *Bering*'s auxiliary boats. They'd contacted the Coast Guard, alerting them to the search grid they'd created based on the information Ted had supplied and the map work Jake had done. Their best bet was a small island ten miles from the day's excursion destination. It would provide a perfect drop location—isolated, uninhabited, and close enough for Clint or Jeremy to run a victim over, or even for someone on the other end to head over for a pickup.

The rest of the McKennas and what security personnel the *Bering* was willing to lend fanned out in the rest of the boats, each taking a different island on Jake's grid.

"We're going to find her," Jake said as they headed out into open water.

Gage gripped the wheel. "I pray you are right."

* * *

Darcy squinted at the boat in the distance. Was it the man Clint had called to pick her up? She wrestled against her bonds, her hands tied to the post, the rope burning her skin each time she tried to wriggle free. The boat grew closer, and panic set in. She squeezed her eyes shut.

Please, Lord.

"Darcy," Gage screamed.

She opened her eyes, relief crashing over her as Gage jumped from the boat, sloshing through the remaining ten feet to shore.

He raced to her side and, kneeling beside her, kissed her fiercely. "I thought I'd lost you."

"We need to hurry." Her breath came in shallow pants. "Someone's coming."

"What?"

"George said they would call for someone to pick me up. I think . . ." Bile rose in her throat.

Gage pulled the utility knife from his pocket. "We need to get out of here."

"No. Wait."

"What?"

"Leave me here."

His eyes widened. "Are you crazy?"

* * *

Gage knelt beside Jake in the bushes. They'd agreed to Darcy's cockamamie plan against his

357

better judgment and hidden their boat in a nearby cove.

"This better work," he murmured to Jake as a boat came in from the east.

"I won't let anything happen to her," Jake promised.

The boat drove right up to the beach. A man jumped out, pulling the small craft up on the sand, and then strode to Darcy.

"Now," Jake said, pulling his Sig .375.

Gage followed.

Jake paused just shy of the man bending to cut Darcy loose. He cocked the gun, and the man stilled. "Turn around."

The man turned slowly, his hands lifting. "You're making a big mistake."

"Funny," Jake said. "I don't see it that way."

* * *

The man refused to talk, but it didn't matter. The GPS in the boat held the coordinates they needed.

"You really think Abby's still being held there?" Gage asked as they climbed in.

"I pray she is," Darcy said. "Regardless, some women are, and we need to rescue them."

Jake lowered the radio he'd been using. "Coast Guard is on its way, as are the rest of the searchers. I told them we were leaving our friend here." He gestured to the man tied to the same post that moments ago Darcy had been secured to. "I let them know he's been subdued."

"That was a pretty good knock you gave him with that oar," Gage said, squeezing her shoulder.

"It was my pleasure." Darcy smiled. They couldn't risk his getting away or warning whoever was in charge they were coming.

Darcy rubbed her arms as the boat sped toward the island fixed in the GPS's coordinates. "What if we can't find them? What if . . . ?"

Gage clasped her hand. "We should pray."

She looked up in shock. "*What* did you just say?"

"We should pray."

"I thought . . ."

"So did I, but God had different plans."

Her eyes narrowed. "Are you saying . . . ?" Had she been right? Had God been at work in Gage's heart?

"I spent our last night aboard the *Bering* on my knees, begging God to forgive my bitterness and anger toward Him for all these years."

"And?" Hope sprang in her eyes.

He swallowed. "I've asked Him to be my Savior."

Tears welled in her eyes, and she hugged him, clinging to him without saying a word.

"You okay?" He rubbed her back.

She burrowed into his hold. "I'm so grateful."

"Are you crying?"

She sniffed. "Don't worry. They are tears of praise. I've been praying—"

"Ever since we met," he said, kissing the top of her head. "I know, and I'm not sure what I did to deserve your prayers, especially considering how I treated you when we first met or even over the past week, but I am so glad you offered them."

She gazed up at him, so overwhelmed with love. "So am I, but I can't take any credit. I may have offered the prayers, but it was God who answered them."

He clutched her hand tightly against his chest. "Let's pray He answers our prayers now."

They poured out their prayers for a miracle to occur. For Abby to be rescued, for enough evidence to mount to bust up the trafficking ring and convict the men behind it.

43

The low-lying island was dotted with hills—a combination of brown tufa and cinder cones—several nearly a hundred feet tall. From their vantage point in the boat bobbing along the rocky coastline, Gage could see the hills provided ample coverage for a house or compound to be nestled behind, out of sight from any passersby. Though, in this region of the Bering Sea, only fishing vessels trawled.

Gage confirmed the coordinates to the rest of

the McKennas, the Coast Guard, and the FBI agents en route. Hopefully, they'd arrive soon.

"We have no idea how many men are on this island," Jake said.

"Or how armed they are," Gage added. "Should we wait for backup?"

"We can't," Darcy said. "They're expecting that man we left on the island to return with me. The longer I'm delayed, the more suspicious they'll become. If Abby or any other women are being held on the island, we need to move now."

Jake nodded. "I agree. And if they hear the boat approach, they'll assume it is their man arriving with Darcy."

Trying to find a place to pull ashore proved tricky—the majority of the coastline was rugged and interspersed with sheer cliff headlands swathed with nesting seabirds. Gage finally spotted a small cove sheltered from the breakers, but they still had to wade through several feet of rock-strewn water to reach the shore.

Having not been greeted by gunfire, they hoped the island's remote location had lulled any guards into complacency and they would be able to approach without confrontation.

"I'll climb that hill." Jake pointed to the nearest mound. "It should give me a good view of the island. If there's a structure here, we'll be able to assess what we're facing."

"All right, let's go," Gage said.

"You two should wait here, in case someone spots me."

Gage wavered.

"Trust me," Jake said.

Gage nodded, watching Jake hike up the hill littered with lichen-covered rocks as Darcy paced beside him. "We're taking too long."

"We need to know what we're walking into."

She balled her hands into fists, her skin paling to an ivory blue.

Gage clasped hold of her. "Give me your hands."

She held them out, and he pressed them between his, trying to warm her. It couldn't be much above freezing. The Bering Sea climate was Arctic Maritime, and with the constant lashing southern wind, it felt it.

Within ten minutes, Jake was back. "Okay, we've got a building about fifty yards northeast. I spotted one man outside. I didn't see any windows, so I couldn't get eyes inside. I think the best course of action is for you to lead Darcy in just as they're expecting her."

"They aren't expecting *me*."

"Keep her in front of you and your head down. Even though they probably know there was trouble on the ship, they have no reason to expect anything out of the norm out here. I'll flank around and overtake the man when his attention is directed on you two."

"And then?" Gage couldn't allow anything to

happen to Darcy. Couldn't even think about . . .

"We use him to figure out what's next."

Gage led Darcy through the knee-high grasses swaying in the breeze.

The man ahead was tall but scrawny; his attention was fixed on a magazine, his gun in its holster at his side. "About time," he said, not bothering to glance up at the sound of Gage's approach. "Don't tell me she gave you a hassle." He flipped to the end of his magazine and turned to Darcy, a smile curling on his bearded face. "The boss will be pleased. She's perfect."

Gage kept his head low.

"Steve?" The man cocked his head, trying to see around Darcy.

Jake took the opportunity to sneak up behind the man and relieve him of his weapon, handing it over to Gage.

"How many men in the house?" Jake asked.

The man raised two fingers.

"How many doors?"

The man raised one finger.

"Thanks." Jake knocked him over the head, and they moved for the house. "I'll go in first," he said, hovering outside the entrance. "Darcy, wait out here until we signal it's okay."

To Gage's amazement, she agreed.

Jake went in first and Gage followed.

A large man sat at the table, dealing out cards in a game of solitaire, his broad back to them.

Jake approached, the man shifted, and Jake leveled his gun at his head.

Noise stirred from the rear, and Gage headed toward it, gun in hand.

The hall was dim, a series of doors lining each side of the narrow passage. He peered into the first room. It took a moment for his eyes to adjust. A woman lay on a mattress on the floor, a tattered blanket covering her. Her hair was dark, her face covered. She shifted with a moan.

Something cracked, then splintered in the room at the end of the hall. Gage rushed to it and jiggled the handle. *Locked.*

A crash sounded and light burst forth beneath the door. "I think we've got a runner," he hollered, kicking in the door.

The room was dank and cold, and he saw another woman lying on a mattress. Her bare arm was littered with puncture marks.

Jake rushed in and glanced at the opening. "A hidden door." The boards blocking it had been kicked to the ground. "I'll go. You stay and check on the women."

"The man in the front room?"

"Secure, as is the rest of the house. We have a total count of three women, including her." He gestured to the woman balled up on the mattress.

"Abby?"

"I didn't look that close. I was just making sure the rooms were secure."

"I'll get Darcy."

Jake nodded and headed outside, while Gage moved to the front, signaling Darcy it was safe to enter.

"Where's Jake?" she asked, hesitating at the sight of the large man bound and gagged in the room off the entry.

"We had a runner. He's tracking him now."

"And Abby?"

"There are three women. From your description, I don't think the two I saw are her."

"And the third?" Darcy asked, heading for the back hall.

"Second door on your right."

She ran into the room and Gage followed. He entered as Darcy's breath hitched.

Abby lay on the makeshift bed, needle marks in her left arm, her eyes dilated, her head swaying.

"Abby." Darcy rushed forward, enveloping her friend in her arms.

Abby looked so frail, so weak, so cold. When she spoke her voice cracked. "I . . . I . . . kn-knew you . . . not . . . give up . . . on me-e-e-e." Her head drooped to the side.

"Never," Darcy said, cradling Abby tighter.

"How is she?" he asked from the doorway, trying to assess the best course of action.

Darcy smoothed the hair from Abby's brow, studying her face. "Semiconscious."

"I'll go look for medical supplies. See if we

can't start flushing the drugs from her system until the Coast Guard medics arrive."

* * *

Jake sprinted up the hill, trying to avoid the jutting rocks.

The runner had a good hundred-yard lead on him and was racing for the south shore—where he probably had a getaway boat stashed. Seeing him disappear over the next rise, Jake increased his pace—his heartbeat whirring in his ears, his legs burning. It felt good to be back in pursuit.

Reaching the top of the ridge, Jake surveyed the landscape while maintaining his brisk pace. It took a moment for his eyes to fasten on the movement ahead—the man darting in and out of his line of sight, weaving around the volcanic mounds. Jake continued pursuit, gaining ground with each stride.

"Kayden, stop!" Piper's shriek echoed over the ridge.

Jake scanned the space, fear welling. *What is she . . . ?* Panic rose in his throat as he spotted her racing along the lower edges of the hills at a perfect angle to intercept. "Kayden, no!"

She was fast—record-shattering fast. He'd heard as much, but he'd never seen her in action, not like this. Within seconds she'd be between an armed criminal and his bid for escape.

Jake lost visual as he neared the bottom of the hill, his heart firmly wedged in his throat. As he cleared a thicket, they stood not five feet ahead. Unable to stop, he barreled into them midstride, and the wind left his lungs as he collided atop the two on the hard-packed earth.

A shot fired, the retort echoing around them.

Please, don't let it be Kayden. Please, God.

Jake scrambled to his feet, his fingers tightening around the gun's grip. Something cracked into his jaw, lashing his head back. Blood pooled in his mouth, the sun overhead flashing bright in his eyes.

He straightened, blinking the sunspots from his eyes until he saw Kayden wrestling with the man on the ground. The man kicked, knocking her back, and lunged for his gun mere inches from his reach.

Jake cocked the hammer, ready to fire. "Stop!"

The man stilled, his gaze fixed on his weapon.

Jake kept the barrel aimed directly at his head. *"Don't* do it."

After a moment's hesitation, the man's shoulders slumped and he lifted his hands in the air.

* * *

"What were you thinking?" Jake asked as they trudged back to join the others.

Kayden wiped dirt from her mouth and swallowed, trying to settle what seemed like a swarm of bees swirling in her stomach. Piper and Landon escorted the now-handcuffed prisoner

367

far enough ahead to be out of earshot. "I was trying to help."

"By chasing down an armed criminal?"

"I . . ." She'd had a plan, hadn't she? "I stopped him before he could escape."

"Yes, but if I hadn't arrived when I had . . ." Jake's face tightened, true fear edging his eyes.

She'd never seen that depth of concern on his face before. She'd missed a lot of things about him in the midst of her distrust—how strong he was, how powerful in his element. What else had her stubbornness caused her to miss the past three years?

What *had* she been thinking?

"I don't even want to imagine what could have—"

"Nothing happened. I'm fine. You're fine." She winced at his swollen jaw. "Well, mostly fine. And now we may finally get some answers."

* * *

Darcy remained steadfastly at Abby's side while Landon and Jake secured the third man in the room where they were holding the other two. Meanwhile, the McKennas tended to the three women as best they could with the minimal supplies available until the Coast Guard arrived.

A half hour later the Coast Guard medic said, "She's going to be fine," and offered a reassuring smile as he hooked up Abby's IV.

"Thank you." Darcy clasped Abby's clammy

hand. "See, Abby, you're going to be all right."
Thank you, Lord.

Gage signaled to her from the doorway, and after a moment's hesitation, she left Abby and joined the McKennas along with Jake and Landon in the front room.

"Federal agents should be here within the hour," Landon said. "Since the women aren't in critical condition, they've requested that the Coast Guard wait to transport them until they've had a chance to assess them on scene."

Darcy nodded, rubbing her arms, anxious to get back to Abby.

"You okay?" Gage asked, wrapping her in a hug.

"Yeah. I just hope we're able to catch whoever is behind this."

"I've questioned the men here," Jake said. "They aren't talking. Period."

"But we have to discover who's running this network, or all we've managed to do is cut out a few of his players."

Jake took a seat at the long narrow table. "Why don't you tell me more about what you saw in the lockbox."

She glanced back at the hall.

"Abby's in good hands," Gage assured her.

"You're right." She nodded. Abby was safe now. The medic was treating her, and figuring out who was running this horrific network was vital.

Wearily, she pulled out the chair beside Jake and sank into it. "The lockbox . . ."

She raked a hand through her hair. That had seemed so long ago, and yet it had been less than twenty-four hours. "I grabbed the ledger but left the photos and drugs, thinking maybe they wouldn't notice the ledger missing if they checked the box because it had been stuffed in the bottom."

"This was before we knew Clint was part of the first rescue crew," Gage said.

"Right. We figured if we pulled the box, Ted would know for certain someone was on to him."

"The pictures?" Jake asked. "Any of our known victims?"

"None of Abby," Darcy said, "but I'm pretty sure I recognized Jessica Matthews from the missing-person flyer you gave Gage."

"I printed off a news article covering the Bowen case earlier." Landon handed her the printout. "What about her?"

"Yes," Darcy said. "I definitely saw her in one of the photos."

"You're positive?" Landon asked.

"As sure as I can be with the time I had, but like I told Gage, I have a knack for faces."

"That's good."

"But it hardly helps any. Clint or Mullins has no doubt destroyed the contents of that lockbox.

It's probably resting at the bottom of the ocean somewhere."

"Let's look at what we do have, what you know," Jake said.

"Not a lot," Darcy said. "Somebody took the black book off of me while I was knocked out, and I'm sure all the evidence we pointed out to Mullins has been destroyed. I still can't believe she was involved."

"I can't believe we totally missed that." Gage shook his head. "I feel like a fool."

"It doesn't matter now," Landon said. "I informed the FBI agents of Mullins' involvement, and they are moving to detain her as we speak."

"Well, that's something," Darcy said.

"Do you still have copies of Clint, Ted, George, and Jeremy's employee files?" Landon asked.

"They're in Gage's cabin," Darcy said, "if Mullins hasn't gotten to those as well."

"Did you find any connections between them?" Jake asked.

"Yes, actually. Alaskan Adventure and Travel Employment Agency."

"What?" Landon arched a brow.

"Alaskan Adventure is the employment agency that supplied all the men in question."

"Alaskan Adventure?" Kayden said, shifting in the chair beside Piper. "That sounds more like a travel booking agency than an employment one."

Landon pulled it up on his SAT phone. "Alaskan

Adventure and Travel Employment Agency. A full-service Alaskan travel agency, providing dream vacations as well as Alaskan-travel professionals to inquiring companies and ventures. Fully screened and highly professional personnel."

"So it books vacations and provides travel personnel?" Jake said.

Landon lifted his chin. "Are you thinking what I'm thinking?"

Jake smiled, then winced. His poor jaw was still swelling. "We may have just found our network source."

"Alaskan Adventure?" Darcy said.

"It's the perfect cover." Landon exhaled. "The person running it books vacations for single women, couples, etc. He keeps on the lookout for women he knows will be in demand, books them on the right vacation, keeping in mind to diversify the carrier or locations, and on the flip side, he plants employees at these places—on the ships, in the wilderness lodges, spas, and on excursions, so they can handle the kidnapping and deliveries."

"From a criminal perspective, it's genius," Jake said, shaking his head.

"And from a human perspective, utterly terrifying." Darcy cringed.

"Every woman who has gone missing while vacationing in Alaska now becomes a possible victim of this network," Landon said.

"Kyle Trent is listed as CEO of Alaskan Adventure," Jake said, studying the screen over Landon's shoulder. "No photo."

"I'll make a call." He stood and stepped from the room.

"How on earth did they pull Mullins in?" Darcy asked, shifting back in the uncomfortable wooden chair, the cold still biting at her.

"Maybe she was tired of working so hard for so little pay. Along comes a man offering her a lot of money to look the other way," Jake suggested. Clearly he'd seen it before.

"That's disgusting."

"It's just a theory, but I bet if we search Mullins' file we'll find a connection to Trent."

"You cold?" Gage said.

He was always so adept at sensing her needs. She nodded.

"Come here." He scooted her chair beside his, engulfing her in his strong arms.

She reveled in the sheltered protection until Landon returned.

"Turns out Kyle Trent has a record—solicitation and assault. But . . ." Landon rubbed the back of his neck. "It looks like he's been clean since nineteen."

"Seriously?" With a grunt, Darcy stood to pace, her muscles tight and sore. "Trent's been clean since nineteen, and Clint, George, and Jeremy have no criminal record?"

"Not as adults," Jake said.

Landon nodded with a smile. "Exactly what I was thinking. I'm going to pull a few strings and call in a couple favors." He again stepped from the room.

"I don't understand." Darcy shook her head. She was thrilled Abby was safe, but the man responsible *needed* to be brought to justice, and so far all they had were a few of his players—all without previous criminal records. How could that be?

Jake reclined with a curious expression. "I think we just figured out what ties the men involved together."

"Huh?"

He stood. "Let me go take another stab at those three." He headed for the room off the entry.

Darcy looked at Gage with confusion. "Are you following this?" She was tired. Hadn't slept since . . . she couldn't remember, but what was she missing? How would juvenile records, if they even existed, help them?

* * *

"Still not talking," Jake said, returning with a grunt.

Darcy balled her fists, wondering if she should take a swing at them, both figuratively and, at the moment, literally—her anger was so riled.

Landon skidded back into the room, nearly breathless, a smile on his rugged face. "Our hunch paid off."

"Juvie?" Jake sat forward.

Landon nodded. "Clint, Jeremy, and George all served time in the Washington State juvenile system."

"Washington?" Gage asked.

"Guess they figured Alaska provided better hunting ground—larger area, more remote, no one knows them or their history."

"Guess who else did time in Juvie?" Landon said.

Jake smiled. "Kyle Trent?"

"Yeah, and his younger brother, Steve, who just happened to share a cell with Jeremy."

"When the brother had finished serving his stint," Landon continued, "Clint became Jeremy's new bunkmate."

"Sounds like Trent started his network way back then. Who knows how far it spreads?" Jake lifted his hand to his chin and grimaced. The medics hadn't had the chance to check out his injury yet.

"I'll see if I can find some ice," Kayden said.

Had Kayden just offered to do something nice for Jake?

Jake shook his head, then winced again. "It's fine, really. But thanks."

"And have we figured out a connection to Mullins?" Gage asked, echoing Darcy's thoughts.

She still couldn't figure out how they tied together. She was quite a bit older than the men involved.

"I got the *Bering*'s head of security to pull her records while I was waiting to hear back from my colleague," Landon said. "Guess who was listed as her previous employer?"

Jake smiled, more tentatively this time, paying heed to his injury. "Alaskan Adventure and Travel Employment Agency?"

"You got it," Landon said. "And Trent's DMV photo should be arriving any minute." He glanced at his SAT smartphone again. "Well, soonish. Then at least we'll know who we are looking for."

"So . . ." Darcy said, running through what they had pieced together. "Mullins works for Kyle Trent. He sees a new opportunity with the launch of Destiny's *Bering* in his own backyard. But he needs to make sure his guys get hired. He figures, why not give her a cut of the profits and get her hired as employee liaison on the *Bering*? And, of course, he provides a stellar recommendation."

"She gets the job and hires whomever Trent tells her to," Gage said.

Darcy snapped. "That's how she did it."

"Did what?" Gage asked.

"Abby's roommate, Pam, said Mullins had a way of filling openings really fast."

"Of course, she'd just call her boss and get a new employee—sometimes legit, sometimes to increase or fill in their network."

"How could a woman knowingly be a part of

selling other women into sexual slavery?" Piper asked, her expression aghast.

"As horrific as it is, even mothers have sold their own children into prostitution," Jake said with sorrow. "Happens all the time, particularly in poorer countries."

Tears spilled down Piper's cheeks, and in an uncharacteristic gesture of physical affection, Kayden clasped her sister's hand tight.

44

"Sheriff Grainger." The clean-cut FBI agent stepped forward and shook Landon's hand. "I'm Special Agent Stan Jackson. We spoke on the phone. This is my partner, Special Agent Will Turow." He gestured to the man beside him.

"Good to meet you." Landon turned to Darcy. "This is Darcy St. James, the reporter who started this entire investigation."

"Nice work, ma'am," Special Agent Turow said.

"Thanks, but it was my former colleague Abigail Tritt who really started the undercover investigation."

"We've cleared the Coast Guard to transport your friend and the other two women to Dutch Harbor Regional Medical Center."

"I'd like to go along."

"We'll get you there, but we have some

questions for you first. Please, have a seat." Agent Turow held out a chair for her.

Darcy started at the beginning, relaying everything she, Gage, Landon, and Jake had learned or speculated.

"Russia has to be the final drop spot," Agent Turow said to Agent Jackson.

"More likely it's the funnel," Agent Jackson replied.

"Funnel?" Darcy asked.

"Kind of like the middleman in business. The product . . ." Agent Jackson cleared his throat. "Forgive the crudity of my words, I'm just trying to explain it as the men involved see it and how the business—vulgar and evil as it is—runs."

Darcy nodded. "I understand."

"So the product is brought to Russia either directly or via holding locations, like this one. They smuggle the women in, process them through the host house, and then use them locally or sell them throughout Europe and Asia to the highest bidder."

"It's the reverse of how the sex-slave trade typically works," Gage said. "Instead of smuggling women into the U.S., they are smuggling them out."

Agent Turow nodded. "In much smaller numbers, but it makes the practice no less evil."

The depths of Abby's story were far deeper and

uglier than Darcy ever imagined when she'd first answered her friend's plea for help.

"The FBI has been tracking the Bratva in Moscow for years, focusing on its American interests," Agent Turow said.

Darcy's brow furrowed. "American interests?"

"This trade network across American borders."

"I'll call our attaché office in Moscow, pass this information along to them," Agent Jackson said, standing and excusing himself.

"What about Trent and the rest of his network?" Darcy asked. "Is there any chance of finding Clint and George?"

"Don't worry. We'll get them," Agent Turow assured her.

Landon's phone dinged. "Finally." He clicked on the attachment and shook his head.

"What is it? What's wrong?" Darcy asked.

"Looks like we've already met Kyle Trent." He turned the phone to face them all. It was the runner Jake had chased down. The man in charge of the entire operation was sitting bound in the next room. No wonder no one was talking.

Darcy smiled. "Gotcha."

45

When they finally arrived back in Dutch Harbor, Darcy entered Abby's hospital room, glad to see her friend's pale cheeks had regained some color as the IV fluids and medication flushed the drugs from her system.

Abby lurched forward, vomiting into the pan the medic held. Perspiration dotted her brow.

A nurse dabbed her forehead with a cool, damp cloth. "Let it out. You'll feel better, honey."

Abby looked up at Darcy, utter gratefulness etched on her damp brow. "How did you find me?"

Darcy explained between Abby's vomiting bouts.

Finally Abby sat back, spent but so much more alert. The nurse wiped her brow with a fresh cloth and offered her mouth rinse, which Abby gladly took.

When the nurse and medic stepped out, Darcy moved to sit at Abby's side.

Abby clasped her hand. "I owe you my life. Seriously. When Jeremy threw me overboard, I thought I was dead. Then I was pulled from the water and I thought I'd been rescued, only to find it was him." She went on to explain how they'd held her on the boat until another arrived and then how they'd transferred her and Jeremy had been shot.

Darcy held Abby as she trembled. "That must have been terrifying."

"I was too scared to fight after that." She swallowed. "They brought me to that house, and then . . ." She squeezed her eyes shut, crying.

"You don't have to," Darcy said. "It's okay."

Gage paced periodically by the door, trying to be sure she was okay while still allowing them some privacy.

Abby sniffed, swiping the tears from her cheeks with the back of her hand. "I'm so thankful you came when you did. I'm pretty sure they were getting ready to move me . . . to Russia, I think. At least initially, from what I could gather." Abby shook her head. "I'm so sorry I pulled you into this. If anything had happened to you . . ." Tears streamed down her cheeks.

"But it didn't. God protected me and led me to you."

* * *

The next couple days were spent briefing the FBI agents while Abby and the two other women were treated. Abby was the only American woman who had been found, though during her short time in captivity, she'd learned others had passed through—no doubt including Jessica Matthews and Christine Bowen.

Clint's and George's bodies were discovered in

the wilderness not far from Dutch Harbor's ferry station—both shot in the head. Kyle Trent remained in FBI custody along with Theodora Mullins—who, in an effort to save her hide, offered to cooperate and was providing vital information on Trent's network. Ted had been questioned, but since he had not played a direct role and there was no hard evidence tying him to the ring, chances were he'd walk.

On the morning of Abby's third day in the hospital, though she was weak, the doctors were satisfied with her progress and had approved her release. While Gage and Jake arranged for their flight to Anchorage, everyone had joined Darcy and Abby as they waited for her final release paperwork to arrive.

In the midst of a cleansing bout of group laughter, Special Agent Stan Jackson rapped on the waiting room door.

Landon stood up. "News?"

"We've talked with the FBI legal attaché office staff at the U.S. embassy in Moscow, and they say that the Bratva, the Russian mafia translated as the Brotherhood, are the major Russian players in the sex-slave trade. They are a huge funneling market for bringing women into Europe and Asia, as well as smuggling sex slaves into the U.S. Working in conjunction with local authorities, they know of several Bratva houses in Moscow and the surrounding area."

"Houses?" Darcy asked.

"They are a combination brothel and processing center," Stan explained. "The women are brought in, and those they feel they can sell for a good profit, they arrange to sell to the highest bidder. The embassy had heard the occasional rumor of an American victim being in Russia, but they've never had any proof. They believe if American women are enslaved, they are sold very quickly to other countries for an obscene price."

"So that's where they were going to take Abby?" Darcy gripped Abby's hand, fear and disgust tracking through her.

"Most likely."

"I've passed along all the information we've gathered on this end to the FBI attaché. Hopefully, it'll be of help on that end."

It was too horrific. They'd saved Abby and two other women, but she shuddered to think of all the women still enslaved.

"Don't worry, ma'am," Stan said. "We'll stay on this, and we'll keep you in the loop, Deputy Grainger."

Landon shook the man's hand. "Thanks. I appreciate it."

"Thank you, all of you, for your help." Stan looked around the room. "I realize by getting Trent and his gang, we may have only caused a small dent in Bratva's trafficking organization, but we cut out one of their major American suppliers. It's a great day for the good guys."

* * *

Darcy settled in beside Gage for the flight—content to simply spend the journey wrapped in his sheltering arms.

Abby was traveling with them as far as Anchorage, and then she would be taking a flight back to California from there. Piper sat beside her, the two deep in conversation.

Gage threaded his fingers through hers. "You doing okay?"

She nodded. "I'll be fine. Do you think she will?" She lifted her chin in Abby's direction.

"I pray so."

Darcy clutched his hand tighter. "Me too. Maybe this experience, all she's been through, will make her more receptive to talking about God."

He smiled. "I think Piper's already on it."

She looked back over to find Piper with her Bible in hand and Abby glancing at the pages as Piper spoke.

Please, Father. Let this horrific experience draw her to you. Let it draw us all closer to you.

46

Securing a flight from Anchorage to Kodiak and then taking the ferry into Yancey took the better part of the day.

Abby caught her flight home from Anchorage, promising to stay in touch. Darcy prayed God would use the ordeal to strengthen their friendship and to allow deeper conversations with Abby about the God who loved her.

Bailey and Cole were waiting to greet them at the ferry station when they finally arrived in Yancey. One look at their welcoming faces and Darcy felt genuinely at home.

They quickly retreated to Piper and Kayden's place and enjoyed a typical McKenna meal filled with love and laughter, and then ended up in the family room chatting over coffee and dessert—amazing individual chocolate soufflés Bailey had spent the afternoon making.

"So is the FBI finding a case against Trent?" Cole asked.

"Yes. They are going through all his financials, business records, business associates, every employee he ever hired," Landon said. "And I don't know about you"—he looked at Jake—"but I think Stan and Will are more than up to the task."

Jake smiled. The swelling in his jaw had diminished nicely. "I agree."

It was weird seeing everyone's shift in attitude toward Jake, subtle as it was. With the exception of Kayden, they'd all accepted, loved, and respected him for years. All had sought his counsel before, but now they finally understood the depth of his knowledge and the years of experience behind that counsel.

Kayden's shift was far more dramatic. She looked at Jake differently, responded to him differently—almost with admiration or genuine respect in her eyes. If Darcy saw the shift, surely it wasn't lost on Jake.

Darcy took another delicious bite of the soufflé, warm liquid chocolate dancing in her mouth.

So much had happened in the months since she'd left Yancey last winter—especially in the last couple weeks—what some might consider a lifetime's worth, and yet she was content to simply sit and enjoy being surrounded by the family she'd come to love so dearly.

"Why don't you bunk here?" Piper said when Darcy finally stood to go.

"Thanks for the offer. I would, but it's nearly ten, and I don't want to cancel my reservation at the Caribou so late."

"That makes sense," Piper said. "But how about tomorrow night? It'll be fun. We could make it a girls' night. What do you think, Kayden?" She smiled at her future sister-in-law. "You too, Bailey."

"I'm in," Bailey said, appearing eager for the girl time.

"Yep," Kayden said, clearly trying to be gracious. Her idea of a girls' night hosted by Piper had to be on par with Darcy's idea of a night spent cage fighting.

Jake seemed to smile at the notion of Kayden participating in a girls' night.

"So are you in, Darcy?" Piper asked.

"Absolutely."

"Great. I'll pick you up at the Caribou when I finish my shift at the shop tomorrow. Should be around four."

"Sounds good. I'll look forward to it." She'd sleep in, spend time in God's Word, go for a jog, and enjoy the Caribou's fabulous afternoon tea. The Caribou was by far her favorite bed and breakfast in Alaska.

Gage grabbed his car keys off the hook. "I'll drive you back."

"Thanks."

He held the door for her as she stepped outside. Temperatures in Yancey were far warmer than they'd been in the Aleutians. Even at ten o'clock at night it was still near fifty.

"You're staying for Cole and Bay's wedding?" he asked once they were in his Land Rover.

"Of course. I wouldn't miss it. I can't believe it's only two weeks away."

"I know." He sighed. "I think we could all use an honest-to-goodness family celebration."

"And then there's Piper and Landon's in August."

"Yes, it's going to be a good summer." He turned on the ignition but left the Rover idling, then shifted to face her. "I realize it's kind of short notice, but I was wondering if you had a date?"

She smiled, butterflies tingling through her. "For Cole and Bailey's wedding?"

He nodded with a charming smile.

"No. I do not." She arched a brow. "Was that an invitation, Mr. McKenna?"

His smile widened. "That depends, Miss St. James."

She shifted to face him fully. "On what?"

"If it can be the first of many."

Joy filled her as he leaned across the space separating them and pressed his lips to hers. *Definitely the first of many,* she prayed.

Acknowledgments

God: Thank you, Father, for carrying me through.

Mike: For being the love of my life and my best friend.

Kay: For being the sweet, kind, hilarious, and occasionally fiery girl that you are. I love you beyond measure.

Doug: For being there for us when we needed you most. Love you.

Dave Long and Karen Schurrer: Words cannot express how grateful I am to be paired with you two, and considering how much I talk, I hope you know that says A LOT. You are both phenomenal!

Debra Larsen, Noelle Buss, Steve Oates, Paul Higdon, Dave Horton, and my entire BHP family: Thank you so much for your tremendous support. It's a joy working with you all.

Dave Lewis, Scott Hurm, Bill Shady, Nathan Henrion, Max Eerdmans, Rod Jantzen, and Rob Teigen: Thank you for getting the ALASKAN COURAGE series into the hands of readers. I deeply appreciate all you do.

Dee: Thank you for your continued friendship, support, encouragement, and advice. I am so blessed by you.

Lisa, Maria, and Donna: Thank you for your abiding friendship and love.

Kelli: For being the amazingly creative and super-talented woman you are. You never cease to amaze.

Rel Mollet, Nora St. Laurent, Casey Herringshaw, Melanie De Jong, Katie McCurdy, Renee Chaw, Nancy Kimball, Susan Sleeman, and Suzanne Kuhn for your amazing support. I deeply appreciate you all.

To my dear readers: Thank you for your kind notes of encouragement, your enthusiasm for the McKennas' stories, and for sharing the ALASKAN COURAGE series with your friends and family. I'm so very grateful for you.

About the Author

Dani Pettrey is a wife, homeschooling mom, and author. She feels blessed to write inspirational romantic suspense because it incorporates so many things she loves—the thrill of adventure, nail-biting suspense, the deepening of her characters' faith, and plenty of romance. She and her husband reside in Maryland with their two teenage daughters.

Visit her Web site at www.danipettrey.com.

Center Point Large Print

600 Brooks Road / PO Box 1
Thorndike ME 04986-0001 USA

(207) 568-3717

US & Canada:
1 800 929-9108
www.centerpointlargeprint.com